HISTORY OF CREATION

HISTORY OF CREATION:
THE ANNOUNCEMENT

JKM MBDW

235, 16 Midlake Boulevard S. E.
Calgary, Alberta T2X 2X7
CANADA

An AfriCalendar Publications' Book
Published by AfriCalendar Publications Company Inc.

Name: Mbdw, jkm 2025 - Author.
Title : History of Creation: *The Announcement*
Description: First edition | Alberta, Canada: AfriCalendar, 2025.
ISBN 978-0-9731038-3-0 (trade paperback) | ISBN 978-0-9731038-4-7 (ebook)

First Edition: December 2025
Cover Art and Design by Rodney Hazard, Le Loup Studios
Book Interior Design by Iram Allam

For the women who lovingly spoiled me!

'Not through height does one see the moon.'

— AFRICAN

CONTENTS

TRUTHS OF CREATION

First   The First, the Self-Generator, exists

Second   There is only one First, the Self-Generator

Third   There were no witnesses to creation

Fourth   There is no before the First, the Self-Generator

Fifth   All of creation is one within the First, the Self-Generator

Sixth   Only the First, the Self-Generator, knows what *It* might or might not do

Seventh   Things created by the First, the Self-Generator, last forever and a more

Eighth   To know the First, the Self-Generator, is to know 'nothing'

Ninth   The First, the Self-Generator, has no form, shape, or image

Tenth   There are no hierarchies in creation, no greater than or lesser than, no consciousness above another; but none that is independent of the First, the Self-Generator

Eleventh   Everything is possible for the First, the Self-Generator

Twelfth   The First, the Self-Generator, is always there and there is both everywhere and nowhere

Thirteenth   Things created from 'nothing' are the creations of the First, the Self-Generator

Last   The First, the Self-Generator's truths are eternal; they are truths forever and a more

CIRCULAR ASSEMBLY

HUMAN'S DESCRIPTIONS AND PLACES OF GLORIFIED

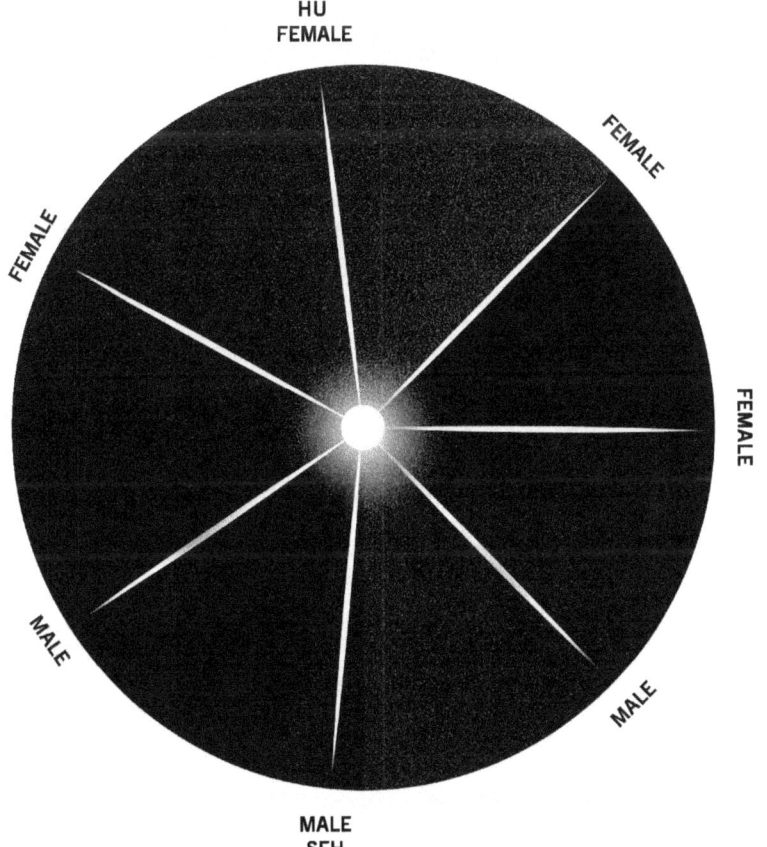

HISTORY OF CREATION

CHAPTER 1

THE RAPTURE

The Glorified Seven existed for many whiles before uncovering the Rapture. The Rapture answered the question: 'Is it possible to be in seven places, spaces, or times at once?' They first experimented with speed, moving quickly through the Realm. They would vanish from one space and appear in another. Then, they would move to another and another, until they journeyed through the seven sections of the Realm. The Glorified, who were created with full knowledge and mastery of their abilities, stretched themselves to a limit, trying to be everywhere at the same while. It took just moments to make the journey through the Realm, but to the Glorified Seven, those moments seemed endless.

After a while, the Glorified reasoned that to be here, there, and everywhere required something other than speed. They wondered if they could divide themselves, so each part could be in a different section of the Realm. That notion might appear strange to humans but in the beginning—when there were only the Glorified—any idea which had not been explored was thought to be possible—since failure was not yet a teacher. They knew the Spark had been separated into parts, and that any number could be represented by fractions. They wondered if that was true for a Glorified as well. Could a Glorified be represented by his or her parts? They explored the thought. They considered how to create fractions of themselves. Should they gain that knowledge, they would station fractions of themselves in different sections of the Realm. This way, they could be in seven different places, spaces, or times simultaneously.

Since their beginning, the Glorified have pursued many ideas and created many things. They even uncovered how to change their form of creation into any shape or size, but they did not know how to divide themselves into fractions. They thought dividing themselves into fractions might be similar to creating the *true gift*. They were discussing the possible steps when a Glorified suggested that they should first try to connect to each other while stationed in different sections of the Realm. 'Simultaneousness'—the ability to be everywhere—should be an expansion of consciousness and will, she said, concerned that fractions of themselves might be a reduction of the whole. 'The sum', she added, 'might be greater than its parts.'

The others did not know if fractions of themselves would be a reduction, but her suggestion was simpler. Each Glorified would station themselves in one section of the Realm. If it worked, the Glorified would connect to each other across the Realm. That might allow them to see, hear, and feel what was happening in each section. They were uncertain whether they could connect to each other in that way, but they started along that path together. They stationed themselves in different sections. They tried to see, hear, and feel for each other by pushing their thoughts outwards. Instead of finding each other, they physically moved from section to section of the Realm. In essence, they were doing the same thing they had done. They had gotten into the habit of moving quickly among the sections, and, like humans, they found it easier to travel a familiar road than to uncover a new path. After many attempts, the idea of physically connecting to each other across the Realm was abandoned. In its place, they began to consider connecting through another 'part of being'. They knew there were three 'parts to being', the physical was not the only path.

The Glorified did not know how to achieve the outcome of being everywhere. They set aside the idea that they could connect the physical 'part of being' to each other and began exploring whether another 'part of being' could lead to 'simultaneousness'. They were sitting in a circular assembly with their legs crossed, storming through different ideas. Their hands rested on their knees with their palms open and facing upwards—the formation the Glorified always used when exploring ideas together. The circular assembly allowed each Glorified to see the others and observe the Spark within each other. They discussed the concept of connecting across the Realm. The notion of stationing a Glorified in each section, whether physically or in some other form of existence, was thought to be the key. They just needed to stop moving among the sections of the Realm and find a way to connect to each other.

They were certain 'simultaneousness' was within their will but after attempting to uncover its path, they would lay the idea aside to partake in merriment. They would sing, clap their hands, and stomp their feet. After the merriment, they would again gather in a circular assembly to explore the idea of being everywhere. Merriment—especially the drinking of ale—drew them back to the idea of physically being in the seven sections of the Realm. They would wonder about the fractions of themselves and how to perform such a division. They discussed the things they had tried, acknowledging that they had no answer to the question: 'Is it possible to be in seven places, spaces, or times at once?'

There were many attempts at being everywhere, followed by many gatherings with eating, drinking, and dancing after the idea had been set aside. It was after one of these gatherings that the Glorified searched the endowment. They were searching for any truth that could contribute to gaining 'simultaneousness'. The endowment was silent. There were no references suggesting the outcome might be gained. From the endowment, they learnt that 'the Spark leads the Spirit'. They had decided the path to 'simultaneousness' might be through another 'part of being'. They wondered whether the Spark leading the Spirit could assist them in opening the path to being everywhere in the Realm.

The Glorified had tried to be everywhere by using speed. They had attempted to connect to each other by pushing their thoughts outwards and they had tried to access the other 'parts of being' by focusing their energy inwards. They could not connect to each other or access the other 'parts of being'. Instead, they moved their physical forms, leading them to assume the physical had dominance over the other 'parts of being'.

They held circular assemblies on how to overcome the physical. They discussed how to deny the certainty the physical provides. They explored the meaning of 'the Spark leads the Spirit' and decided to let the Spark lead. They thought the Spark might connect their Spirits to each other. Once more, they positioned themselves one in each section of the Realm. They arranged themselves as in a circular assembly and closed their eyes to reduce the effects of the physical. They had one thought: 'Remove the physical so the Spark could lead.' Each sat with their back straight, legs crossed and their hands–the vessels of the Spark–resting comfortably on their knees. The vessels were held with two fingers touching each other to form a circle and the other three fingers curved slightly upwards. Held in this manner, the vessels symbolised the 'nothing' and the three 'parts of being'. It allowed them to focus. But even with their eyes closed, the Spark would not lead. Their physical forms were again hurled across the Realm.

They put the idea aside again, only to find themselves after much ale, discussing being everywhere. They searched the endowment for references to the Spark and the Spirit. They were searching for how to cause the Spark to lead. They knew no words that could cause the Spark to lead nor what actions might animate the Spirit. The endowment affirmed that the Spark could not be commanded, but it revealed that the Spirit could roam. The Glorified had tried; they could not cause the Spark to go or to come, start or stop. Still, the Glorified were certain that 'simultaneousness' was within them. Once again, they stationed themselves throughout the Realm, wondering how to let the Spark lead. They thought that by reducing the effect of the physical and finding the quiet within themselves, they might be able to gain 'simultaneousness'.

The Glorified were no longer trying to physically be in seven places, spaces, or times at once. Instead, they wanted to share with each other, to participate in the oneness of creation. They had noticed the Sparks glowed brighter at the gatherings when they were sharing. They thought that if they placed the purpose of creation above everything, the Sparks might brighten their glows. It might lead their Spirits to connect to each other, allowing them to share with each other—to be one and yet seven, or, as humans would say, unity and plurality. With a sense of beginning again, the Glorified put aside the thought of being everywhere and replaced it with the contentment that comes from sharing. They wanted to be of service to each other. They wanted to share with the others in any way the Spark might choose. That allowed them to focus their energy inwards, creating a calm and denying the certainty of the physical. It caused the sounds of the Realm to fall away. The need to give, to share, and to commune with each other grew. They had chosen the purpose of creation. That choice allowed the Spark to lead. In that moment, in the quiet, the physical was abandoned; it fell away like the far-off sound of distant thunder.

The transition from the physical form to the Rapture seemed to require no effort on their part, except choosing the way of creation. The Spark spread its glow over the physical form like a flame, changing it into particles. The halves of the Spark joined to form a golden disc. The particles, in the shape of a four-sided structure, sat in the middle of the disc. Nothing in the human world resembled the mound of the particles of the Rapture. The particles were small and could not individually be seen by the physical eyes. Yet together, they resembled the Mystery of Creation.

The Raptures would have been identical but for the colours of the particles. In their physical form, the Glorified Seven resemble humans. Their faces are round; not like a circle, but in the way that faces among groups of people are round. Their faces appear flat as the forehead protrudes very slightly over the eyes. Both the mouth and the nose would be considered broad. Their eyes are bright, and their full lips have a distinct edge that outlines and enhances the lips' size. In the form of their creation, the colour of the Glorified could be described as the colour of rich and fertile soil. However, the colours of the particles of their Raptures cannot be described in human terms. There are no duplicate or parallel colours in the human universe. The sum of the colours of the particles equals the colour of rich and fertile soil, which is the opposite of what would take place on Earth. Where the sum of the colours would equal the colour of light. Since the History of Creation can only be told from the limited perspective of humans, not much more can be said about the colours in the Rapture.

The Spark waited before each particle separated from the mound, drifting off in a slightly different direction. The particles spread until they were in each of the seven sections. The Glorified described the experience as opening a door to a warm room and feeling cool air flowing into the room. The feeling of cool air flowing over the human body is similar to what the Glorified felt as the particles drifted into the different sections of the Realm. They drifted off, but the particles remained connected to each other, with none detaching from the Spark. The Glorified were everywhere. Yet they felt no different than in their physical form. Even though the physical had crumbled, the Glorified still felt like they were sitting in the circular assembly position. Each Glorified could see, hear, and feel what was happening everywhere in the Realm. The Spark led, but it did not connect their Spirits. They expected 'simultaneousness' would require them to be one and yet seven. They did not expect individual 'simultaneousness'. The Rapture was beyond their expectations.

The limitations of the physical form were no more. They uncovered a new way of being, transforming from physical form, Spark, and Spirit to just Spark and Spirit. The Spark is separated into two, each half resided in its vessel. During the Rapture, the halves became a whole. Other than that, the Spark was unaffected by the Rapture. It gathered and arranged the particles in a straight and narrow path. There were seven straight and narrow paths, each with a different colour, parallel to each other, forming a broad, many-coloured path. After lining up the particles, the Sparks separated, with each half attaching to one end of its straight and narrow path. The weight of the Spark caused each path to arch, forming a bow. The arches were stacked one on top of the other. If humans had seen it, they would have described it as a beautiful bow. Within the bow, the particles flowed along the arches as if greeting each other for the first. At each end of the arches, the Sparks were radiant and golden. Fragments from this part of the History of Creation can still be found among the tales and myths of humans. Humans have stories where golden vessels could be found at the end of many-coloured bows. These stories, though altered to meet the needs of the storytellers, have their origins in the Rapture of the Glorified.

The Rapture was disorienting for the Glorified. As the particles spread throughout the Realm, the Spirit's eye opened, and they were everywhere. Humans know the Spirit's eye. They refer to it as the 'all-knowing' or the 'all-seeing' eye. These are appropriate descriptions of the Spirit's eye, as it is both knowing and seeing. The Glorified had grown beyond their knowledge and Raptured into 'simultaneous beings'. There was so much to see, hear, and feel, so much to share with each other—so much more than there was before.

The arches were straightened into narrow pathways again, separated by a fixed distance from each other but *crossing* at a single point. At the *crossing*, the seven colours of the Rapture met and became the colour of the Glorified. That was the place where the Glorified found each other. They described it as sitting in a circular assembly, except everywhere. They did not know how they were able to see, hear, and feel. The Spark led and created the particles but the Glorified were not seeing through each other's eyes, hearing through each other's ears, or feeling what each other felt. They had no knowledge of the Rapture; they had only uncovered that the 'Spark leads the Spirit'. They did not know that letting the Spark lead would lead to the Rapture. The Spark entombed the physical form in its glow and replaced it with the particles. It spread the particles, allowing the Glorified to be everywhere, but the Spark did not connect the Glorified to each other.

The Glorified reached for each other to discuss the outcome but in the Rapture, communication occurred differently. They would say that it is more difficult. Prior to the Rapture, communicating in the Realm involved sound; whether at work or play, there were always meaningful sounds. The Glorified could speak from the moment—as humans have defined that word—of their creation. They had a common set of symbols to share thoughts. Those symbols were included in the endowment. They were the only symbols or, as humans would say, words, of the First, the Self-Generator, that exist in creation. *It* created the symbols, but no creature, neither Glorified nor humans, in any place, space, or time, has ever heard *It* utter any of those words. *It* has communicated with the Glorified in the way the Glorified have indicated. The Glorified cannot summon *It*, nor can *It* be commanded. Human ritual societies, knowing the First, the Self-Generator, is always there, would preach that *It* could be commanded to grant wishes. That preaching is not a truth. It is not found among the truths of creation. The First, the Self-Generator, has never come when *It* has been called. *It* has never given when *It* has been asked.

'*It* is always there' is a truth found among the truths of creation, but *It* does not grant wishes. The Realm—or *Amenta*—as humans would call it, is a voiceless place, space, or time in the Rapture. A Glorified in his physical form knows not how to communicate with a Glorified in the Rapture. That is similar to the relationship between the First, the Self-Generator, and every consciousness in creation. Beings, creatures, or consciousnesses know not how to communicate with the First, the Self-Generator. Yet among the many truths of creation, the twelfth truth says, 'The First, the Self-Generator, is always there and there is both everywhere and nowhere.' *It* sees, hears, and feels creation, but neither Glorified nor humans could see *It*, hear *It*, or feel *It*. That is the reason humans have said, '*It* is the secret one—the one who is everywhere and who is everything.'

The Rapture gave the Glorified another way of being. As they looked upon creation, they asked, 'Is this the Realm?' They each asked the question or thought the question. The Glorified heard the question, saw the question, or felt the question. It was not clear how they heard, saw, or felt the question. What was clear was that no sound was made. Communicating in the Rapture is voiceless. They speak without sound; they hear without ears, and they see without eyes. It is the story of the Rapture humans reference with the words: 'The dumb can speak, the deaf can hear, and the blind can see.' Humans are unable to understand communicating in the Rapture. There are no parallels in the human world that could explain what takes place at the *crossing*. The History of Creation uses the terms seeing, hearing, and feeling because humans understand these symbols. What humans cannot understand is that communicating can be seen in the Rapture. It can be heard, it can be felt, and it can be touched. It is like being part of sound or being the sound. If humans could comprehend communicating in the Rapture, they would be able to see life differently, similar to how the Rapture allowed the Glorified to exist in a different way.

The Glorified knew the Realm, but they did not know that the Realm had a Spark, nor did they know that everything in creation shared the same Presence. That knowledge was not included in the endowment. The Glorified knew all of creation was one within the First, the Self-Generator, because the endowment said so. It is the fifth truth of creation, and the Rapture with the Spirit's eye affirmed it. Before the Rapture, the Glorified could see the Spark in each other and thought it was the Spark that made them one with creation. In the Rapture with the Spirit's eye, they could see a Presence within the Sparks and they uncovered that the Presence within the Sparks is the foundation of the oneness in creation.

After the Rapture, the Glorified spent many whiles, or as humans would say, a long time, in solitude, wandering in the Realm. They walked with their arms spread wide, touching as many things as possible. They let the particles spread everywhere, making themselves one with the Realm. They joined the Mystery of Creation as it flowed along its path, listening to its melody, hearing it in new and different ways. In the Rapture, they became open to sound. They could hear it, feel it, and see it. They made themselves part of it. They flowed along with it like a leaf on a stream; with their particles, they fell upon it like dew in the early morning and embraced it like air in a bubble.

The Rapture gave the Glorified a new way to exist, and for a while they existed in that way. They laid the particles one on top of the other to see if each stack would create a *crossing*. Stacking their particles, the Glorified could not find each other. The *crossing* could only be created in the way indicated by the Spark.

The seven colours of the Rapture sum to the colour of rich, fertile soil. The Glorified marvelled at the mysterious ways of the First, the Self-Generator, when they realised that any two of the colours sum to the same colour as all seven. There is nothing like it in the human world or in the rest of creation, where the sum of seven is the same as the sum of any two within the seven. They experimented to see if they were all seeing the same thing with the Spirit's eye. One Glorified would start by describing what he was seeing, hearing, and feeling. The others would then identify what he described. Humans are still familiar with this part of the History. Among humans, there is a form of relations where one human would start by saying, 'I see with my little eye.' The others would identify the thing that he or she described. Humans used to know this example of sharing was first practiced in the Realm.

There were many circular assemblies held at the *crossing*. Those circular assemblies were used to discuss outcomes, ask questions, and suggest areas to explore further. At one assembly, the question was asked: which form of being the Glorified preferred—the form of creation or the Rapture? The question was asked in an uncertain tone, suggesting there may not be a clear answer. The Rapture gave the Glorified insight into creation. It made them 'simultaneous beings'. They could see a Presence in everything. They could be everywhere at the same while. Yet they could not say they preferred being in the Rapture to existing in the form of their creation.

The Spirit of the Rapture and the Spirit of the physical form are not the same. From the endowment, the Glorified knew there were 'three parts to being'. They did not know what the differences might be. In the Rapture, they learnt that the Glorified could not act upon creation. They could not affect or change the Realm in any way, as they could in the physical form. They could let their particles flow with the Mystery of Creation but could not change its path or use it to create things. They could hear sound and be part of the sound. Yet they could not make music or any type of sound. They could not create their favourite foods or special colours to bring to the *crossing*. Even though they were 'simultaneous beings', they could not act upon creation. That distinguished the Rapture from the form of creation. The Glorified could not raise their voices, as humans say, unto glory in the Rapture. There is no laughing, singing, or other precious sounds. That 'part of being' is silent. Over the whiles, as the Glorified experimented with the particles, they began to think of the Rapture as a way to be with the First, the Self-Generator.

In the physical form, their Spirit could act upon creation. In the Rapture, they could not affect it. That's why there was no clear answer to which form of existence the Glorified preferred. The Glorified would prefer to have both. They were certain the Rapture started with the entombing and crumbling of the physical, meaning they could not exist in both ways at the same while. This is why the Glorified who found herself the focus of the First, the Self-Generator, was confused to find her physical form and her Rapture within reach of each other. She did not know she could stand beside herself and look upon herself. She thought she had uncovered a new way of being. She thought she had found a way to expand beyond the limitations of either form or Rapture. It was the first that Hu had seen both her form and Rapture at the same time, to use a human reference. The particles were in the shape of her physical form. It was the colour of her Rapture. It looked as though it was made from the Mystery of Creation. She looked at the Rapture and realised she was also looking at her physical form from the Rapture. It was similar to how humans look at their reflections, but Hu was also looking at her physical form from the reflection.

The Rapture form stood in the kind of stance the human body is made to stand in without pain or pressure. Her eyes were opened, her shoulders rounded, and her arms fell to her side in a relaxed manner. She looked at the Rapture, and her sight found the hands, the vessels of the Spark. Her gaze moved down the form, noticing the knees were slightly bent, and the feet were firmly planted. She was looking to see if another Glorified had created the form with the particles, but she did not see a Spark. She knew that the Rapture occurs when the Spark leads the Spirit. In the physical form, the Spark is often found in its vessels, which the Glorified use for giving and receiving. Her gaze drifted towards the feet, knowing that the parts of the Spark combined into a disc in the Rapture. The Spark was not there. She waited to see if others would join her, even though she sensed she was alone. She tried to spread the particles to use the Spirit's eye to understand what was happening. She knew the path to the Rapture well. She had spent many whiles following the Spark along the path to the Rapture. She did not know the Rapture could be gained without the entombing and crumbling of the physical form. She tried to spread the particles of the

Rapture. Seeing through the Spirit's eye would reveal whether she was truly alone or if others were there in their Rapture form. She looked straight ahead, seeing her physical form where it lay, while her physical form looked at her Rapture where it stood. She could see, but only with the limited sight of the forms. The greater sight of the Spirit's eye was not at her command.

After a while, she became conscious of her efforts to spread the particles. She recalled the first Rapture and tried to find the contentment that came with sharing. She was certain she was looking at the particles of her Rapture, which was unexpected. The particles were always in motion, and they could not be seen with the physical eyes. A Glorified entering the Rapture would be there and then not there. From a human perspective, it is like looking at a person and in the blink of an eye, he disappears. She could not move the Rapture form, spread the particles, or open the Spirit's eye. There was an emptiness within her, a void, which the History of Creation described as the 'nothing'. She felt it. She thought it was in the place of her will and strength. She looked at both the Rapture and her physical form. She did not know what to think about the physical form. The Glorified thought both 'parts of being' could not exist at the same while. They assumed the physical form was crumbled to allow the particles to exist.

Hu had followed the Spark along the path to the Rapture. She had seen how the Spark spread its glow, first to the thumb and the index finger. Those fingers touched to form a circle, and from there the glow moved to the other three fingers. The vessels of the Spark held in that way symbolised both the 'nothing', which the First, the Self-Generator, used to create *itself*, and the 'three parts of being'. The Spark then moved its glow up the arms towards the shoulders and the head. Finally, the glow flowed down the form and into the crossed legs towards the feet with the soles facing upwards. That process has not been witnessed by any Glorified in the physical form. The entire form vanishes from the physical eyes once the Rapture starts.

A Glorified in the Rapture can see the Spark following its path. The Spark follows the same path whether the Glorified entered the Rapture in the form of creation or some other shape. The Rapture starts where the Spark resides and covers the entire form with its glow. The process has been described to humans as a flame upon a bush. Humans understood that description. Flames can change a bush into ashes—similar to the Rapture changing the physical form into particles. The Glorified have the ability to change the particles back to the physical form, similar to the human myth about the phoenix. A flame upon a bush, from the perspective of humans, is an appropriate symbol for how the glow of the Spark spreads and creates the particles of the Rapture. Humans still know this symbol. It was carried from the village, the place where humans began, to the mountains and valleys as humans spread themselves about the Earth. But similar to other stories, that symbol has been changed to suit the purposes of the storytellers.

Hu knew that a Glorified could not be in the physical form and Rapture at the same while. The Spark always changed the physical form into particles. The Glorified would be everywhere, and the form of creation could not be found in the Realm. That knowledge led Hu, in the announcement, as the focus of the First, Self-Generator, to conclude she had uncovered a new way of being–a way of expanding beyond the limitations of either form or Rapture.

CHAPTER 2

IF AT FIRST ...

The Rapture appeared to be within the will of the Glorified. They no longer thought about the Spark leading the Spirit or the purpose of creation when they transitioned from the physical to the Rapture. They entered the Rapture with ease and gave no thought to its path. After many whiles of entering the Rapture, of being everywhere, Hu began to wonder if there were more to entering the Rapture, if the Glorified, in their haste to gain 'simultaneousness', were hurdling over parts of the journey. 'The Spark opens the way, the Glorified chooses how to be', a Seven told her, dismissing her thoughts. The others did not know if that was true. The Rapture appeared to be at their command, so they entered the Rapture without considering what they were doing. Hu questioned if being everywhere was all there was to the Rapture.

Hu wondered if there could be things to uncover along the path to the Rapture. That thought is similar to humans wondering if there is any meaning in the journey from the marketplace to home. She started to observe the others entering the Rapture, learning that the Spark always followed the same path. She suggested to the others that there might be things to uncover if they followed the Spark as it leads the Spirit. She was not certain there was anything to gain, but she wanted to follow the path slowly. She began to follow the Spark by trying to command it to wait. She tried to get the Spark to wait after it entombed the physical form but before it created the particles. Neither Hu nor the others witnessed how the particles of the Rapture were created. They did not know where along the path the physical form was crumbled into particles. They would enter the Rapture, and the particles would be everywhere. The Glorified would be in full command of the particles. This led Hu to assume she had the will to command the Spark to wait for her to witness the creation of the particles.

The Spark continued to follow the same path whenever Hu entered the Rapture. Her particles would spread, and she would be everywhere. She would try again. The path to the Rapture seemed to have only two steps. She would position herself as in the circular assembly, and then she would be here, there, and everywhere. It seemed that she had jumped over steps she knew the Spark had taken. She visualised the outcome she wanted. She searched the endowment, wondering if there was a way to indicate to the Spark the outcome to provide. She reaffirmed that the Spark leads the Spirit. She decided that instead of trying to direct the Spark, she would try to follow the Spark along its path.

She arranged herself as in the circular assembly. She held the vessels of the Spark up in front of her face so she could see both at the same while. She focused on the vessels of the Spark as the Rapture began. At first, it appeared the Rapture took a while, causing her to lose her concentration, regaining it only after the particles were spread. Hu was determined to witness at least the steps she knew the Spark had taken—so she started again, and again the particles were everywhere. This continued for a while. She positioned herself, focused on the seat of the Spark, and she would be everywhere in the Realm. She was doing the same thing over and over again. With each attempt, she did not expect a different outcome; she expected a different experience. She knew that the outcome would be 'simultaneousness'. She expected to be able to follow the Spark as it led the Spirit into the Rapture. Humans, too, have learnt from this experience. Those who journey slowly often say to the young, 'If at first you try ...'. That is not the wisdom of age. It is how the tale of Hu's attempts to follow the Spark began in the village. Humans, over the whiles, came to think of the Glorified as knowing and able to do all things. They had forgotten that everything the Glorified gained required a while of trying, of doing, time, and time again. The Glorified are not perfect beings, but they know that perfection comes only with practise.

She continued to practise until she regained her concentration along the path where the Spark created the four-sided structure. She did the same thing and had a different experience. She tried to focus on the base of the structure before realising, at some point along the path, she could not see, hear, or feel—not even in the limited way of the physical form. That was her first realisation in following the Spark. The Glorified had assumed the Rapture was an extension of their physical abilities. What she observed suggested that it might 'remake' rather than extend. She shared her observation with the others. She proposed there might be additional knowledge along the path. The others asked how was it possible for her to know that she could not see, hear, or feel. 'Seeing and hearing could be lost. The ears could be clogged and the eyes blocked, but feeling is to be', they said. They wondered if the Glorified ceased to be along the path of the Rapture. Without feeling, seeing, and hearing, how would a Glorified exist? The Glorified sat in a quiet moment of thought before it was suggested that her sharing was not new knowledge. The Glorified, whose place in the circular assembly is between the two others who humans would consider male, pointed out that they are not 'simultaneous' when the particles sit in the four-sided structure. "The Rapture is the process of transforming into 'simultaneous beings'. Could the path be of more value than the outcome?" he asked. The others had no answer to his question. He thought he knew the answer, but Hu was not certain. She, too, recalled her other Raptures. She knew she had observed something different, even though she did not fully understand its meaning.

After the gathering, Hu sat with her legs crossed, the soles of her feet facing upwards, and she followed as the Spark led the Spirit. She focused on the seat of the Spark. In this attempt at observing the path to the Rapture, the Spark seemed to be in a rush. It might have been the ale, which caused it to appear that the glow of the Spark was travelling the path quickly. She knew the path led to the crumbling of the physical form. She increased her focus as the Spark transformed its glow into a golden tomb. She was aware, following the Spark like a lamb to a shepherd, as humans would say. She thought she was about to witness how the particles were created. She tried to increase her focus, to be with all of her being, but, once again, she found herself in the four-sided structure.

The four-sided mound was exactly the same as in her other Raptures, with a square base and four-sides that taper into a single point at its summit. She felt no difference between the Rapture and her physical form as both her Spark and Spirit were there. She was able to focus on a portion of the journey she had not witnessed. In her previous Raptures, that part of the path was missed, and observing others entering the Rapture showed only the glow as it entombed the form. Inside the glow was unseen and unknown to the Glorified. The Rapture continued along its path and spread the particles. She could see, hear, and feel everything in the Realm. She saw the others each at rest in a *while of quiet.* She made herself one with the Mystery of Creation, and she travelled with it along its path. She saw the Presence within all things and knew as if the Presence itself had spoken that none had any greater value than the other. Everything is one within the First, the Self-Generator. It is solely the First, the Self-Generator, who has value other than one; everything else is one. She then *'remade'* her form of creation and joined the others in a *while of quiet.*

She rose from the quiet, feeling rested. She did not understand how or why she always lost her way along the path to the Rapture. She had followed the Spark as it entombed the form and had expected to see how the particles were created. As she recalled the Rapture, there seemed to be a while missing, a gap in her memory, and yet, she was not deterred. This is the reason this tale started with, 'If at first you try …' in the village. She had learnt it was possible to observe the Spark as it leads the Spirit. She uncovered that along the path, there came a place, space, or time where she was, and she was not. She wondered if that was because the Spark entombed the physical and inside the glowing tomb the ears were clogged, the eyes were blocked, and feelings were numbed. She spent many more whiles, or a lot more time, as humans say, following the Spark.

She followed along for more and more of the path; she felt the glow as it entombed her form. It was a quiet process. The Spark leads in silence. Inside the glow, her physical form was unaffected. She could clearly see that the golden glow was next to the form but not on it. She focused on the seat of the Spark, holding her hands up in front of her face instead of resting them on her knees. That was the point where she would lose her way. She would regain her consciousness sitting in the four-sided structure. After she found her way back to herself, she would remain in the Rapture to observe the Presence in all things;

then, she would try again.

Hu shared what she had learnt with the others. Some of the others started to follow the Spark along its path, but they made little progress. They faced many of the same challenges as Hu, and she could offer no insight other than to say: 'Focus on the seat of the Spark.' That was a hurdle for some of the Glorified. The seat of the Spark, in both Glorified and humans, is the vessels. In the form of creation, the vessels were used for giving and receiving. Hu always entered the Rapture in the form of creation. The others often entered the Rapture in different shapes and forms. The Glorified who had suggested that they divide themselves one to each section of the Realm often entered the Rapture in a form with neither arms nor legs. In that form, this Glorified gained motion by sliding on her belly in a left-right, left-right curvature movement. She would stand upright by raising part of the elongated form, and the remaining part made a circle at its base. In standing up, she would expand the part of the body just below the head, adding half-circles to each side of the neck. That was where the two parts of the Spark would be located. In entering the Rapture in this form, she had difficulty locating the seat of the Spark. She did not know where to focus, nor how to begin to follow the Spark.

Hu tried, tried, and tried again, yet she was not able to follow the Spark without losing her way. After many whiles and many attempts, she expected to lose her focus and concentration. She began paying less and less attention to the Spark and its glow, instead thinking more about the point where she would lose her way. She was focused on losing her way even when she was not entering the Rapture. She continued to contribute to each gathering, sometimes with new foods but often with new shapes and forms. In the quiet that followed the gatherings, she spent less and less of it at rest. She found resting difficult while wondering how and why she lost her way in travelling the path to the Rapture.

She did not know the reason she lost her way. The endowment was silent. She knew only that she had not been able to follow the Spark without losing her way. She did not understand what was preventing her from observing a segment of the path. Humans, in their time, will preach: 'Knock, the door will open; ask, and receive'; those are not truths. There might be doors that cannot be opened; questions which cannot be answered. There might be hurdles which cannot be overcome. Hu did not know this to be true because the endowment did not say so and the Glorified thought any unexplored idea is possible. So, she tried again. She entered the Rapture. Her particles spread, and she was everywhere. That attempt at following the Spark was no different than any other. She let the Spark lead, and she lost her way as she expected. She allowed her particles to join the Mystery of Creation on its journey.

Her thoughts were about losing her way. She tried to recall the path to the Rapture. She saw the glow of the Spark as it entombs the form. The glow was not on the form. It was separated from it by a silvery lining. As she recalled the Rapture, she witnessed a golden part, a dark inner part, and a bright silvery lining inside the entombed glow of the Spark. The silvery lining was like the colour of the Mystery of Creation on a bright, sunny day. Humans often reference this part of the History. In the village, it was described as the silver lining of a cloud—before it was changed by the storytellers. They would say, 'Every dark cloud has a silver lining.' The storytellers attached meaning to that saying and presented it to others as wisdom. Hu was so focused on what she had not gained that she missed what she had done. Like humans would do, she had let the thing which she did not have take away the thing she had. If there were wisdom to be found in this part of the History, that would be it. For among humans, that is often the answer when humans wonder how they lost everything.

Focusing on what she had gained, Hu noticed the dark inner layer growing darker as it expanded. She was not certain whether the inner layer was expanding outwards or the golden part was flowing into it. She was certain, however, that as the golden part grew smaller, the inner layer grew darker, and in between them the silvery lining got brighter. She pushed the thought of losing her way aside. She had followed the Spark for many whiles as it entombed her form. Yet, she had not noticed this part of the journey. She no longer felt the Mystery of Creation or heard its melody as she realised that she may have overcome her inability to follow the Spark. She recalled the dark inner layer caressing her form in a gentle and tender manner, much like a mother's touch. There was no sound. The Spark travelled its path in silence. It was not the kind of silence that occurs when the ears are clogged. It was the kind of silence that occurred when the ears are clear, and there just isn't any sound. She examined the dark inner layer as it gently rubbed against her form. It was difficult for her to tell where her form ended and where the dark layer began. She observed the dark layer was made up of particles, similar to those of the Rapture. Like the particles of the Rapture, they were flowing, that movement was what caused the caressing of her form. That told her these particles were more than the particles of the Rapture. The physical form had never been able to feel the particles of the Rapture. Even if the particles completely covered the form, it was unaffected. The particles which caressed her form were different. If not different in nature, then certainly different in purpose.

The silvery part separating the dark inner layer from the golden part grew brighter. The brightness forced her to look away. It dimmed and darkened her sight. She could no longer see the dark inner layer or observe her form. She tried to focus on her form. She was trying to feel the caressing of the particles, but the gentle touch, too, was gone. Her eyes were darkened and her feelings were numbed. She was certain that was the point where the form of creation crumbled into particles. She focused, expecting to uncover how the particles were created. Instead, she saw the four-sided structure. There was still a gap in her recollection. There was still a part she did not observe. She still had not witnessed the creation of the particles, but she did not focus on losing her way. She had followed the Spark further along the path, and she started again to recall the Rapture, following it until she came to the familiar mound. Then, she recalled it again and again. She was trying to understand how she could have missed such changes in so many attempts at following the Spark.

After examining her attempt at following the Spark, she knew there were things, yet to be uncovered, along the path to the Rapture. She witnessed the darkening of her sight and recalled the loss of her feelings. Brightening her face, she recollected the discussion about the point along the path where the Glorified might and might not be. She slowly drifted back to herself, feeling the Mystery and hearing its melody. She was content with the outcome of following the Spark, uncovering there was more to the path of the Rapture. She had followed it almost to the point where the form of creation was made into particles. She decided to close her eyes before the silvery lining grew too bright in her next attempt. She then gathered her particles and returned to her physical form standing beside the Mystery of Creation. She thought of the forthcoming gathering and decided to create a new form for it.

CHAPTER 3

THE UNKNOWN

Hu did not know that she could exist in both the physical form and the Rapture at the same while. The Glorified had tried, but the *duality of being* was beyond their will and strength. They were certain the physical form was crumbled into particles; during the Rapture, the physical form could not be found in the Realm. So, they concluded that it *'became'* the particles of the Rapture. As the whiles passed, the assumption, like many human beliefs, became a truth among them. That certainty contributed to Hu's confusion in the announcement, since both ways of existing were within reach of each other. She focused her thoughts on the seat of the Spark, trying to raise her physical form into the circular assembly position. She was attempting to take control of the announcement in the same way she had done in following the Spark. She tried to symbolise the 'nothing' and the 'three parts of being'. She wanted the particles to spread, she wanted to use the strength of the Spirit's eye, but her physical form did not obey her command; the particles did not spread, and she realised she did not know that section of the Realm.

That part of the Realm was unknown to her. It had a Presence she had not felt in any other section of the Realm. The Presence felt wholly perfect. It felt more than her—it felt as though it was that section of the Realm. She wondered if the Presence was the reason she was restricted. She had never been restricted by any shape or form. She had existed in many different types of form. She had spent many whiles in the shape of her favourite form. It had a long stem, and atop the stem sat a circular bulb made of delicate red pieces. She would plant it in the Mystery of Creation. At whiles, she would let the red pieces drift along with the Mystery like petals floating on top of a stream. She would collect the Mystery of Creation by drawing it up through the stem and, reverting to her physical form, she would hold it in the cup of her hands. In making and changing shapes, in jumping from one form to another, Hu knew no limit to the command of her will. But the announcement was different. In that section of the Realm, the parts of her being were divided, like the Spark being divided into two but, unlike the Spark, restricted. The Rapture form seemed frozen. The particles seemed trapped within some kind of vessel. She waited to see if the Spark would complete its journey, but the Rapture form stood there, gazing into the distance.

The announcement was certainly a new experience for Hu. The History did not say so, but in the village, humans called it 'a frightening experience.' The Rapture and the physical were unmoved. They gazed off into the distance as silence enveloped her. She thought that the announcement was another attempt at following the Spark along its path. She did not know where along the path she might be. She knew the Rapture only waited in the mound of the particles, and the *duality of being* was beyond her will. In following the Spark along its path, she had never come to a point where both the physical and Rapture coexisted, but she had not been able to follow the Spark without losing her way. She wondered if she could be at a point along the path after her eyes were darkened but before the making of the four-sided structure.

Her physical form rested on its back, with her arms comfortably at her side. Her eyes were closed, giving her the look of someone meditating or peacefully at rest. A warm, calming, and welcoming light appeared around her face and head like a halo. The gentle and pleasing aura that graced her face did not betray her confusion. She continued to observe herself from outside herself. Her fingers and toes were in perfect proportion to the rest of her form. Her hands were open and seemed soft and gentle. There was slow and deliberate movement in her chest. She marvelled at the consciousness that could create such perfection from 'nothing'. 'It is a perfect creation', she said. Humans in their while would think of the Divine and add, 'He is great' or 'Praise him'. That is not the way of the Glorified.

Hu gazed off into the distance as far as she could, and with closed eyes, looked around her. She knew the Realm as if it were an extension of herself–a place, space, or time where the Glorified created bread, ale, and music; where she attended gatherings, laughed, and danced with the others; and where in the *whiles of quiet*, she wandered freely, contemplating the purpose of their lives and the reasons for their existence. She had seen the Realm through the perspective of many forms and shapes. Yet she could not identify this part of it. The idea that there might be a section of the Realm which has not been explored filled her with anticipation, but it did not last. It was not possible that the Seven had missed a section of the Realm. They had explored it at ever-increasing speeds. They travelled through it so slowly humans would have thought they were standing still. Yet she did not recognise this part of it. She did not know where she was and wondered if that, too, could be a reason for the restrictions.

The Glorified had never known any restriction. In the announcement, Hu was both more and less at the same while. She existed in both the physical form and the Rapture, even though she knew that type of *duality* lay beyond the Glorified. Motion is characteristic of the Glorified, yet she could not raise her physical form. The Rapture always completes its journey, but she could not cause the particles to spread. She wondered if the *duality of being* was a reduction of 'self', recalling the notion about fractions of themselves. She was confused. She did not know how she had gained the *duality of being*. She surveyed the physical form and observed the Rapture at the same time. She waited to see if it would complete its journey. She could not raise her form, the particles did not spread, but for the first since she began existence, she looked upon the Spark within her.

Her hands were perfect images of each other: two halves that made a whole. They were open, with the thumbs resting beside the palms. Her fingers were slightly raised, forming a small cup. Every human can make a cup with their hands, used for giving and receiving. Looking at herself from above herself, she could see that the palms were vessels–not just for giving and receiving, but also the seat of the Spark. In each palm, reclining as if in a state of comfortable rest, was an opposite image of the Spark. The Spark flowed gently into the fingers and the thumb as if it were a creature with four legs and one arm. The fingers on each hand held the same part of the Spark. The History says that either hand can represent the Spark, and in the endowment, it is said, 'The Spark indicates the way towards *nia*.' Hu knew a Glorified could not look upon the Spark within him or her, so she started to consider other explanations. She could not recall entering the Rapture, and it had not completed its journey. There were no sections in the Realm that felt so full of 'nothing'. She searched the endowment, wondering what she had done to open this path.

She recalled that she had just returned from a gathering which she attended in a shape that required her to walk on four legs. The form had a long tail with a tuft of hair at the end. Its body was sleek and supported by four muscular limbs. There was hair around its neck that looked like an overgrown beard. The thick mass of hair fell over the front legs, resembling a chest plate. This form, with its hair mainly behind its ears and around its neck, had a thin, lipless mouth. Its face was flat with deep-set but keen-looking eyes, and its mouth displayed an impressive set of teeth. The mouth could open wide. In front, as if to mark corners, were four long teeth—two on top and two on the bottom. The size of the four teeth gave the form a fierce appearance when Hu smiled. It was a unique form that Hu had created, but the Glorified Seven hardly noticed her contribution. She was outdone by another of the Seven and was practically ignored during the gathering.

The other Seven also created a four-legged form with a much shorter tail. The form was huge. Everything about it was large or overgrown. Its legs were overgrown and heavy, designed to carry a very heavy body. The ears were big, and the others thought the ears might provide enhanced hearing. However, the Glorified did not have any additional hearing. The ears were simply for show, and he used them to amuse the others. He created quite a storm by moving his ears back and forth, blowing over food and drinks. The form and its oversized ears held the attention of the others, including Hu. She shared in the joy of the merriment. She felt no lack of contentment at being outdone. Even more amazing than the ears were the two large teeth that protruded from its cheeks, which measured three bits long. The other Sevens wondered how it could use its teeth. The teeth were complemented by a nose of similar length. He used it in the manner of a hand to put food and drink in his mouth, which was hidden beneath his nose. He amused and entertained the others with his ears and nose. The glows of the Sparks brightened with the sharing of creativity, and there was much eating, drinking and dancing.

Recalling that she had drunk much at the gathering, Hu was about to dismiss the announcement as an effect of ale. She knew the Realm had only seven sections. She knew she could be either in the physical or the Rapture, not both together; she knew a Glorified could not look upon the Spark within him or herself; but above all, she knew ale could have unknown and unpredictable effects. Hu allowed her gaze to drift back to her form as she listened to the silence in the announcement. She was thinking about the gathering, about the form the other Seven had created. She was starting to brighten her face when she saw a Creature—or a Being—whom she had never seen before standing on her physical form. She tried to move her Rapture form closer to the Creature. She attempted to raise her physical form, but again, she could not. She did not have the strength to move her form, and once more, her limitedness surprised her.

CHAPTER 4

THE ANNOUNCEMENT

The Creature standing on her ribs forced her to reconsider her assumption that the announcement was an effect of ale. The Creature was real. She felt its sharp toes gripping onto her form. That, in itself, was new for her. The toes pressing into her form gave her an uncomfortable sensation for the first since their beginning. That was the first any feeling of touch, of life, could be described as unfamiliar. The sensation was gone as quickly as it came. The Creature spread its limbs and leapt off her form, leaving her to wonder about the unfamiliar sensation. She looked at the Creature, which seemed to be waiting. She saw that it had five toes on each foot. The toes were not like the toes of the Glorified. The Creature's toes were thin, pointy— almost bone-like. They looked like fingers that had been misplaced and used as feet. The Creature's feet resembled the human hand if the thumb pointed towards the body and the fingers pointed outwards. The toes were connected directly to the shin. The legs were stick-like and covered with scaly yellow skin. The head was unlike any Hu had ever seen. None of the forms the Seven created had a head resembling this Creature's head. Its face had two distinct sides, each with a nostril, and its beady eyes, brown and clear as the Mystery of Creation, looked in opposite directions. The Creature looked off into the distance and also kept an eye on Hu.

The Creature's mouth was not like the mouth of the Seven or humans. It was not broad, but narrow; not soft, but hard and pointy. Hu tried again to move her form to pick up the Creature. She wanted to see if she would experience the unfamiliar sensation again. The Creature's entire body was covered in a strange material. The material added mass to the body, but not weight. There were individual pieces that lay on top of each other, covering the body. Hu could see each piece was stuck to the body like leaves on a branch. The Creature did not stand upright. Its body was elongated. It seemed like it should be standing on four limbs, not just two. Half of its body was in front of its legs, and both its head and hind part, which could be considered a tail, were the same height. Hu had difficulty focusing on the Creature. 'If the Creature is real, then this experience is real, not just an effect of ale', she said in a confused tone. She started looking for the seat of the Spark in the Creature. It occurred to her that if the Creature was a form created by one of the others, she would be able to recognise the Spark. The Spark is that part of the First, the Self-Generator's creations that cannot be concealed. The Glorified used the Spark to identify each other. Even though it could choose to locate itself anywhere in the form, the Spark is most often found in its vessels.

The hands were not where they were supposed to be, so she thought the Spark might be in the feet of the Creature. Once more, she tried to move her form to get closer to the Creature. Her inability to reposition herself caused her to be slightly confused at her lack of motion. Never before had she been denied motion. In the village, humans added to this part of the History. They would say, 'Fear nothing but the secret one.' That indicated to them that if Hu were human, she would have suspected danger and fear would arise in her. The very idea of fear never occurred to any of the Seven. It was not until a while after the birth of humans that trepidation as a condition was given meaning. Equally, the idea of happiness never intruded upon their thoughts. That is because fear and happiness are human emotional conditions arising out of need and want. Those conditions would be among the ebbs and flows of human beings. They have led to false truths, causing the loss of the wisdom in hesitation. Fear is the foundation of hate, and happiness stands on the shoulders of love; both overpowered the will of humans, blinding them to the truth. What human beings say, do, or believe is coloured by either fear or happiness.

Those conditions were unknown to the Glorified. The First, the Self-Generator, did not include symbols for them in the endowment. There are no words in the endowment or among the Glorified to describe love, hate, fear, or happiness. Those are purely human emotions. There is no reason for those conditions among the Glorified. The Glorified need not, and they want not. They were created with full mastery of their physical and spiritual abilities. It could be said that they have peace in being and add joy to their peace through sharing. They share in each other's creativity. They give without expecting to receive. They have without wanting. The Glorified exist in the Realm, a place of freedom from the human burdens, where abundance is far greater than need. Fear did not arise in Hu. Even though she was restricted, she continued to search the Creature for a Spark.

In place of arms, the Creature had limbs, which were folded close to its body. The limbs were where the shoulders would be if the Creature stood upright. Their shape and size did not suggest they could be used for giving and receiving. In both Glorified and humans, the Spark has its vessels, which are used for giving and receiving. Hu wondered where the Spark resided in this Creature. Unable to locate the seat of the Spark in the Creature, she began to wonder if the Creature had a Spark, turning her attention to its eyes.

She did not know a creature could exist without a Spark because there were no other creatures in the Realm. There were no birds, no creatures of the sea, no cattle, and no creeping things. She had no knowledge of any other forms of life, except the first truth of creation. The Glorified are not the First, the Self-Generator, so they do not know everything in creation. The First, the Self-Generator, is a knowing Being; only *It* knows everything. The Creature was unknown to Hu because the First, the Self-Generator, did not include knowledge of it in the endowment.

Hu gazed into the Creature's eyes, searching them as if the eyes were windows to the Spark. As she did, she felt a change in the Spark within her. She wondered if the Creature's eyes affected her Spark's Spirit, but the feeling continued to grow even after the Creature looked away. She looked at the vessels of the Spark. It was the first she had seen the Spark within herself. The Glorified cannot look upon their Sparks, which was one of the reasons she had assumed the experience was an effect of ale. She could see her Spark was slightly different from that of the others. That was how the others recognised her. The Sparks were not all the same; each had a slight variation. This variation in the Spark was how each Seven was known. As she looked at the Spark, there was a sudden wave of contentment within it. It was filled with anticipation beyond anything Hu had experienced. It felt as if the Spark was approaching a *beginning again,* much like human beings nearing the end of a journey.

The anticipation in her Spark continued to grow. The Rapture form began to change into the colours of the 'three parts of being' as the particles started to drift back towards her palms. They started slowly, like morning mist being blown by a gentle breeze. As more and more particles re-entered the vessels, the process became faster and more forceful. She noticed the Spark within her had grown not in size, but in presence. She had followed the Spark, felt the gentle caress within its glow, but had never felt the Spark itself. The vessels of the Spark knocked, and her vision dimmed, then darkened. It reminded her of the path towards the Rapture. As the particles were forced back into her, the knocking in the vessels intensified. Humans still reference this part of the History. They expect to receive when their palms knock. In their beginning, they expected to receive a task. That, too, has been changed to meet the needs of the storytellers. Humans no longer think of their Sparks when their palms knock or as humans say itch, instead they expect a reward to come. All around her was a medley of colours as the particles were forced into their vessels, and the knocking intensified.

She always recalled the moment, to use a human term, when her Rapture particles were forced back into her physical form because she felt the place, space, or time closing in on her. That told her that she was not alone, even though she saw no one, heard no one, and her physical form did not move; she knew she was not alone. The particles flowing back into their vessels caused her to feel whole again. The emptiness, the void she felt within her was no longer there. She was at peace; the movement in her chest did not change. She tried again to rise to her feet but found she could only raise her form to a sitting position. She bent her knees and sat on her heels. Then, she positioned the vessels to symbolise 'nothing' and the 'three parts of being', while the feeling in the Spark grew more intense. The Creature seemed to recognise the symbol. It spread its limbs and started to jump around in circles, as if dancing to the beat of its own drum. The Creature knew. It was waiting, and the beginning was almost upon them. Hu's thoughts, on the other hand, were drifting like the particles of the Rapture. The Spark drummed, and the Creature danced while Hu was on her knees, having an experience she did not understand.

She was on her knees, not because she needed to humble herself, but because the space above her had been filled by a Presence. The Presence was on her, and she held herself firm to prevent the 'nothing' from closing in any further. She wondered if she would be pushed from this place, space, or time. Had she intruded upon it, as light intrudes upon darkness or sound upon silence? She braced herself against the Presence, yet she felt that she was moving. She sat up straight with her weight on her heels, as she started to expand outwards. She was no longer outside herself, looking upon herself. She had joined a greater Presence or been given a greater 'self'. She affirmed that her kneeling form had not moved. It was covered in a glow, as if she had entered the Rapture. The glow seemed to mingle with the colour of 'nothing', brightening the place, space, or time. At this point in the telling of the History, humans have always asked, 'What is the colour of nothing?' That question reflects the restriction upon human beings. Something that is 'nothing' yet has a colour seems just beyond their reach. Before ritual societies, humans would remember their limitation before usurping the divine, before speaking of It in vain as though It has compulsions.

Hu had grown beyond herself. She was a part of creation in a way she never thought a Glorified could be. Despite her abilities, despite knowing that she was one with the First, the Self-Generator, she never thought she could be creation. With her greater 'self', she felt she could rise to her feet or spread the particles, but she knew standing, sitting, or lying down did not matter. She knew spreading the particles would give her no more, for there is no beyond the First, the Self-Generator. Expanding in all directions, the place, space, or time was widening.

The 'nothing' seemed to be moving away, creating space for her greater *self* to fill. She saw everything she knew to be creation, including the Presence. She saw the other six members of the Seven as they rested. She was outside of the Realm, and yet she was in the Realm. She flowed throughout the Realm and became part of it. She was the generator of plenty. She had travelled with the Mystery of Creation, but in the announcement, she became the Mystery. She was the Presence within it, not merely her particles drifting along with it. She could hear its voice. The sweet, rugged melody—which even humans are familiar with—is its tongue. She focused on the Mystery and understood its sounds to mean, 'Creation began with the First, the Self-Generator...' She wanted to dwell with it, to listen to its tales, to ask and be answered by it. She repeated the sounds of the Mystery. She did not know that the Mystery of Creation told a story of the beginning. She wanted to wait, to listen, but she felt she was drifting away. Her focus shifted as she continued to expand outwards.

There were more and more circles of her *self*, with her form of creation on its knees in the middle of it all. When human ritual societies preach that a humble man must be on his knees in the presence of the divine, they are referencing this part of the History of Creation. That is not a truth—not for the Glorified, and not for humans. It is not found among the truths of creation. The First, the Self-Generator, has made no request for humans to be on their knees in *Its* presence. Such a request would require humans to live their lives on their knees. That preaching is not part of the purpose of creation; it is usurping the divine, speaking of *It* in vain.

Hu looked upon each of the Seven. Each was still at rest from the last gathering, and their thoughts shifted between what had happened at the gathering and what their contribution to the next gathering should be. She could see, hear, and feel everything the Seven were thinking and planning. That was what she expected when they thought they could connect to one another to gain the 'simultaneousness of being'. They could not connect to each other, and as she lingered with the Seven, she understood why. She was connected to the others by the Presence in all things. They needed to *be* the Presence in each other to see, hear, and feel what one another was seeing, hearing, and feeling.

She was surprised that even at rest they were still thinking and planning. She recalled the last gathering. She was certain the form with the oversized ears and elongated nose was more creative than the form she had contributed. The Seven who contributed it was less certain. He thought Hu's form might have been more creative than his. He liked the sound she made when she laughed. She smiled, then heard him resolve to be more creative for the next gathering. He began to focus on creating a form which would again have four legs. She caught a glimpse of the form in his thoughts. It had a short tail and a small head perched on top of a long neck, but there was something else about this Seven. He was not simply trying to make the best contribution he could to the gathering. There was something that Hu had not felt in herself. It seemed he was in need. He had a need which appeared unfulfilled. Whatever it was she knew it was empty, and yet, he coveted it. She tried to wait to see if she could understand what such a thing could be. Her focus shifted again, like with the Mystery of Creation, but not before wondering what a Glorified could possibly need that had not been provided by creation.

Hu recalled her own thoughts during the *whiles of quiet*. She did not plan her contribution to the gathering while at rest. She spent the *whiles of quiet* in thought, letting her mind flow freely—mostly contemplating the purpose of their being. The gatherings always filled her with contentment. She loved—to use a human emotional symbol— the gatherings, and contributed to each one. She especially loved the whiles of 'collective creativity'. The creation of the *ndo* was an example of the *harambe* of 'collective creativity'. The Seven pulled together and brought into being something that did not exist. In fact, it was Hu who started the process, which ended in the creation of the first *ndo* or musical instrument, as humans would say.

That instrument would also be created on Earth, but it was first created in the Realm. The Seven were created with an affinity for music. There would be groups of human beings who others would say 'have rhythm and can sing and dance.' That statement would equally apply to the Glorified. Hu and the others were singing. She wanted to add to the sound, so she started to clap her hands. After the others started clapping, she added more sound by stomping her feet. The clapping and stomping were slightly out of step. That was how the first musical instrument was created. The story of the *ndo* was one of the first stories the Glorified told to human beings. It was among the stories found in the village. Fragments of it could still be found, even in this present while.

The Glorified were singing, which humans interpreted to mean they were happy. Happiness and sadness are human terms and ought not be used in reference to the Glorified or the First, the Self-Generator. The Glorified sang and danced at their gatherings. Their singing voices accompanied them as they worked. In the whiles of 'collective creativity', they would sing as they explored and created together. Humans use singing in the same way. Every human—from nursing mothers to work gangs—can testify that singing makes the work easier.

The human story recalling the creation of the *ndo* was often passed down in the form of a song. That, too, was a result of the Glorified singing. The song started with the line: *'If you are singing and want music, clap your hands.'* Most humans have never heard this song because it has been changed by the storytellers. It became about happiness, about clapping and stomping if they were happy. Though much has been lost since the story was first told, the instrument—the drum—was carried from the village to the mountains and valleys of the Earth. Like other stories, the story of the first musical instrument would first be changed to meet the needs of the storytellers. Then, after humans spread themselves far and wide, the tale was no longer passed down, but the drum would be found in every nook and cranny of the Earth. Everywhere humans found themselves, the drum would also be there.

The story humans were told about the first instrument was actually the story about how the idea of the instrument occurred to Hu. The tale referenced what Hu had done. After the others clapped their hands and stomped their feet, Hu bent her knees and started to tap her thighs. She tapped the outside of the thigh, then moved her hand over her thigh, tapping the inside of her thigh with the back of the hand. She did the same on the other thigh, and then both together. She heard a different sound from tapping her thighs than from clapping her hands. The human song said, *'hands and thighs together.'* The song may have been lost, but hands clapping and thighs tapping to make music are still found among humans.

The instrument was not created at the gathering where the Glorified were clapping, stomping, and tapping. Hu made the instrument after she rose from a *while of quiet*. She brought the first instrument to a gathering to contribute to the merriment. It had a thin membrane, stretched over a circular base. The middle was a circular shaft, half the diameter of the top. Both ends of the instrument had the same shape and size, but the membrane on each end was of different thickness. When this musical instrument was created in the Realm, it was called *ndo*. The *ndo* had three distinct parts. The two ends looked similar but produced different sounds. Each end had pegs to secure the membrane to the top. The Glorified not only beat on the membrane to produce sound, they also pulled on the strings and tapped on the pegs.

That gathering was all about sound. Each Glorified took turns playing the *ndo*. After taking turns, they played it together. They drummed on the membranes at both ends, then tapped on the middle—which sounded as the tapping of the thighs—and they also pulled on the strings, and beat the pegs. One end of the *ndo* was beaten, then there would be a slight pause as though it were waiting for a response. The other end would answer, picking up where the first end left off. They explored the *ndo*. They beat it fast and slow. They created patterns in the drumming. They clapped and stomped, and sang and danced. They moved their feet in accordance with the drumming. They gyrated their waists, bent over and shook their shoulders. They did that while facing each other. They leaned in and shook their shoulders, and then they leaned away and whined their waists. They drummed loud at one end and answered at the other with a soft, slow tempo. The rhythm of the *ndo* seemed to shape the motion of the Glorified. They moved their whole body—fast or slow—depending on how the *ndo* was beaten.

Whether fast or slow, the *ndo* sounded as if it had something to say, and they took turns participating in its conversation. They called with one end and responded with the other, repeating and adding to the pattern, back and forth between the ends until it seemed like the *ndo* was telling a tale. Humans would discover how to do that as well, but it was in the Realm the drum was first made to speak. That gathering lasted a while. They were tired from the stomping, shaking, and gyrating. Before the gathering came to a close, a Glorified Seven declared, 'This was the best gathering, and Hu', she said, looking at her, 'is indeed a master of sound.'

The Glorified left the gathering for a *while of quiet*, with the sounds of the *ndo* echoing in their heads. Only Hu rested through the entire while. The others wanted to explore the *ndo*. They discussed the different parts of the *ndo* and the sound each part made. In those discussions, they returned to the basics of clapping their hands and stomping their feet, but it was the tapping of the thighs that held their attention. It was the sound that could be made to resemble the *ndo* most closely. Those discussions helped the Glorified prepare their contributions to the next gathering. There were five other *ndos* at the next gathering, each made by a different Seven and each designed to produce a distinct sound. There was a big circular *ndo* which made a deep and distinctive sound. One *ndo* was played with pegs instead of hands. They all thought of expanding on the *ndo*, except the Glorified who became known as Seh. He would be the one to create the form with the oversized ears. He would be the one to say, 'The Spark opens the way, but the Glorified chooses how to be.' He did not rest during the *while of quiet*. He spent that while working on his contribution for the next gathering. He was trying to do something none of the others had done. At the next gathering, he arrived last, so that the others would notice his contribution as he joined them.

The others were playing their *ndos* when Seh entered the gathering. Presenting his contribution required all of his focus. He began moving with the rhythm of the *ndos* but, when the others saw his contribution, they rose to their feet. For the first, there was a form unlike the Glorified in the Realm. They did not recognise Seh. He had transformed himself into a form that walked upright with a long tail. The form was tall when measured upright. Its height was half its size when it was measured from the tip of the tail to the top of the head. The head had an oblong shape and was attached to a neck that seemed to be made of only muscles. It had a big mouth with over sixty teeth. The others were astonished they had not known the Glorified could altered their shape. Seh had forced his form of creation into another shape, confusing the others. The form had two strong legs with three toes on each. Its arms were small—undersized—and appeared not to be usable. The others surrounded him. Their focus was on the form he had created. Seh wanted to make the most of the moment, so he demonstrated how the form could dance. He ran at great speed, pointing the tail upwards. When one of the Seven asked why the arms were so small, he picked up a *ndo*, the large round one, tossed it up, leapt after it, and caught it. He then put down the drum and played it, showing the arms were small but usable.

The Seven examined the form. Seh offered to share 'know-how', even though he was having difficulty maintaining the form. There were moments when he lost control of parts of it. Those parts melted back into the shape of their creation. After seeing the form, Hu wondered if she could transform into that shape. The Glorified knew, as it is with humans, that what one has done, the others can do. She ran the vessel of her Spark along the tail where the Spark within Seh had located itself. As her hand passed over his Spark, she saw a slight twinkle in its glow, then, without thinking, she transformed into the shape. She alone among the Seven duplicated the form and held it for a while before returning to her form of creation. Hu's form differed from Seh's only in size.

Her form had all the same features: the large mouth with many teeth, the tail, the muscular legs, and the tiny arms. Both forms standing next to each other would remind a human of an adult and a child. Hu was surprised at the ease with which she had gained the 'know-how'. She was content not because she had uncovered the path to the knowledge of forms, but because of the immense outpouring of creativity among the Seven. There were five other *ndos*, and 'know-how' to transform their forms of creation. She stepped back, brightening her face. She wanted to observe the Seven in that moment of giving and receiving—in that while of sharing.

The others were only able to create parts of the form Seh had created. One Glorified created the legs, another the tiny arms, and one Seven just managed the mouth with the teeth. Those were amusing to the Seven, and they laughed, ate, and drank before trying again. Seh, on the other hand, was not amused, and as the gathering continued, he had more difficulty maintaining the form. That disturbed Seh's peace. He had spent the while since the last gathering acquiring the 'know-how'. He was surprised that Hu had gained the knowledge. He found a kind of contentment in the struggles the others were having. As the others ate and drank, their efforts became less focused, and after a while, they stopped trying to gain the 'know-how'. They were back to playing the *ndos*, eating, drinking, and dancing. That was not what Seh had envisioned. He envisioned leaving the gathering in his new form and the others saying that he is indeed 'the master of transformation'. He expected to ask the others to spend the while gaining the 'know-how' and to come to him for further guidance. Instead, the others commented on the ease with which Hu had gained the 'know-how', and they asked Seh why he pursued the knowledge by himself.

The Seven did not understand the knowledge of forms. They did not see it as an outcome of 'collective creativity'. *Harambe* was not part of its uncovering. 'Is it not', they asked Seh, 'the way of creation to discuss an idea and uncover its path together?' Seh pointed out that the idea was mentioned at a circular assembly. The Glorified were discussing the creation of bread and the conversion of the Mystery of Creation into ale. In that discussion, he had wondered whether it was possible to convert their physical forms into something else. That was the only mention of it, and then the discussion moved on to the limitless possibilities for creativity within creation. The others did not recall the passing mention of transformation. They wondered if Seh had mentioned it or just thought of it. Seh answered their question about the way of creation by saying he wanted to offer the knowledge as a *gift* to them. Seeing their confusion, he added, 'In the same way Hu gave the *ndo* as a *gift*.' The Glorified were even more confused. They said Hu did not build the *ndo* as a *gift*. The *ndo* is merely a contribution to the gathering, much like the various breads and numerous ales, created during the quiet and brought to the gathering as an addition to what was already there. The *ndo* is an addition to the clapping of hands and the tapping of thighs. It is an expansion of the sounds the Seven made together. It is not a *gift*. *Gifts* are not things the Glorified can give.

Seh said his actions were not different from the actions of any other Glorified. Then he offered to share his knowledge, but the others knew transformation ought to have been a shared experience. Pursuing the knowledge together, the Seven would have acquired the knowledge at the same while. Only Seh and Hu had the 'know-how' at the gathering. It was the first that the knowledge of the Glorified was not the same. The Glorified were created with the same endowment. They were the same, except for male and female parts. It appeared they acquired knowledge at the same while when it was pursued together. Seh's actions departed from how knowledge was uncovered in the Realm. In the many whiles that followed, the Seven would continue to question Seh as to why he pursued the 'know-how' by himself. In those whiles, Hu would transform into Seh's original form. She would say, 'The knowledge is a valuable contribution to the gathering.' On these occasions, the others would be reminded that Hu had gained the 'know-how' at the gathering. They would comment on her creativity, saying she was 'not only a master of sound but also a master of forms.'

Hu's thoughts slowly drifted back to the announcement and what was happening. She was around and about the Realm. The Realm with its seven places, spaces, or times was itself small and minor compared to the depth and breadth of creation. She wondered about the size and shape of creation. Was it flat? Would she fall over the edge if she continued to expand outwards? Like a child who had been given too much information, Hu was dazed by creation. 'How many Realms could fit into creation?' she asked. She had grown beyond herself. She realised her thoughts were hers and not hers. Once again, she thought about the Creature, wondering whether creatures and beings could exist without Sparks. She felt the answer, heard the answer, and saw the answer. The omnipresence of the announcement was much greater than the 'simultaneousness' of the Rapture. 'Simultaneousness' allowed the Glorified to be everywhere, but it limited them to their own experience. They could see the Presence in creation, but could not hear it, join it or be it. She was not certain how to interpret the experience. Was she a part of creation, or was she creation? She glanced at her physical form. She noticed the Creature was once again standing on top of her form, but she could not feel its touch, as her form was covered by a glow.

The Creature's limbs were spread. Hu could see the same Presence in it as in everything, but the Creature did not have a Spark. Her thoughts were unclear and unfocused. She did not know where to begin to consider what was happening. Her thoughts drifted from the idea that the Creature had no Spark towards the question of, 'How?' How was she expanding beyond herself? She knew there was a 'nothing' there, which she felt was beyond her comprehension, but did not think of that which is greater than herself. Her initial reaction was that she had found a new way to exist. She had found a way to transcend being either form or Rapture, to be both at the same while. She knew the first truth of creation, but the First, the Self-Generator, was not part of Hu's ordinary thoughts and actions. The Glorified had not thought of the First, the Self-Generator, in any significant way before

48

the announcement. They knew they were created by *It*, but they had never called on *It* for help. They had never sought *Its* guidance. They had never attributed any of their actions, whether success or failure, to the will of the First, the Self-Generator. Yet they knew the first truth of creation: 'The First, the Self-Generator, exists.'

Hu was on her knees, with the vessels of the Sparks facing upwards. If she focused, she was the Glorified in the Realm, she was the Mystery of Creation telling its story of the beginning, and she was the Realm itself. If she concentrated, as she did while following the Spark, she was all those things. Yet she was still just herself, a small and minor part of creation. The omnipresence of the announcement connected her to the rest of creation. Her senses were inundated and she tried to search the endowment, but she was too unfocused to comprehend what was happening. Her *'self'* was expanding. Her form was entombed in a glow as her consciousness and senses flowed outwards. She could feel the warmth of the glow she thought was protecting her from the touch of the Creature. The Creature had settled on top of her entombed form. It seemed keen, as if it was again expecting an outcome. As Hu expanded outwards, she saw that there were several distinct rings surrounding her form; within the rings were spheres, each following its own path or orbit as humans would describe it. Hu brightened her face at the pattern, noticing the motion of each sphere. They were moving around her form, and the Creature without a Spark was observing them as if studying a plan.

Hu's thoughts drifted back to the *duality of being* as she noted the places and positions of the spheres in the rings around her form. She recalled the eleventh truth: 'Everything is possible for the First, the Self-Generator', before realising she was no longer flowing outwards. She had come to the edge of the glow that entombed her, and she had stopped expanding. Beyond the glow was 'nothing'; not the kind of nothing that humans know, but the kind of 'nothing' that is the First, the Self-Generator. The History says, 'Nothing' is the First, the Self-Generator's most favoured instrument. *It* creates things from 'nothing', including putting words in *Its* mouth, making *itself* the creator. That is how the First, the Self-Generator, came to be. Hu's senses and consciousness simply stopped expanding, as if the greater '*self*' she had been given had ceased growing. She did not know why she stopped. She sensed there was so much more to creation than what she had been shown. She stopped growing just beyond the glow that entombed her. Beyond that, everything was in darkness.

CHAPTER 5

AT THE END OF EVERYTHING

Hu's physical form was entombed in a glow. Yet she felt as though she stood at the end of everything she knew and at the beginning of 'nothing'. Her expanded '*self*' had ceased flowing, her thoughts, a little clearer. She was everything there was in creation—except the 'nothing'. At the edge of the glow, she knew what was happening in the Realm. She was the Realm—the generator of plenty. She was the seven sections and the seven Glorified. She was everything. She was everywhere—and yet she was merely herself on her knees, amid an experience she did not understand.

The 'nothing' stood just beyond the edge of the glow. It seemed separate from her as if it were an individual. Beyond the edge of the glow, there was no shape or form, just darkness of infinite width, breadth, and depth. She felt the contentment in the Spark—like making it home after a long journey. She listened while her Spark, consciousness, and senses stood before the 'nothing'. She stretched forth her hands, but the 'nothing' was beyond her reach. There was no sound, just an overwhelming sense of peace. Her knowledge of creation had grown. With the Rapture, the Glorified uncovered a Presence in all things. In the announcement, she was connected to that Presence. It revealed there is only one Being in creation, one Consciousness.

It cannot be heard, nor touched, yet it dwells in all things, like a second 'self'. At the end of everything and at the beginning of 'nothing', she said, 'Creation is a work of wonder, for out of one came many.'

Her face lit up as she heard, felt, and saw that a task was to be done. She understood it to be a new realm. It was the reason for the announcement. The Creature broke the silence with a loud 'cock-cock-koo', repeating it twice —as if in celebration of her insight. Her focus turned to the pattern revealed as she expanded outwards. It was still moving around her form. The glow that entombed her—like the golden sphere at the centre of the human universe—was to be part of the task. She noticed the things in the design. There were orbs and areas of darkness, resembling the *crossing*. Her thoughts drifted to the eighth truth: "To know the First, the Self-Generator, is to know 'nothing.'" She looked again upon the 'nothing', which surrounded her and all of creation. She did not understand how to begin to know the 'nothing'. The Glorified knew the First, the Self-Generator, only through the first truth of creation. The First, the Self-Generator, never walked with them nor talked with them, and there were no troubled waters for *It* to carry them over.

The announcement was a new, different experience. It gave Hu insight into creation, but she still did not know the 'nothing'. Though she was everything, she was not the 'nothing'. Only the First, the Self-Generator, could be everything and 'nothing'. As Hu stood at the end of everything and at the beginning of 'nothing', she knew that beyond everything, there is only 'nothing'. She paused, brightened her face, and beheld her form—and the Spark within her. She knew a Glorified should not be able to see the Spark within themselves. Then she recalled another truth about the First, the Self-Generator. As she consider that all things are possible for the First, the Self-Generator,

Hu concluded that this was the reason she could see the Spark within herself.

As she thought of the eighth truth, she realised she had not considered the First, the Self-Generator, when the announcement began. She had first looked to herself, thinking she had uncovered a new way of being. She had even thought of ale. She felt childlike for not considering the only thing that was more than her. She smiled—or she was smiled at. That reminded her that her thoughts were her thoughts and not hers as though she had a second 'self'. Her own thoughts began to wonder whether she could accomplish the task. She had failed to follow the Spark along its path without losing her way. She still did not uncover how the particles were made. Her thoughts drifted again like random ideas flowing into a human's mind. She saw the others preparing for a gathering. They were creating forms. The long-necked form she saw in the thoughts of Seh was almost complete. She saw him adding patterns to the form, with no two patterns the same. It was the form he planned while he rested.

A sparkle in her eyes enhanced her brightened face, recalling that her thoughts during the *whiles of quiet* were mostly about the reason for their being. She had failed at that as well. She had found no reason for their being other than that being is a *gift*. Her thoughts were brought back to the task at hand, as if her own thoughts about the reasons for their being did not matter. She set aside the thoughts about her failures and looked at the Creature as if they were entering a pact—a promise to fulfil the task together. She observed the pattern with the rings, spheres, and dark areas. She did not know how to create the design—especially the dark areas—nor how the Presence in all things would become part of it. She thought: the First, the Self-Generator, is always there and would be there in the outcome.

At the end of everything, Hu knew her knowledge had been expanded. 'Existence', she said, 'is a *gift*, but creation is the First, the Self-Generator.' "*It* opened a place, space, or time within creation to share the '*gift of being*'", she added, as her thoughts again rambled away from the task. Human beings once understood creation in that way. They no longer know creation as the First, the Self-Generator. The knowledge that *It* opened a place, space, or time for them to journey from the marketplace to home over the whiles had been changed to suit the purposes of the storytellers. Humans think *It* created heaven and earth, but they lost the knowledge that what the First, the Self-Generator, created was '*Itself*'. That was what Hu understood in the announcement.

Her expanded '*self*' began to flow again. The 'nothing' began to gently push her, moving her back towards her form. She was still at the end of everything and at the beginning of 'nothing', but it was the 'nothing's' turn to expand. The place, space, or time, which the 'nothing' opened so she could grow and become one with the Presence in all things, was now closing. The 'nothing' was pushing her like a shepherd driving his flock. As she was slowly pushed back towards herself, her thoughts were mostly her own. She wanted to be the Presence in all things for as long as she could, to be creation forever and a more, but the announcement was coming to a close. She started to think about the glow of her Spark. Would it brighten the whole section for the task? She heard the Mystery of Creation again saying, "In the beginning, the First, the Self-Generator, created *Itself* from 'nothing' and the First, the Self-Generator, was all that there was; *It* was everything and *It* was 'nothing'. *It* was creation, and creation was without form and covered with darkness." She listened as the Mystery told its tale, and she called the Mystery her favourite thing in creation. She had spent many whiles with it, but she did not know it told a tale of the beginning.

She knew the story of creation, but the Mystery had been a witness to creation for a while before the Glorified. 'After creating the Mystery, the First, the Self-Generator, hovered over the Mystery for a while. A while could be a long time, a short time, or no time at all. In creation, there were only the First, the Self-Generator, and the Mystery', it said. Hu looked at the pattern again to see where the Mystery would fit. There were no signs of it in the design. She was moving back towards herself like the particles moving towards the dark depth at the *crossing*. She was trying to be with the Mystery. She wanted to hold on to it for as long as she could, but she knew the announcement had to close for the task to begin. Humans understand how she felt as the announcement came to a close. They reference this part of the History by saying, 'When one door is closed, another is opened.'

The 'nothing' surrounded Hu like it surrounds creation. She was standing at the end of everything she knew and at the beginning of 'nothing'. As the 'nothing' closed in around her, she felt cuddled as in a mother's arms. If this were to be the reason for her being, she would long for the Mystery and the gatherings. She again felt as if she were smiling or being smiled at. The Creature perched on top of her began to drum at the glow, entombing her form. The Creature bumped its mouth against the glow as Hu took another look at the Spark within her. She wondered if her Spark was bright not because it had returned home after a long journey, but because it had been asked to be of service. She knew from her own experience that Sparks are most noticeable in whiles of sharing. The Creature continued to peck at the glow as if it wanted Hu to be free. It bopped its head up and down, and the glow began to crack and chip away. She looked at the

Spark as her senses and consciousness were once again limited to her form. She was no longer the Presence in all things. The sense of standing at the end of everything and at the beginning of 'nothing' was gone. She was entombed in the glow. She could not rise to her feet or enter the Rapture because the place, space, or time that had been opened for her had been closed. She saw the Creature as it interrupted its drumming. She stretched forth her hands, reaching for the Presence in all things. But she lost her way as if she were following the Spark into the Rapture. She regained consciousness in her physical form. It was as if she had risen from a *while of quiet*. Hu felt rested. She felt new, like she had been created again. She looked at the vessels of the Spark to see whether she could see the Spark within her. She did not expect to see the Spark, but the Creature standing a short distance away intruded upon her inspection. Its presence affirmed the announcement. It reminded Hu that there was a task to be done.

CHAPTER 6

ALL THINGS COME TO AN END

The Creature was waiting. Hu moved towards the Creature and offered it her hand. Without hesitation, the Creature stepped onto the vessel of the Spark. Hu expected to experience the unfamiliar sensation of touch once more. The Creature's touch was neither unusual nor unfamiliar. She felt its pulse, and she heard the rhythm of its heart. She searched the Creature again for a Spark. She knew the Creature had *nia*, and a part in the task. She wanted to affirm that a creature could exist without a Spark. After searching the Creature, she looked at the object which stood next to it. The object was rectangular, with a light brown colour. It was open at the top; and the sides were solid but thin. Inside the object was the pattern from the announcement. She picked it up; a design was imprinted on it, outlining the task to be done. Hearing this part of the History, humans would ask Hu: Did she know then that she had the whole world in her hands? Hu would say, 'That is not possible. Only the First, the Self-Generator, could have the whole world in *Its* hands.' Then Hu would remind humans of the sixth truth of creation: 'Only the First, the Self-Generator, knows what *It* might or might not do.' She was referring to the Creature and the object, which seemed to be the last things created from 'nothing'. There would be nothing else known to the Glorified or humans that would be created from 'nothing'. Why the First, the Self-Generator, created so few things, the endowment does not say. It could only affirm the truth: that 'no one knows what *It* might or might not do.'

Hu put the object and the Creature down so she could follow the Spark into the Rapture. She entered the Rapture and found herself in the four-sided structure. Again, she did not uncover how the particles of the Rapture were created, but for the first, she sensed she knew the reason. She easily opened the Spirit's eye. The others were at a gathering; she visited the Mystery of Creation, looking at it as if she had never seen it before. She thought that this Rapture might be the closing of one place, space, or time before the opening of another.

She gathered her particles and allowed them to fall upon the Creature. She was trying to be one with the Creature in the same way she had been one with other things in the Realm. The Creature jumped with a loud sound—similar to clucking—and shook its form to rid itself of the particles. Hu then let her particles fall upon the container and spent a while observing the Creature. She noticed that the Creature was looking directly at her. It was as if it could see her in the Rapture. She moved behind the container to hide herself from the Creature; the Creature followed. She saw the same Presence in the Creature as in everything. The Creature carried a Sphere, and there was an additional Presence within it. The Sphere resembled the Spark in colour. It had not been there in the announcement, and she knew it was not a Spark. If it were a Spark, it could not be kept out of sight, and it would brighten its glow in the presence of the Spark within her. She recalled the Creature drumming on the glow that entombed her and the glow cracking and chipping away. She did not see what the Creature did with each piece. She wondered if part of the Creature's role was to entomb her in the glow, like the 'nothing' had done during the announcement. She did not know how that would be done, but she thought the Creature's golden Sphere also had a part in the task.

She felt the Creature's eyes on her. It was eager, as if it knew they had an appointment—and that it would be a long journey. Hu again offered the Creature her hand; it flapped its limbs and landed on her shoulder. She picked up the container and began what she thought would be her last journey in the Realm. She walked in silence, considering how she would position herself and arrange the spheres. She glanced at the design on the container to reassure herself she knew how the spheres should be placed, and how they should flow around the bright, glowing centre. The Creature might have other insights into the task, and about the place, space, or time for the design. The first part of the task, she thought, is the breaking of the seal. The seal must first be broken before entering the place, space, or time that has been prepared. Once the seal is broken, she would let the Spark lead, and journey beyond the Realm. She looked at the Creature, reaffirming their pact to carry out the task together. She then took a step, and another, as she chose her path through the Realm.

The Glorified had spent many whiles in the section where the seal was to be found. It was the section where the Mystery of Creation began its journey. They always marvelled at how the Mystery of Creation appeared. In their physical form and with their particles, they had followed it until it *began again*. They had tried to uncover its source. It seemed never-ending. The further they travelled, trying to see the first drop, the further away it seemed to be. They said, 'The Mystery has no beginning and no end; the last of it is the first of it, like creation itself, without beginning and without end.' She wondered how a seal could exist within the Realm and yet remained hidden from the Glorified. Her walk slowed as she searched the endowment to see whether there were any indications of a seal before the announcement. She wondered if the seal was newly created or just being revealed for the Glorified to see. She decided that, before breaking the seal—before becoming the centre of the First, the Self-Generator's design—she would enter the Rapture to see whether the seal could be seen with the Spirit's eye.

The Creature started jumping from her shoulder to her arm. She brightened her face, recalling that in the announcement, she was not smiling alone. She had gained insight into creation, a better understanding of how places, spaces, or times came to be. They exist because the First, the Self-Generator, exists. *It* created the place, space, or time—filled with creation—by withdrawing *Itself*. It is similar to the way darkness withdraws itself from a place, space, or time so that light can have a place to be. Hu knew the first truth of creation: 'The First, the Self-Generator, exists', but the announcement gave substance and meaning to that truth. Hu thought the design would be similar to being in the announcement. It would fill the place, space, or time which had been created for it.

The Creature continued to jump from her shoulder to her arm without disturbing her thoughts. The glow of the Spark within her could not fill a section of the Realm. She wondered if it would be bright enough to light the entire place, space, or time of the design. She wanted its glow to reach the farthest points—so it could be upon everything in the design. She thought about being the centre of the plan and quickened her steps, as if she, too, had decided that they had an appointment with destiny.

The Creature settled on her shoulder. It looked at the path already travelled and the road still to come. They were both filled with anticipation. In the distance, they heard the sound of a *ndo* like humans having a party. The Creature tilted its head slightly as it listened. Hu knew the sound. It was the sound of a gathering. She had not thought of the others since beginning the journey towards the seal. She wondered if she should put aside the task to join the merriment. As they neared to the sound, the Creature seemed settled, as if deciding that, although it would be wonderful to meet the others, to attend a gathering, and to share the tale of the announcement, they should not delay. Hu picked up her pace as they passed the gathering. She recalled the *duality of being*, the *gift* of the greater '*self*', and the contentment of the Spark in the announcement. She longed for the omnipresence of the announcement. She wanted to be the Presence in all things again, and she exhaled slowly, saying to herself, 'All things come to an end.'

She had not thought of an end in that way before, 'Is that true?' she asked herself. 'Do all things come to an end?' She knew there were things in creation without end. The Mystery of Creation had no end, and the First, the Self-Generator, is the beginning without end. There are things that have not ended, but could all things come to an end? The announcement ended. The place, space, or time created for her, ended when she was shepherded back towards herself. She quietly began to explore the meaning of 'coming to an end', leaving the sounds of the gathering behind.

She was deep in thought, walking quickly, when someone asked if she had not heard the sound of the *ndo*. Seh had told the others to start the gathering without her. Yet he wondered why she had not arrived. After a while, he stepped away from the gathering to find her. He could have entered the Rapture and used the Spirit's eye, but instead chose to maintain the form he had created and moved quickly through the Realm. Seh thought Hu might still be resting due to the strength of the ale he had prepared for the last gathering. She was not far from the others. She had passed the place where the others were gathered, when Seh found her. He did not know what to think— she had not created a form like he expected. He assumed she would be more creative for this gathering, given that her last contribution had been almost as creative as his. This was her chance to do better than 'the master of transformation', he thought.

At the last gathering, they both created forms with four limbs. Hu's form had hair around its shoulders that fell down in front of its chest, while Seh's form was big and heavy with oversized ears and an elongated nose, which functioned like a hand. He thought her form was creative, but it was his form that was the centre of attention. He used the form to amuse the others, and he noticed the others were more focused on him. He knew she had noticed too, and assumed it would inspire her to be more creative for this gathering. Seh was more concerned with himself and did not notice the Creature. He wanted to ensure his contribution was better than any other form at the gathering. He stood behind her in the form with the long neck, the four almost-straight legs, and the short tail, just like Hu had seen during the announcement. He wanted to confirm he had been more creative than her.

'The gathering has started', he said. Hu turned to face Seh. She recognised the form as the one she had seen in the announcement; it was another confirmation. She searched his form for the Spark. She wanted to see if that strange tinge of need was still there. Seh's Spark was bright and seemed to be growing brighter. She commented on the form. Seh appeared content with her comments. But, he waited a while to see if she would call him 'the master of transformation' before spreading the front legs apart, bringing his shoulders forward and his long neck down in order to bow for her. She smiled at the form, an awkward, odd-looking, disproportionate form, knowing it matched exactly what she had seen in the announcement. The small head, the pointed ears, and two short poles between the ears. The neck of the form was angled in such a way that it could not reach down without spreading the front legs apart. She commented, 'Such sharing, a wondrous form', but, as if to remind her that they should not delay, the Creature began jumping from her shoulder to her arm again. Seh had not noticed the Creature or the container in her hands. He was taken by surprise and shaken back into his form of creation. It had been a while since Seh had lost control of a form. The Glorified could transform into any shape or form they chose. Seh had not had any difficulty maintaining a form since the knowledge of forms was revealed. Over the whiles, nothing had caused him to be shaken back into his form of creation. Seeing the Creature jump from Hu's shoulder to her arm caused him to take a step back, as he lost control of his form and melted back into his form of creation.

Seh had uncovered the knowledge of forms, which he called the 'knowledge of transformation'. The others questioned him as to why he pursued such knowledge by himself. Seh always responded in the same way: he wanted to provide the knowledge as a *gift*. The others would conclude that *gifts* were not things a Glorified could give. There were no symbols among the Glorified to properly describe what Seh had done in pursuing transformation by himself. He drifted away from the path, making the straight crooked, the broad narrow, and hindering the purpose of creation. He had departed from the way knowledge was uncovered, and the others did not know why. Humans would call it an act for himself, but there were no symbols among the Glorified to describe it in that way. Seh wanted to be set apart and be acknowledged as 'the master of transformation'. He did not share that desire with the others. He would simply say he offered the knowledge as a *gift*.

Compared to the *ndo*, transformation had not grown, nor had it been transformed by the others in any way. It had not been explored neither alone nor together. The *ndo* grew through sharing; it was seen as the outcome of 'collective creativity'. The Glorified gathered in small groups, in combinations of twos, threes, or fours to discuss, play, and experiment with the *ndo*. In these small gatherings, new ways to replicate the clapping, stomping, and tapping were explored. A variety of other musical instruments were created. It was a small gathering, which led to the first instrument with a string. Even that instrument was explored in the circular assembly and in small group gatherings. It started with a single string; more strings were added to capture as many sounds as possible. One of these instruments would be recreated among humans. It has a score and one string. This instrument, where the strings are played with the thumps of the vessels, passed from father to son and can still be found among humans. Its soft, soothing sound was said to be life-giving by the storytellers and at times they restricted it, allowing it only to be played for their royals.

Some of the small gatherings, the duets, trios or quintets, combined the *ndo* and string instruments to participate in conversations. These gatherings built upon the knowledge of the *ndo*. They added different versions of each type of instrument to broaden the conversations. That was not the case with the knowledge of forms. There were no similar collaborations with transformation. *Harambe* was not part of its beginning; no two Glorified gathered to explore the knowledge. Each Glorified simply followed the path Seh laid in uncovering the knowledge of forms. The only mention of transformation at the circular assembly was the question to Seh. He always answered in the same way, and Hu would transform into the original form, and say, 'Transformation was a valuable contribution to the gatherings.' The knowledge of forms was not recognised as an outcome of 'collective creativity'. It had no foundation, no point of common departure among them. Each Glorified created a number of different forms. Some of these forms, humans are familiar with, but no matter the shape or form, whether it had four limbs or two, whether it walked or slithered—the Glorified remained the same as before transforming. There were no additions to the endowment other than the knowledge of a new shape.

Seh thought the other Glorified would not be able to uncover the path to transformation. He had spent a while uncovering the knowledge and thought the others would need him to lead them along its path. The only Glorified to acquire transformation when Seh revealed it was Hu. She was able to copy Seh's complete form. The others acquired transformation as Seh had by him or herself during the quiet that followed the gathering. The three Glorified whom humans would consider females waited until after the *while of quiet* before attempting to acquire the full knowledge of forms. The other two acquired it before beginning the *while of quiet*. They were able to gain the outcome without being led along the way. After the *while of quiet*, the Glorified gathered in small groups, but there were no discussions of transformation. It was not until the next gathering that it became known all of the Seven had acquired the knowledge of forms. At that gathering, as with the *ndo*, there were several new forms. Each Glorified attended the gathering in a form he or she had created. Seh wondered if they rested, or did they use the entire while to gain the knowledge of transformation? Acquiring the knowledge for them was different from what Seh expected. The others wondered why they did not acquire it at the gathering when it was revealed, but no discussions were held among them. They each demonstrated they had acquired the knowledge by presenting a form as their contribution to the gathering.

Transforming into different shapes had no impact on the Glorified, except for the sounds they made. The Glorified whose favourite form had no arms nor legs and gained motion by sliding on its belly made a hissing sound. In transforming their shape, the Glorified still spoke the symbols from the endowment. The sounds they made differed depending on the shape of the form. In that particular form, the tongue had a separation, a kind of fork at its tip. This, along with the shape of the neck and throat, caused her to make a strange sound. The sound was the only noticeable difference transformation caused in the Glorified. It should have been a subject of a circular assembly. Such strange sounds could have contributed to their knowledge of sounds. The Glorified did not discuss it, nor did they attempt to understand the reasons for it. Unlike their other outcomes, there have been no circular assemblies to discuss the meaning and purpose of transformation. There was only the question to Seh, as to why he pursued such knowledge by himself. Seh did not disagree that he pursued the knowledge by himself. He insisted he simply wanted to do as Hu had done: offer transformation as a 'gift' to them.

The others did not understand what Seh meant. Seh had heard the others refer to Hu as 'the master of sound'. He thought the others had set Hu apart and above them. He wanted to be set apart; he imagined the others would refer to him as 'the master of transformation'. He was determined to be set apart, to be 'the master of transformation'. He attended fewer small gatherings and, even as the others found new things to contribute to the gatherings, Seh contributed only forms. He continued to contribute only forms until the Rapture. After the Rapture, he started to make other contributions again. As the whiles passed, he saw value in transformation only as far as the others could use it to set him apart and above them. The others recognised little benefit to transformation, other than a form of creativity—a way to add to their merriment. They did not know the purpose of transformation and it would be many whiles before the knowledge of forms would seem to have served a purpose.

No Glorified thought to call Seh names. Over the whiles, they recreated each other's forms and used them as their contributions to the gathering. Many forms were recreated, but none of the others recreated Seh's original form. The form with the many teeth and long tail was only seen in the Realm when Seh recreated it. That form reminded the others that transformation ought to have been a shared experience. They would question Seh about pursuing transformation by himself. It was on these occasions that Hu would transform into the original form and say, 'Transformation is a valuable contribution to the gathering', but even Hu's form was not a copy of Seh's original form. She would transform into the form she had created when Seh revealed transformation. Her form was not the same as Seh's. Her form reminded the others that she was able to acquire the full knowledge at the gathering. This led them to call her names, saying of her that she was not only 'a master of sound' but also 'a master of forms'. After many of these encounters, hearing the others refer to Hu as 'the master of forms', Seh ceased recreating his original form. It was as if his original form had come to an end. The form with the long tail, strong legs, and small arms was the first form ever created by a Glorified, but after a while, it was seen no more in the Realm.

CHAPTER 7

SHARING OF KNOW-HOW

If the circular assembly had a purpose, it would be *'sharing of know-how'*. That was what the Glorified did when they shared how they created their favourite things. What ingredients were combined to create their favourite colours or which combination of strings made the instrument to speak its truth. *'Sharing of know-how'*—similar to human females sharing recipes—had always been part of the Spirit of the Glorified. The Glorified, who created what humans call spicy, needed an entire gathering to demonstrate how the ingredients were changed so a heated feeling could be left in the mouth. All kinds of 'know-how' were shared. The term *'sharing of know-how'* is from the endowment. The Glorified interpreted the term to mean knowledge should be shared so each Glorified would have the same knowledge, as in their beginning. That was the rule of the Spirit Seh broke. The question posed to Seh was ultimately about *'sharing of know-how'*. If Seh thought transformation was within the will of the Glorified, *'sharing of know-how'* required that he starts the exploration of it at a circular assembly. The Glorified gained the same outcome, but they did not know whether they followed the same path. They did not know what obstacles were overcome. Were they the same obstacles for each Glorified? Did they overcome them in the same way? Other than Hu, each Glorified acquired transformation individually and alone, working out whatever difficulty by themselves. Gaining the outcome allowed the Glorified to assume they had acquired the same knowledge.

The Glorified did not know each other's experiences in gaining transformation. They especially did not understand Seh's journey. After a while, they assumed the purpose of transformation was to contribute to the merriment at the gatherings; nothing more came of it. It was not explored in the way other outcomes were explored. There were no discussions of the steps in transforming. They did not observe each other during the process. There were no attempts to understand if the process always followed the same path. They did not try to determine whether some forms were easier than others. Many different shapes were created, and as the Glorified used transformation, a *false truth* grew among them.

When Seh revealed the outcome of his exploration, they all thought they could do what Seh had done. They could create that particular form. That was why they started their journeys by copying Seh's form. As they uncovered how simple transforming could be, each Glorified knew he or she could recreate any form he or she saw. They were certain that if they could see it, they could recreate it. That was because they did not know that hearing and seeing were the same in transformation.

Even though the certainty that they had to see the form to recreate it was not explored, it became a truth, and for a while it remained a truth among them. It was part of the reason the Glorified created forms by themselves. The Glorified would say, 'Transformation is used out of sight, but the outcome is revealed in the glow of the Sparks.' Humans have a similar saying with the same meaning. They say, 'What is done in the dark must be brought into the light.' The Glorified knew that once the form had been revealed, each Glorified would be able to recreate it. Some of the Glorified wondered if that was the reason

Seh had pursued transformation by himself. As more and more shapes were created, more and more the Glorified were out of sight. The simple knowledge of transformation affected the Glorified in ways they could not see. The *false truth* about seeing the form before recreating it led the Glorified to spend more of the whiles alone. Fewer small group gatherings were held. Fewer things were created together, all so the Glorified could create forms out of sight of each other.

The Glorified started to occupy different sections of the Realm to create forms. They wondered if creativity with transformation had any limits. They were slowly drifting away from 'collective creativity'. In some whiles, the Glorified only saw each other at the gathering in the forms they created. During the quiet, whether at rest or doing some type of creative work, the Glorified would be alone, accompanied only by the sounds of the Mystery of Creation. On occasion, throughout the Realm, the aching tone of a lonely *ndo* would be heard. It would be the mournful sound of speech without having a conversation. It would be a beckoning to the others, an invitation to participate. On occasion, it would be heeded. The Glorified would gather in groups and be together for a while. That behaviour was new, but no one questioned or wondered about it. It was understood that it was part of the method for creating forms. Contributing a form to the gathering meant being alone. Forms became a common feature of the gathering. It was expected that each Glorified would contribute a form. That was especially true if the Glorified was not seen during the *while of quiet*. It was assumed he or she was working on a contribution for the gathering. For a while, it seemed the gatherings were all about forms, and the *whiles of quiet* were all about hiding themselves away to create forms.

That was until Hu chose not to contribute a form to a gathering. She attended the gathering in the form of her creation and did not transform to a different shape. Instead she brought a new kind of food for the gathering. Humans call this type of food fruits. The fruit, to use the human symbol, had a large brown seed in the middle, with skin of similar colour, and a mealy orange body. Hu chose to contribute food instead of a form and the others asked whether she was unable to think of a new form. She was asked if she had reached the limit of her creativity with transformation. Hu responded by describing a form she considered creating. She described it and the others transformed from the shapes they created to the one she described. Each Glorified was able to create the shape Hu described, even the unusual skin covering, which was white, and she described it as similar to the tightly curled hair on the heads of the Glorified.

The turning of Hu's thoughts into a physical form was surprising. The glow of the Spark brightened as each Glorified created the form. Each Glorified created the same form—even the size of the form was the same. It had an elongated head with big eyes, a neck that was connected to the body at a slight angle, and a short tail. All of the details were identical. The feet of the form, created six times, were created exactly the same in each case. The form had four legs but did not have feet like the Glorified. The front legs were different from the back legs. The front legs were straight, while the back legs bent at the knees. Each Glorified had all of the details of Hu's description, even the split at the end of each leg, which divided it into two parts that could be considered toes. Every Glorified created Hu's description exactly as if they had seen it. For the rest of the gathering, they remained in that form.

The Glorified did not need to see the form in order to recreate it. The assumption was *a false truth*. It should have prompted a circular assembly to explore how it was possible that each Glorified could create the same form by hearing. A circular assembly would have given each Glorified an opportunity to describe what they heard. Did they hear the symbols, or did they see the symbols? There were many unanswered questions, unexplored characteristics, of transformation. While the others were surprised and in wonder at the *false truth* that had been revealed to be false, Seh thought he saw another reason why he had to pursue transformation by himself. He was always looking for ways to justify choosing a path other than the *'sharing of know-how'*. His attempts to say it was similar to the creation of the *ndo* had fallen on clogged ears. He pointed out his actions were no different from the actions of the others when they created their favourites. The others saw it differently. Seh had missed the point, for he thought he was justified in pursuing transformation alone. He thought the others needed to see that his choosing was the same as Hu's. He continued to answer their questions in the way he always had. He also looked for opportunities he could use to demonstrate he was just in his choosing. The others turned away whenever he attempted to show his actions were just. It was the same on this occasion. He spoke, 'Bah, bah,' the sound the form made into the silence, saying, 'This is why transformation had to be pursued alone—because together the Seven would be limited to one thought.' Seh was speculating. He did not know. While the others were in the form Hu had described, she transformed into Seh's original form. The other Glorified, realising Seh was attempting another justification for his choosing, turned their attention to the fruit Hu had contributed.

That was the only occasion any Glorified ever shared an idea for a form with the others. Seh's comments cut short any further discussion; that opportunity to explore the characteristics of transformation was lost. None of the Glorified thought Seh was justified in his choosing but they continued to create forms out of sight. They created forms in the same way Seh had created the first form, hidden away. In revealing a form, they would indicate that it was a contribution to the gathering.

There were many contributions to the gatherings. Things that added to their merriment, and were part of sharing. There was no need for the Glorified to indicate that they were contributing to the gathering. With forms, the Glorified took the additional step because Seh said he was giving the knowledge to the others as a *gift*. He used the idea of a *gift* to justify his actions. The others responded by saying *gifts* were not things the Glorified could give. In transforming, the Glorified replicated Seh's actions except the notion that the outcome was a *gift*. The phrase 'This is a contribution to the gathering', was used not only to indicate transformation but also to remind themselves that transformation was not a *gift*. They did not know the place or purpose of transformation. They did not understand what Seh had done to uncover the knowledge. They only knew he had not chosen the '*sharing of know-how*'. While the others attempted to separate the creation of forms from Seh's failure to '*share know-how*', Seh thought the others had failed to uncover the value within transformation.

If Seh had chosen '*sharing of know-how*', the Glorified would have travelled the path together. They would have uncovered the same knowledge and transformation would have been an outcome of 'collective creativity'. Hu sharing her idea for a form showed that a simple description of a form allowed the others to create it. The description was somehow heard in the same way and they added the same value to their knowledge. That sharing was an example of 'collective creativity', of creating things together. It also showed that transformation could have been a shared journey, and might have led along a different path to the same outcome. If Seh had chosen the '*sharing of know-how*' transformation could have been uncovered together.

73

There were many missed opportunities to explore transformation. They were missed not only because of Seh's behaviour but also because the Glorified were trying to give meaning to the outcomes of transformation. The forms were created for no particular reason, no Glorified, except Seh, could identify a purpose for their form. The only reason for their creation was that it added to the Glorified's merriment. Once the form was revealed, it existed only as knowledge to be used occasionally. They made many attempts to infuse—meaning and purpose—if not into the knowledge itself, then into the outcome of transformation. At some gatherings, the Glorified would not only reveal a new form but would create contributions made in the shape of the form. These decorative forms—contributions to the gathering shaped like their favourite forms—were attempts to give the outcome of transformation a presence beyond the Glorified. Forms existed only in knowledge, real only so long as the Glorified remained in that shape. The Glorified contributed their favourite foods shaped as their favourite form. After a while, these attempts to give forms presence faded and no other uses were developed for the knowledge of forms.

There was always wonder—and delight—when a new form was revealed. The Glorified would use the same form on different occasions but would alter it by changing one or two features. They examined the form to discover where the Spark had located itself. In Seh's form with the long neck, which Hu saw in the announcement, the Spark located itself between the ears along the two poles atop the head. The Spark could locate itself anywhere within the form and it always brightened its glow with giving and receiving. The endowment did not provide the reason the Sparks always brightened on occasions of sharing. The Glorified thought it was how the Spark recognised 'sharing of know-how'. Unlike humans, who say, 'It is better to give than to receive', the Sparks valued both giving and receiving equally. Giving and receiving are the two sides of sharing—like coming and going from the marketplace to home—they are the pillars of 'collective creativity'. Over the many whiles of sharing, no Glorified ever said the thing shared was offered to the others because giving among the Glorified had always been part of sharing and it had no more value than receiving.

The words of Seh when he revealed the knowledge of forms had never been heard in the Realm before. The others had never heard those symbols expressed in that way. The idea of offering a thing to another as a *gift* was brought into being by Seh. That was his most favoured explanation for pursuing transformation. He said he wanted to offer the knowledge as a *gift*, like Hu had offered the *ndo*. Except, Hu did not use those symbols when she introduced the *ndo*. The *ndo* needed no introduction, as everyone including Seh recognised its place and purpose in the Realm. Seh first saw the *ndo* as an outcome of 'collective creativity'. Unlike the *ndo*, transformation was not an outcome of *harambe*. None of the Glorified could say he or she shared in its uncovering or contributed to its meaning and purpose. The *ndo* recreated the sounds the Glorified made together. Where the idea of transformation came from was a mystery.

There were many circular assemblies about the transformation of things, but no Glorified saw in those discussions the outcome that Seh saw. They could not see through the eyes of Seh; to them, the source of the idea remained unknown. Seh, on the other hand, said he had never forgotten the idea after it was mentioned. Though he suggested he had thought about the idea for many whiles, the others asked why he did not bring it to a circular assembly. In explaining, he did not truly share; it was only after the introduction of the *ndo* he thought of the idea again. He had no thoughts about transformation for many whiles. His preferred occupation during the *whiles of quiet* had been to expand the knowledge of ale. He did not say he wanted to be set apart; instead, he said he pursued transformation, so he could give the others a *gift*.

The *ndo* was created by Hu, but she did not offer it as a *gift* to the others. She made no comments about the *ndo*. The *ndo* spoke for itself. She used the *ndo* to accompany the sounds at the gathering. The Glorified sang and clapped their hands at their gatherings; to that, she added the voice of the *ndo*. After they had taken turns playing the *ndo*, a circular assembly was held, and none of the others asked Hu why she made it. In that circular assembly, Seh held the *ndo*. It sat across his lap, allowing him to tap on both ends in support of the discussion. He was the first of the Glorified to have a turn at playing the *ndo*. He provided Hu with ale he had made, and while she tasted it, he took over playing the *ndo*. He started out by playing one end and then beating on the other end, examining the differences in sounds. He then played both ends together. During the gathering, there were discussions about whether it sounded more like the clapping, stomping or tapping. Seh was certain it sounded more like tapping the thighs. 'With tapping, different sounds could be made with different positioning of the hands', he said, 'and the same is true with playing the *ndo*.'

After the circular assembly, the gathering moved towards a close. Seh stood up playing the *ndo* and said, 'The sounds of the *ndo* have been at every gathering.' He then suggested that the rhythm he was playing should be played at the beginning of each gathering. To the others, it appeared Seh had embraced the *ndo*. They expected Seh to expand on it to create other types of *ndos*. As the gathering closed and the beginning of the *while of quiet* was almost upon them, a Glorified said of Hu, 'She is a master of sound.' The others seemed to agree but Seh stopped playing the *ndo*. He paused in thought and, if Hu's senses had been expanded as they were in the announcement, she would have seen a slight change in Seh. Like the others, she thought nothing of the name-calling, and they continued towards the *while of quiet*. It was those words, the calling of a name, that led Seh to uncover the knowledge of forms. After he heard the Glorified call Hu 'the master of sound', he stopped playing the *ndo*, put it down, and left the gathering.

The name-calling stirred something in Seh. It caused him to spend a portion of the while in thought. He was thinking about 'the master of sound' and how that name distinguished Hu from the others. He wondered what he could do to distinguish himself. It was in that while of thought, looking for a way to set himself apart, that he recalled transformation.

Seh was stooping, his chin resting on his fist, his elbow planted on his knee, listening to the quiet of the Realm. The others were at rest. Seh did not rest; he was unable to put aside the thought that Hu had uncovered a way to distinguish herself. He thought about the Mystery of Creation, how it was used to create things. He wondered if the things created with it were not merely a transformation of form. If the Mystery could be transformed, he said, his voice uncertain but determined, maybe the physical form could also be transformed; after all, both were the creations of the First, the Self-Generator. With that thought, he searched the endowment for reference to transformation. He found no reference to anything like it, but he did find the reference to the '*sharing of know-how*'. Seh felt the weight of his head in his knees as he considered whether he should wait until the next circular assembly to discuss the idea of transformation.

If not for the name-calling, he would have waited so they could all travel the path together. He reasoned that Hu had not become 'the master of sound' by waiting for circular assemblies. He thought since the idea had already been presented at a circular assembly, he could add to the idea by expanding on it. He thought again about *'sharing of know-how'*, but brushed it aside, by saying he did not know if an outcome could be gained. If he gained an outcome, he thought, feeling the weight of his chin in his wrist, it could be offered as a *gift*.

He paused; it was the first, he had used the symbol *gift* in that manner. He too knew *gifts* were not things a Glorified could give. That was how Seh started down the path. 'If an outcome is gained, it would be the same as the *ndo'*, he continued. As Seh spent more of the while in pursuit of a way to distinguish himself, he started to think of the *ndo* differently. The idea of distinguishing himself grew and he did not realise the *false truth* he was creating. He was following the path of his choosing when the *false truth* entered him, as humans would say, like a needle, then spread like a mighty oak.

After a while of questioning and answering of himself, Seh settled on the idea of experimenting to see if any outcome could be gained. He thought, if he brought transformation into being, it would set him apart from the others—he would become 'the master of transformation'. He was certain he had found a path forward, even as *'sharing of know-how'* intruded upon his thoughts. He would share the outcome in the same way the *ndo* was shared. The *ndo* was a *gift*, he thought, a *gift* of sound.

His reasoning was false. The *ndo* was the same as the other contributions to the gatherings. It was an expansion of something the Glorified did together. Seh thought the ideas of the *ndo* and transformation were similar, since music has no physical presence. He was trying to find a way around the path that led to the *'sharing of know-how'*. His thoughts flickering like a flame in the breeze, he convinced himself that Hu did not share the idea of the *ndo* because she wanted to distinguish herself from them.

He was certain his choosing was no different from Hu's choosing. He wondered if she did not know about the *sharing of know-how*. Seh was following where his Spirit led. He had embraced the *ndo*, but he no longer saw the *ndo* as an expansion of 'collective creativity'. Instead, it became a departure from the Spirit of the Glorified, from the way of creation. As he spent that while searching for a way to distinguish himself, he drifted away from his behaviour at the gathering. He began to see the *ndo* not as a contribution, not as an expansion of 'collective creativity', but as a method that Hu had used to set herself apart. He thought her Spirit had strayed from the path. She should not have created the *ndo* by herself—she should have brought the idea to a circular assembly. These thoughts were new for Seh; in the loneliness of that *while of quiet*, they quickly became *false truths*. They caused him to see the *ndo* as a departure from the Spirit of the Glorified—opening the path for him to pursue transformation by himself.

At the gathering, Seh had embraced the *ndo*, recognising both its purpose and its place among them. He was the first and the last to play it. He suggested the *ndo* had been at every gathering. He recommended a rhythm to be played at the start of the gatherings. He played the *ndo* while the others danced. He participated in the circular assembly. There were no indications that Seh did not fully embrace the *ndo*. As Seh journeyed along the path towards transformation, he thought less and less about sharing and more about the name-calling. The calling of a name caused Seh to put down the *ndo* and prevented him from resting during the *while of quiet*. After the others rested, they used a portion of the while to expand upon the *ndo*. For them, there was nothing different about the creation of the *ndo*. Hu had not departed from the way of creation, and it was Seh who spoke truth when he said, 'The *ndo* has been at every gathering.' The *ndo* was just an outcome of 'collective creativity'—a mere contribution to the gathering. Hu had not forsaken sharing, and referring to Hu as 'a master of sound' was neither *false truth* nor evidence of a change in their Spirit. The Glorified—as humans would come to know—are all 'masters of sound', including Seh. Seh was looking for a way to gloss over his choosing; thinking of these things as departures from the way of creation allowed him to feel he had reasons to pursue transformation by himself.

CHAPTER 8

SUM OF WRONGS EQUALS NOT ...

Before transformation, the Glorified were often together in the same section of the Realm. They were with each other as they worked, suggesting ideas or questions for circular assemblies and collectively contributing to the gatherings. On occasion, they wandered alone, following the paths throughout the Realm. They were often in pursuit of their favourites, sometimes attending small group gatherings or just in thought. As transformation took hold, those aspects of their behaviour began to change. Slowly at first, the whiles together became shorter, small group gatherings became fewer and the whiles alone became longer. Transformation was separating the Glorified from each other. They were not only creating forms out of sight, but other things were created as well. Hu was unable to discuss the food, which humans called a fruit, before contributing it to the gathering. The others were out of sight, and no Glorified heeded the beckoning of the *ndo*. Transformation—which appeared purposeless—was affecting the outcome of the Spark and the form of creation. That is the other side of the Spirit: action begets reaction. It was difficult to discern the influence upon their Spirit. Using transformation to create was easier than creating with other things. The process was simpler. There were no assemblies or discussions, no small group gatherings, just the Glorified with his or her thoughts, alone, and each Glorified chose to follow that path.

The others did not know Seh's experience nor understood his comments about a *gift*. They could not feel what he was feeling. His actions had drifted away from '*sharing of know-how*'. He thought giving could be elevated above receiving. His offer to give a *gift* to the others caused him to lose his place in receiving. His focus blinded him to the Sparks of the others, to the twinkle in Hu's Spark—when he revealed transformation. Over the whiles, he gave many reasons for pursuing transformation, but he never said he wanted to be 'the master of transformation' or to be elevated above the others. His explanations never met the needs of their questions, and Hu often interrupted the questioning of Seh. She would transform and say, 'Transformation is a valuable contribution to the gatherings.' Seh did not acknowledge her assistance. Instead, he rolled his fingers into tight balls and planted his feet firmly. His entire form would heat up; he would become rigid and energy would flow through him. Those feelings only grew, because those occasions often ended with the other Glorified calling Hu names.

Even recalling those occasions would cause Seh's ears to become warm. He did not know the meaning of those sensations. Seh did not discuss them with the others. He searched the endowment, but it provided no insights. Something in him had changed. The name-calling was meaningless to Hu; it did not disturb her peace nor add joy to it. She had no need to be a master of either sound or forms. She never thought there could be any difference among the First, the Self-Generator's creations, which could set one above another. Seh was the only Glorified who had such a thought. He thought he could be above the others as the First, the Self-Generator, was above creation. Seh recognised changes in his Spirit and looked to see if there were similar changes in the Spirits of the others. He did not understand what he felt, but he chose not to discuss them with the others. He waited to see if any other Glorified mentioned similar sensations.

It took Seh a while to uncover transformation. As he uncovered fragments of the knowledge, he began to envision himself being positioned above the others. He thought the others would not be able to uncover the path to transformation without his guidance. He could lead them along the path, showing them a new way to live. That, he thought, would cause them to call him 'the master of transformation'. Seh did not know where the path would lead. He knew only that he should be set apart from the others. They should follow his guidance as he leads them towards a new way. He would indicate the way like the Sparks showing the way towards *nia*. He would give them the knowledge like the giver of *gifts*. Seh, following where his thoughts led, did not seem to grasp the implications of his path.

He questioned and answered himself until he was certain the others had departed from the way of creation. He did not realise that he had abandoned a truth to convince himself that he could be set above the others. The behaviour of the others had not changed. The name-calling was not a departure from the indications of the Spark. Even if the Spirits of the others had forsaken the way of creation, Seh knew 'A sum of wrongs equals not a right.' The Glorified are the creations of the First, the Self-Generator, and none can be elevated above another.

Seh had not only spent the while alone but he had also spent the while focusing on himself. The Glorified were the same except for what human beings would describe as male and female parts. They had no need to focus on themselves or on each other. They recognised each other not by their physical appearance but by the Spark. It was the Spark that allowed the others to recognise Seh when he revealed transformation. Hu searched the Creature in the announcement for a Spark for the same reason. Seh not only made transformation about him but also placed his physical self at the centre of being. No Glorified had travelled that path before. *Harambe*, the *'sharing of know-how'*, put the purpose of creation at the centre of being. His purpose, and the focus on altering his shape caused transformation to become about his physical form, allowing him to put the tenth truth aside. He was certain Hu had been set apart, which is what he coveted. Calling Hu 'a master of sound' was a gesture that acknowledged her creativity. The gesture held no meaning to the others; they showed no reaction and their Spirits remained at peace. Seh failed to see a gesture and the idea that a Glorified could be elevated above the others manifested into being.

Seh had been alone for a while, considering ways to distinguish himself. He saw that four of the Glorified had different parts than his. He wondered if it were possible to transform his shape to be the same as theirs.

The Spark within him did not brighten and he began to see his form differently, envisioning himself as separate from the others. He attempted to change his shape and after a while he added a new part to his form of creation. The part was a long piece added to his back, which appeared to be an elongation of his backbone. Though his intention had been to replicate the female parts, he instead added length to his backbone. If he focused on it, he could move it around as if it were a leg. His experiment yielded more than he expected. He had not expected an outcome at all. He pushed aside the purpose of creation and kept *'sharing of know-how'* from intruding on his thoughts. He had been working at it for a while and reminded himself that Hu did not wait to become 'the master of sound'. He did not know how he had gained the outcome, but it was enough to assure him that he had grown above the others. He began to see himself as 'the master of transformation', even though what he gained was fleeting. He did not know what thoughts or actions caused his form to change. Seh did not know if he could recreate the part, but he knew that transformation was possible. The part he added to his form was not found on the forms the First, the Self-Generator, had created. His thoughts were focused in one direction and the outcome was in another. He could not make the connection, yet he thought the outcome would set him apart from the others.

He began thinking on how he might introduce this new knowledge to the others. He was leaping ahead of himself, planning his entrance into the gathering—showing off his new knowledge before he had acquired it. As he travelled the path, he would return to the idea of being 'the master', setting himself apart, again and again. He had to force himself to put that thought aside. He focused on the part to change, yet found his arms were replaced with smaller arms instead. He could not control the outcome but saw that his parts could not only be grown but also reduced. That second, haphazard result added to his confidence, and again he searched the endowment. He found no reference to transformation but was reminded of 'sharing of know-how'. Seh continued, slowly travelling further along the path by changing other parts of himself. He combined the parts into one unified form. First the elongated piece at his back, then the small arms, followed by the legs until his whole form was altered. As he transformed his parts, he wondered if the others would be able to uncover this knowledge. He then considered not sharing the outcome. The others knew not that a path existed which led to transformation. Again he found himself questioning and answering his own thoughts. 'How would the knowledge serve its purpose?' he asked. Only the others could make him 'the master of transformation', just as they had made Hu 'the master of sound'. Not revealing transformation would serve no purpose. Giving it to the others might lead them to call him names, to set him apart—and above them.

Transformation was not found in the endowment, and no Glorified knew it was possible. Seh wondered: *if things not found in the endowment were unknown to the First, the Self-Generator.* That stood as a first in creation. It was the first any Glorified had questioned the depth of the First, the Self-Generator's knowledge. The Glorified knew the first truth of creation, yet none had any thoughts about *It*—save that *It* exists. He reshaped his head, his neck and his shoulders. The more Seh changed his form, the more he assumed that he stood above the others, almost on the level of the First, the Self-Generator. Human beings called what Seh felt after gaining the outcome, *pride.* They say it is a *sin,* but both *pride* and *sin* were unknown to the Glorified. It was that feeling that caused Seh to wonder about the knowledge not in the endowment. He was certain that no other Glorified would be able to gain transformation without his instructions and directions. After all, it took him an entire while—without rest—to uncover its path. He wanted the others to see him in a new way. He wanted to appear changed by the knowledge. He wanted his presence to be bigger than the presence of the others. He held his head up and pushed out his chest. That became his new way of carrying himself, but before revealing transformation, he again considered if there was any purpose in knowledge known only to one.

Seh wondered if transformation should be a secret, something known only to him. There are many secrets in creation, knowledge known only to the First, the Self-Generator. Transformation was not a secret, even if Seh were the only Glorified who knew its path. He was concerned that if another Glorified recalled the idea of transformation, his purpose would be lost. The opportunity to be set apart, to lead the others into a new way of being, would be gone. He reasoned that the only path to gaining his purpose started with revealing transformation. He had not chosen 'sharing of know-how', but as he considered how to gain his purpose, he thought he could go beyond sharing. He could offer the outcome as a *gift* like the First, the Self-Generator. He had found an explanation for his choosing, even though it meant he must put aside the meaning of both '*gift*' and '*sharing of know-how*'.

Over the whiles, '*sharing of know-how*' had come to mean the sharing of a journey, taking a path and together uncovering the unknown. He gave no thought to the meaning of those symbols, to the two-sidedness of the Spirit, to how the others might react. Gaining the outcome for him meant the actions he had taken were the appropriate steps. All other questions and thoughts were put aside and he *began again* to plan how to reveal transformation, so he might be called a name.

The name-calling was a meaningless symbol to the others. For Seh, it was as if a storm had knocked him from the path. He had begun to expand on the *ndo* even at the gathering, suggesting the *ndo* could be divided into two. That was indeed his intention before the name-calling. From the moment—to borrow a human reference to a while—those symbols were spoken, he dismissed the idea of adding to the *ndo* in favour of finding a way to set himself apart. While the Glorified created other types of *ndos*, Seh pursued transformation of his physical shape. The others were playing his tune—the rhythm he had suggested to signal the start of the gatherings. He waited before joining them. He confirmed that he stood in his new posture: chest pushed out, head held high. He had not considered what the others would see—or how they would see him in his new form. He assumed the others would be able to recognise him. He waited until Hu asked about him before entering their midst.

The others did not recognise Seh. The sound he made was like no other in the Realm. It caused Seh to pause, to hesitate. He had worked in silence and did not know that in transformation the sounds made were unlike those of the Glorified. Seh assumed the others would hear his voice and look for his Spark to affirm that it was him. The others got to their feet and Seh tried to communicate. It was difficult for the others to recognise him. As they stood up, Seh tried to speak again except louder and more forceful, thinking this would cause them to comprehend. The force of his voice caused him to lean forward, pointing his head and spreading his small arms. He made a loud, thunderous sound, filling the Realm, and the others stepped back, puzzled.

Seh, in attempting to speak, lost his focus. Parts of his form reverted to the shape of his creation. He quickly regained control of those parts, changing them back into the shape he wanted. He continued trying to speak, but his peace was ruffled by a subtle thought of sameness. He did not want to lose control of his form in the presence of the others. He wanted the others to think that he was 'the master'. Having to recreate parts of his form, he thought, reduced him to their level. The others started to look for the Spark after the parts reverted. The Spark affirmed that the strange shape was Seh. They began to examine the form. The Glorified walked around the form, touching it and looking closely at some of the peaks and valleys on the skin. They asked Seh how he had gained such knowledge. They searched the endowment for references to this unknown. The new form added to their merriment. The Sparks lit up and the entire section of the Realm shimmered with the glow of their joy. As the others questioned Seh and he offered his explanation, the Spark within him dimmed its glow—but no one noticed. It was not until the announcement that Hu would see a slight change in the glow of the Spark within Seh. He was about to instruct the others on how to gain the outcome when Hu changed into a form that resembled his. Her form was like Seh's, and that encouraged the others to attempt to gain the knowledge as well.

The others gained less of the outcome than Hu, but Hu's outcome meant that Seh's opportunity to lead, to guide, and to point towards a new path was lessened. The others would return to playing the *ndos* or eating, drinking, and dancing between their efforts at transforming. They were looking to Seh for an explanation of the source of the knowledge, not for direction on how to gain the outcome. After a while, the others no longer attempted to transform. They played the *ndos* while Seh stood apart in his new form, feeling his opportunity slipping away. The others were focused on what they knew rather than on what they did not understand. They took turns playing the *ndos*. They sang, danced, and partook of ale. There were no more attempts at transformation and the *ndos* grew louder and the tempos hotter, before they all stopped playing.

After the heated tempos of the drums, the Glorified sat in their places as the voices of the *ndos* drifted through creation. Seh stood at a distance from the others, gazing upon the whole circle. The circular assembly was incomplete without Seh; his place was there but empty. The Glorified always sat in the same order with Seh in between the two males. Seh chose not to join the others even though he saw that his place waited for him. He chose to stand at a distance with his head held up in such a way that he had to cast his eyes down in order to see the others. He wanted to look at the others and still hold his head up. He slowly walked around the others as they sat, ensuring they were able to observe him as he tried to make himself bigger. It felt unnatural to Seh to hold his head up and still look down on the others. He was holding his head in such a way that he saw parts of his face when he looked down. Others would have simply held their heads in its natural position. Seh, instead, practiced looking down past his nose and mouth to see the others. Humans have heard this part of the History. Their suggestion that it is wrong to look down your face—or, as humans would say, look down your nose—at others, referenced the History of Creation. Seh was focused on himself; he wanted to be acknowledged for the outcome he had gained, and looking down his nose was simply a way of setting himself apart and above the others.

As Seh walked around the circular assembly, the others asked him to take his place. The *ndos* had spoken their truth and the gathering was coming to a close. Seh, in his new posture, continued to stand apart. Each of the Glorified searched the endowment to see if there were any references to transformation. They asked Seh about the source of the knowledge. Seh, still standing apart, said it was discussed at a circular assembly. The others could not recall transformation of self as the subject of a circular assembly. It was only mentioned in passing, he added. Seeing that the others were puzzled, he reminded them of the discussion about converting the Mystery of Creation to ale. That's when the question of whether it was possible to change the form of creation was raised. He admitted there was no further discussion, but thought that it was possible. The Glorified asked why he did not bring the idea to another circular assembly. He responded with his prepared explanation. He wanted to offer the knowledge as a *gift*, like Hu did with the *ndo*. The others did not understand. The only *gifts* the Glorified knew were *gifts* from the creator of existence. Seh's pre-planned explanation seemed empty, minor when spoken out loud, and he recognised he was redefining the symbol '*gift*'. Yet he persisted with his explanation, insisting Hu had offered the *ndo* as a *gift*. The others knew she only used the knowledge the Glorified possessed. There had been many circular assemblies discussing sound and its elements—how its elements could be brought together. The beating of the *ndos* was no different from clapping hands, stomping feet, and tapping thighs. Any Glorified could have made the *ndo*, they said. Each Glorified had the same knowledge of sound. The Glorified had explored not only the elements of sound but had also considered the melodies of silence. They had spent many whiles listening to silence, examining its rhythm, hearing it before and after the intrusion of sound. They pointed out that they had just played their *ndos*. They intruded upon silence but stopped playing to allow silence to participate in the conversation. The *ndo*, the others assured Seh, was an extension of what the Glorified knew about sound. It demonstrated *'sharing of know-how'*.

Seh, standing with his feet firmly planted, heard not—or chose not to hear—the voices of the others. He continued with his planned explanation, indicating he could open the path and guide them along the way. He knew the destination and they could follow him there, he said. The Glorified did not follow one another. They stood together, assisted each other, shared with one another, but none ever led the others into the unknown as Seh was offering. He then said he 'offers transformation as a *gift*.' The others, tired from a long gathering, seemed uninterested in Seh's form and asked him once more to take his place. Instead of taking his place, he started to walk around the circular assembly, transforming back and forth between his form and his form of creation. The others, though tired, were attempting to have a discussion about transformation. Seh remained apart, saying the *gift* he offers is a *gift* of knowledge.

While waiting for Seh to take his place, Hu asked whether there could be a giving that is not part of sharing. It was clear Seh was attempting to create a distinction, to separate 'giving' from its part in 'sharing'. Giving and receiving were the two parts of sharing. The Glorified could not distinguish giving from receiving. There was no giving without sharing and there was no sharing without receiving. Giving meant the '*sharing of know-how*' and receiving was the uncovering of the unknown. The Glorified had never explored the idea of giving without receiving. Although they were weary and the gathering was nearing a close, the question seemed to renew their strengths. They searched the endowment to see if there could be a 'giving' that was distinct and different from 'sharing'. In the endowment, the symbol *gift* referenced only things the First, the Self-Generator, had done. Seh used the symbol in a way the others did not understand. No acts of a Glorified could be the same as the acts of the First, the Self-Generator. In searching the endowment, they affirmed the reference to '*sharing of know-how*', but there were no indications that giving was anything other than a part of sharing. The distinction Seh was making simply did not exist. There were references to *gifts*, as Seh had used the symbol, but only in relation to the creator of existence. The First, the Self-Generator, gave, and creation received. The Glorified did not know what, if anything, *It* received for *Its* giving. The *gifts* referenced in the endowment were created from 'nothing', which affirmed for the Glorified that they could not be the givers of *gifts*.

Giving was what the First, the Self-Generator, did. Every thought, every act, every creation was a *gift*. In sharing the *true gift*, they assumed *It* received, but they did not know. That was not what Seh was offering; he was not the creator of existence, and he did not have the will to create a *gift*. He offered to share the knowledge of transformation if the others attached themselves as in a row, to be led by him along a path. This would allow him to set himself above them. Humans, in their while, would separate giving from receiving. They would say it is better to give than to receive. If what humans mean is that in giving they become the master of the gift or are set above the receiver of the gift, then that is not a truth. It is not found among the truths of creation. In fact, the tenth truth of creation says, 'There are no hierarchies among the First, the Self-Generator's creations.' Creating hierarchy is not, to use a human symbol, a blessed act. Seh did not contribute to the discussion about whether giving could be distinguished from sharing. He too was tired. He had spent the while trying to find a way to distinguish himself and did not rest. He was having difficulty with transformation and maintaining his new posture. After that gathering, Seh would never again have difficulty maintaining a shape—until he saw the Creature jump from Hu's shoulder to her arm as they journeyed towards the seal. When he saw the Creature, he lost control of his form because he thought that she had found a way to create the *duality of being* or a *true gift*.

Seh was not asked to take his place again. They compared a *true gift* to transformation. Hu transformed into the shape that Seh had created and told him, 'Transformation is a valuable contribution to the gathering.' The others, recognising that she had acquired the knowledge while they struggled, called her names, commenting on her creativity. Seh was left standing with his feet firmly planted, his ears burning, and his fingers rolled into tight balls, wondering how she could be 'the master of forms' when she did not uncover the knowledge. When the gathering came to a close, there were no offers to get together in small groups to expand upon the knowledge of forms. They waited because they thought a circular assembly would be held, and they would uncover the purpose of transformation and the reasons Seh had pursued it by himself.

CHAPTER 9

NDOS AND FORMS

The Glorified did not know that they did not all have the same knowledge as Seh. Hu had gained the knowledge in the bright glow of the Sparks. The others followed a path similar to Seh's. They uncovered the knowledge of form out of sight and revealed it in the glow of the Sparks, but their knowledge was not the same as Seh's. They created the same form but the others did not make themselves the centre of being. Their Spark did not dim its glow. In the human beginning, humans would ask if Seh had gained the knowledge but lost his Spark. The Glorified would pause to contemplate the meaning of losing a Spark, before saying, 'A Spark cannot be lost.'

The others were able to bring the form into being because they knew the knowledge existed. Gaining the outcome for these Glorified was similar to creating the *ndo*. They were trying to gain an outcome they knew existed. After the *while of quiet*, the Glorified had the same outcome, but they did not have the same experience. With each Glorified having the ability to create forms, it was easy to assume that each travelled the same path. That was not true. The others' paths were different from Seh's. He started with a purpose. He explored alone, trying to find a path to an unknown, and his Spirit was impacted differently than the others'.

At the next gathering, each Glorified contributed a new form. Five of the forms were almost the same, adding to the assumption that the Glorified had the same knowledge. Hu's and Seh's forms were different. They both wondered if the others explored transformation and created their forms together. As with Seh, the forms were created hidden away and they each attended the gathering in the form he or she created. Unlike Seh, none of the others had the desire to be set apart. Transformation was just another way to contribute to the gathering. They contributed other things as well, and forms were not the only new items at that gathering.

The Glorified were experimenting with the size of the *ndo*, exploring if the size of the *ndo* would cause it to make a different type of sound. They referred back to the clapping of hands, stomping of feet, and tapping of thighs, knowing that a different sound was made with different positioning of the hands, feet or thighs. That was the conclusion about the size of the *ndo* as well; different-sized *ndos* gave different sounds even though the rhythm might be the same, like two people singing the same song. As they explored the size of the *ndo*, the question of whether the *ndo* was the first instrument created was asked. Seh, who had taken his place at this circular assembly, thought he knew the answer. He was certain the *ndo* was the first instrument. The Glorified searched the endowment and found no references to the *ndo*, but, unlike Seh they knew that there is wisdom in hesitation.

The endowment did not mention the *ndo* in the same way it did not mention transformation. That was what made Seh certain. The Glorified, whose place in the circular assembly was on the right side of Hu, asked whether things not included in the endowment existed in creation. They knew the first truth. They did not know whether or not things not found in the endowment existed. This struck Seh as different from his question. He had wondered if the First, the Self-Generator, knew the things that are not mentioned in the endowment. The statement of the other Glorified implied the First, the Self-Generator, knew but had reasons for not including such knowledge in the endowment. Seh was still considering the thought when the others concluded that the only thing that can be said is, 'The *ndo* is the first instrument created by the Glorified.'

Seh did not agree that the *ndo* was created by the Glorified. It was made by Hu. It set her apart, he thought. The Glorified on the right side of Hu broadened their conclusion. Their voices, she said—especially their singing voices—might be the first instrument in creation. She hesitated before contradicting herself, saying, 'It is the voice of the First, the Self-Generator, which is the first instrument in creation. The voices of the Glorified are variations of the first in the same way that these *ndos* are variations of the first *ndo*.' Those comments led to other questions. 'Does the First, the Self-Generator, have a voice?' 'Were the Glorified created by the sound of *Its* voice or by a thought or a method known only to *It*?' That circular assembly drifted into questions the Glorified had never had reasons to ask.

So much about the First, the Self-Generator, was unknown and speculating about *It* could lead to *false truths*. In the Realm, the Glorified were content in saying they did not know. No Glorified would ever claim that they had the answer to the question of whether the First, the Self-Generator, had a voice, or that they had any insight into *Its* methods of creation. There are only a few references to the First, the Self-Generator, in the endowment. The first reference is the first truth of creation. In searching the endowment, the Glorified always paused at that statement. There are other references to the First, the Self-Generator, but that is the only statement that says *It* is.

Humans could not access the endowment in the same way. They

were not born with full knowledge and mastery of their abilities. Human knowledge of the First, the Self-Generator, was first passed to them through the Glorified. They could not search the endowment to find the first truth of creation or any truth. Without knowing how to access the endowment, humans had to accept the existence of the First, the Self-Generator, by believing what they had been told. In the human beginning, when the Glorified recited parts of the endowment, humans would say that they did not know but they believed, while the Glorified paused after the first truth of creation. The Glorified, knowing that the endowment was not bestowed upon humans, would say, 'The burden upon humans is to grow into the knowledge.' That, too, would be changed by the storytellers. They would not understand the Glorified's words. So instead, they would preach that 'The burden upon humans is to believe without knowing.'

Just like the *ndo*, the Glorified whose place is on the right side of Hu, said, 'Forms created with the knowledge of forms are not the first forms in creation.' As she spoke, she rose as if to say her shape, which was created from 'nothing', was one of the first forms in creation. Her comments caught Seh's attention; he had wondered whether transformation was unknown to the First, the Self-Generator. 'There is no reference to transformation in the endowment', he said. 'Transformation is not about creating shapes and forms. It is about taking a shape and changing it into another. That was not what the First, the Self-Generator, did when *It* created the Realm and everything within it.' 'It might be exactly what *It* did', said the Glorified standing next to Hu. "*It* put sound in *Its* mouth and made *Itself* the creator. *It* created *Itself* from 'nothing'," yet, *It* has neither shape nor form. What is the shape of 'nothing'?' she asked. 'The Glorified have shapes even though

97

they too were brought forth from 'nothing'. The First, the Self-Generator, could have created the Seven as 'nothing' and then transformed them into these shapes'. "The Seven were never 'nothing'," Seh said. 'They were not brought forth in the image of the First, the Self-Generator. Therefore, *It* did not use the knowledge of transformation to create the Seven.' 'It is true the Seven are not the image of the First, the Self-Generator. They might be *Its* likeness. But it remains unknown whether the creator of existence used the knowledge of forms', suggested Hu. 'There have been no witnesses to any of *Its* acts. *It* has not shared all *Its* knowledge with creation'. 'It is a truth that there was no witness to creation', added the Glorified still standing. 'It is the third truth'. The mention of the truth of creation caused the Glorified to pause. Then silence was chased from among them by a voice that was soft, smooth, and sweet. It was the Glorified standing on the right of Hu. She said, 'Not everything is known but what is known is that the First, the Self-Generator, created these forms and *It* created these sounds', as she beat on a *ndo*. "*It* created the symbols found in the endowment and *It* created the things in the Realm. Yet *It* has neither shape nor form, and before creating things, *It* was alone—one continuous 'self'—nought existed but *It*. Still, *It* knew what creation needed and created them, for no greater reason than sharing. That", she said as she sat down in her place in the circular assembly, "is the purpose of creation. It is the *true gift*."

That circular assembly, which started as a discussion about the *ndo*, closed with a reference to the *true gift*. While they silently reflected on the *gift* of existence, Hu intruded upon the quiet, saying, 'It is not known why *It* created the Realm and the Seven'. The Glorified refer to the First, the Self-Generator, as '*It*' or by one of the two descriptions found in the endowment: 'The First, the Self-Generator', or 'The First, the Self-Creator'. Later, humans would say there are many wonderful names to call *It* but the truth as found in the endowment is that there are only two descriptions for *It*. Referring to the First, the Self-Generator, as *It* showed the Glorified do not know what the creator of existence is. *It* is described as 'everything' and as 'nothing'. 'It is not known', Hu continued, 'why or how *It* creates things but, as with the *ndo*, the only thing that can be said is that the forms created with the knowledge of forms are the first forms the Glorified have created.' With that, Hu transformed into the shape she had created. As Hu transformed, the others transformed into their contribution to the gathering, bringing the circular assembly to a close. They would hold other assemblies about the *ndo*, but this assembly, as oft occur with humans, drifted away from its purpose.

CHAPTER 10

ONLY TRUE PATH

As Seh created his contribution to the gathering, he assessed how he could gain the outcome of his purpose. He recalled Hu being called 'the master of sound' and, at the last gathering, the others referred to her as 'the master of forms'. He felt heat flowing over him as he rolled his fingers into tight balls. He knew something had changed. He had pursued transformation alone, and his purpose gave substance and meaning to something that was unknown to the others. That was the outcome of the two-sidedness of the Spirit: action gives substance and meaning to reaction. He did not consider the two-sidedness of the Spirit or the reaction the others might have. He looked at the Seven, evaluating their attempts at transformation. He expected the others to seek him out for assistance. He looked at them and none of the others seemed to have developed a new posture. They did not position their heads or their chest in the way he expected. He wondered if they had gained the full knowledge. He did not know what the heating of the form or the energy flowing through him meant. He thought they were beacons—indicating the true path. He had seen nought to suggest that the others had travelled the same path as him.

Seh thought his path was the only true path towards transformation. He had taken his own experience and fastened to it the limitation of certainty. Human beings would do that as well, and, like Seh, they would want others to use their certainty as a cast for their Spirit. Seh was certain there was a true way to gain the knowledge of transformation and only he knew the signs along the path. As he waited for the others to seek his assistance, he practiced how to best lead them. When the gathering began with no request for assistance, Seh experienced again the mysteries he had uncovered in pursuing transformation. He knew not what the others did during that while, but he supposed, guessed, and reasoned. He was certain the others would have challenges, reflecting upon their struggle at the gathering. He guessed they must have asked Hu for her assistance rather than him. He reasoned that one or both of his speculations must be true. As he contemplated those thoughts, he realised he had stood up, his feet firmly planted, and he had formed tight balls with his hands. He uttered in a low voice, 'Ah, the mysteries along the way', calming himself.

The other Glorified created five similar forms. When Seh saw the forms the others contributed, he supposed the five Glorified had gathered with Hu and were led along the same path. Seh was beginning to warm up again then Hu asked the others, 'Had they explored the knowledge of forms together?' The question surprised him. He thought the Glorified would need assistance. It appeared each had gained the knowledge by him or herself. His certainties were false. He dismissed the thoughts as he lifted his head and thrust out his chest, to making himself look bigger.

Seh created a shape with a hard, stone-like cover. It had four short limbs and walked low to the ground. The other Glorified could not see his chest but noticed his head was pointed upwards. It was part of Seh's posture—his attempt to appear greater. They thought it was how the form was designed. Seh felt sure in his command of transformation. He thought his form was the most creative. The hard, stone-like structure was almost a circle. Its small head and short tail were perfectly aligned. Seh imagined this form as a symbol of himself, providing guidance to the others. The form had six parts: the head, the tail, and four limbs, each of which he thought could represent a Glorified. He created the form as he considered how to instruct the others. The body of the form represented him, 'the master of transformation'. The form was a symbol of transformation because the form itself could change. It could be changed from a form with a body and six parts to just a body. Both the top and the belly were hard, and the head, tail, and limbs could be drawn into the body. The hard parts of the form could close to appear circular. In that way, the form itself symbolised transformation and represented how Seh could be set above and apart from the others.

Seh looked at Hu's form, wondering if Hu had gained the knowledge too quickly. Transformation seemed to have no impact on her. She did not grow a new posture. Her form stood vertical, with many fine vines spreading from its base. Seh thought it was too straight, wondering if she would stumble if a Glorified leaned against her. The form had a stem and at its base there were vine-like pieces spread out in all directions; she used them to root herself, ensuring she maintained her balance. Hu would use that form throughout the whiles. The top was circular, with delicate layers. Individual pieces formed a bulb at the top, each overlaid on the next. The Spark flowed gently through the pieces, displaying itself in the three colours of the 'parts of being'. Her creation was unique—but unstable, with limited motion, Seh thought, wondering if she meant to remain still throughout the gathering.

Hu spread the vine-like parts about her and replicated her form. She sprouted other versions of her form, slowly growing them until they became the taller parts of the form. There were shouts of laughter, which were not at first recognised as such. Each Glorified made a different, and oddly strange sound. The others thought Hu had transformed into multiple forms. They soon realised it was a single form with many parts. The Spark within her did not move, but grew brighter. She remained still as she had no need for movement. She spread and grew her form so wide it surrounded the others. They walked though it as humans might through a forest. The Spark within each of the Seven was bright with the Spirit of giving and receiving. Seh's form was heating up; he felt a surge of energy within him, for after their laughter, the others again called Hu names. That disturbed Seh's peace and feelings similar to human emotions boiled in him. He wanted to shout. He wanted to say that he was the one who uncovered transformation, not Hu; not the Glorified, not the First, the Self-Generator. Him! They should have no other master but him!

The others in the forms they had contributed, walked through and about Hu's form. They were careful to step over the vines Hu had spread. Seh was standing apart, while the others who had created similar forms moved about Hu's form as if exploring a new section of the Realm. Among the various stems of her form, the Glorified regarded the knowledge of form as a wondrous uncovering of the unknown, but no one commented to Seh. Instead, one of the others asked in a voice that would cause humans to assume he was thinking aloud or asking a rhetorical question: 'Why did Seh pursue this knowledge by himself?' Seh, still standing apart, offered no answer to the question. He was uncertain whether a question was truly asked or whether the Glorified was simply expressing his thoughts aloud.

Hu's form was the central feature of the gathering. The others, except Seh, seemed comfortable within her form. The Glorified, whose place in the circular assembly was on the right side of Hu, created a form with a shiny silvery streak down her back. Her contribution was the largest among the five similar forms. Her back was broad at the shoulders and narrowed towards the tailbone. The glow of the Sparks reflected off the silvery path on her back, providing an added sparkle to the gathering. She sat beside one of the stems within Hu's form and leaned back against it. She sat there for a while, gently swaying from side to side, causing the silvery streak to twinkle like distant stars. Her bent knees were almost at her chest. Her long arms fell to her side as she rocked gently. Seeing how the silvery streak mingled with the glow, the others asked if she knew the glow of the Sparks would enhance that feature of her form in such a way. She brightened her face and uttered a rough, bark-like sound to say she had not known. 'It must be part of those things to be uncovered with the knowledge of forms', she added. That comment caught the attention of Seh.

'She knows', he thought, 'there are mysteries along the path to the knowledge of transformation'. Before her comment, he had been looking at and pondering Hu's form. As she spoke, he started to examine her form, looking for clues that she had uncovered the mysteries along the way. He examined her face, which was not unlike the face of the Glorified. It was not round in the way that faces are, but more elongated as its jaws were pushed out, causing the lips to become thinner and the mouth to narrow. Seh expected her head to be held up and her chest to be pushed out. These were some of the signs Seh assumed indicated knowledge of the mysteries along the way. This Glorified, who had led the circular assembly about the meaning of a *true gift*, was leaning against Hu's form with her head bowed as if in deep thought.

Everything about the form she had created was like the Glorified, though with a slight variation. She had proposed that the First, the Self-Generator, had a voice and the Glorified's voices were variations of it. The form she had created was like that; merely a variation of the Glorified's form. Humans seeing her form would be forgiven if they thought it had come forth from the form of the Glorified. Seh looked at her form. He did not see any indication that she had knowledge of the mysteries along the way. He said to himself that her form was a poor use of transformation because it was just a variation upon the form of creation. The lips were much thinner than the lips of the Glorified. The nose had been transformed. The two holes or nostrils, as humans say, were widened, made larger to look like barely touching circles. The nose looked flattened on the face, as though the bridge had been removed but it was because the forehead was brought forward, causing the nose and the eyes to recede.

The forehead formed a distinct ridge over the eyes, which were a shade darker in colour than the eyes of the Glorified. Though the face looked similar to the Glorified, it was clearly not the head of the Glorified. The back of the head was moved to the top, forming a crest. The form did not seem to have a proper neck. It could not be distinguished where the neck ended and the shoulders and back began. The head seemed to sit on its shoulders. There were differences between the head of the Glorified and the head of her form. The face seemed to have been fitted onto the head and the back of the head was higher than the top of the forehead. There was a distinct mount on top of the head. There the silver back or the silvery part of her back began.

The Glorified in that form could walk upright, but was more at ease using her four limbs for motion. The hind limbs were the transformed legs of the Glorified only made to seem shorter, with well-defined muscles. The feet had five digits, which could be considered toes, but the great toe was oddly placed compared to the Glorified's. The fore-limbs, which were her transformed arms, were longer than the legs, causing the body to slant upwards when the four limbs were used for motion. Whether in that position or standing on just the legs, her head was not held up in the way Seh expected nor her chest pushed forward. Seh looked at her form and saw no sign she had uncovered mysteries along the way. He noticed her hands had five digits with the great finger—or thumb—oddly placed relative to the others. He wondered what the purpose of so small a change in both the hands and feet could be. In their positions, neither the thumb nor the great toe would point in the same direction as the fingers or toes. That suggested to Seh that her form would need to choose a direction to travel in order to fulfil *nia*. Seh began to wonder about choosing a path towards *nia*, but his thoughts were interrupted when the Glorified rose from leaning against Hu's form.

As she rose, she rolled the digits on her hands inwards as humans do to form a fist. Seh noticed and wondered whether she was feeling the growth of energy within her. Since transformation, Seh had felt changes in himself. He rolled his fingers inwards and formed tight balls with his hands. Sensations would seize him and before he knew what happened—or how it happened—he would be standing with his feet firmly planted, with the vessels of the Spark rolled into tight balls. Seh knew neither the path to nor the meaning of those behaviours. Seeing another Glorified roll her digits inwards made Seh wonder if she only partially uncovered the mysteries along the way, as she had not grown in posture. Partial knowledge, he thought, might be worse than none at all, for it may not lead to the true way. That's the reason, he thought, that the others needed to be guided so they may wholly uncover the true path to transformation.

It would be a while before Seh came to know that the others' experience was not the same as his. He continued to observe the others, looking for signs of change in their Spirits. He saw no difference in them; even the rolling of the digits by the Glorified was not an indication of the mysteries he found. It was, as humans say, 'A means to an end.' The Glorified rose and leaned forward so she could stand on all four of her limbs. She rolled her digits inward because she did not want to use the seat of the Spark as the Glorified used their feet. She knew the palms of the hands were the vessels of the Spark. She did not know for certain that the Spark was in its vessels. She was careful to place her hands facing upwards when she sat. The parts of the Spark were not in their vessels. They had spread across her chest, with a small ridge in the middle separating the halves. She wanted to avoid placing the vessels of the Sparks face down. She made a ball with her hands and used the bony part, the part humans called knuckles, as feet. For that reason, she could have been called a knuckle-walker with silver along her back.

The movement of the form was slow and deliberate. She made her way by putting the weight of her upper body on her knuckles. The feet, with the oddly placed digits, were also slightly different from the Glorified's. Like so many things in creation, the hands and the feet of the form were symmetric. They were not only symmetric in the sense that each was the mirror image of the other, but they were also symmetric in function. The form had four limbs, which could be used as feet. It could also be said it had four hands. The oddly placed digits on both hands and feet allowed the form to use both in the same manner. They were feet suited for walking upright, and they were hands that could be used for giving and receiving. That feature was shared by the similar forms created by the others.

There were no explanations why the five Glorified created similar forms. The forms ranged in size. The largest form was created by the Glorified whose place in the circular assembly is one position on the right of Hu and six positions on her left. The smallest form was created by the Glorified whose place is three positions on the left side of Hu and four positions on her right. That was the way the Glorified referred to one another. They made a reference to his or her place in the circular assembly. Humans would reference Hu's place in the circular assembly as position one. That would be, in part, due to the limitedness of human beings. The circular assembly is a circle and any place within it could be thought of as position one. Seh often thought of his place as position one, especially in the whiles after he uncovered the knowledge of transformation. Within it, Seh's place is three positions on the right of Hu and four positions on her left. The distance between Hu and Seh was the furthest separation possible within the circular assembly.

The circular assembly, also, reflects the symmetry in creation and demonstrates the sameness of the Glorified. Each Glorified's place could be one, and each could be a part of the symmetry that defines the furthest point away from one. Before humans, there were no individual names for the Glorified. The Glorified identified each other by the Spark and they referred to one another by his or her place in the circular assembly. While Seh pursued the knowledge of transformation, he wondered about a structure where each place could be called by the same symbol and there was no clear way to establish a hierarchy among them. In creating his form, he returned to the thought that his place should not be just another position. He should be set apart—above the others.

Seh stood apart while Hu spread her form. She created new stems and shoots from the vine-like parts of her form. She focused on the shoot the Glorified sat beside. She started to grow it, making it taller and giving it a bigger stem. As it grew, other shoots grew out of it. From those shoots came others. It grew taller. The shoots at the bottom grew outwards and new shoots were added above them and then new shoots were added above those and so on, until the top. That particular shoot had shoots attached to shoots, and the attached shoots had other shoots attached to them. All the shoots grew until they were intertwined, forming a kind of bramble. The Glorified whose place in the circular assembly is three positions on the left side of Hu and four positions on her right climbed up into the intertwined and tangled form. That Glorified had created a form which walked on all fours as well. It was the smallest of the five similar forms. The main similarities of the forms were the faces and the fact that they all had four limbs. The forms could stand upright using their hind limbs but found it easier to walk on four limbs.

As the Glorified climbed up into the bramble, it used all four of its limbs to hold on. This small form also had a tail. The tail was an extension of his backbone and he used it like a hand to grasp onto the stem. He allowed his form to hang down from Hu's form like a fruit hanging from a tree. Holding only with the tail, he started swinging back and forth. He called to Seh. Seh had not ventured into Hu's form like the others. He stood at the edge of her form like a human standing at the edge of a forest. The Glorified called to Seh and said to him that he could not have done this with his form from the last gathering. That caused the others to laugh, and the Sparks brightened. Seh's form from the last gathering was big and heavy. Both forms had a tail but the tail on Seh's form could not function like a hand. He would not have been able to hang from Hu's form like a fruit hanging from a tree.

Seh did not notice the similarities until the Seven pointed them out.

The tails were the same except they had different functions. The large and heavy tail was the first part of his form that Seh had transformed. He pointed it upwards when he demonstrated how fast the form could move. Seh's extension allowed him to balance the large form. On the tiny form, the extension to the backbone was almost always up. It appeared the form was created to walk on four limbs. The front and hind limbs were approximately the same length. His back was level, not slanted upwards when he walked. When he stood up, his front limbs appeared to be longer than his back legs because his back limbs bent sharply at the knees. It was easier for the tiny form to walk on four limbs. He did not have the same concern about the Spark as the Glorified one position on the right side of Hu. When he walked, the extended portion of the backbone formed an arch over his back. The curl at the tip of the tail was held just over his head. He held it there, as if he knew the Spark required it that way. Even Seh admitted that he had created a wonderful form.

Similar to how the Spark placed itself in the tail of Seh's original form, the Spark had placed itself along the extension on this tiny form. Upon the form, the Spark filled in the space between the arch and his back, displaying itself in the colours of the 'three parts of being'. When the tail was straight, when he used it to reach, to touch the others, or to swing from Hu's form, it was divided into equal parts by the 'three colours of being', starting with red, followed by black and then green. It is not known—and there are no references in the endowment—whether there is a divine order in which the three colours of the 'parts of being' should be displayed. Is it red, black and green or green, black and red? What is true, like their places in the circular assembly, is that the colours of the 'parts of being' are always displayed with black in the middle. On the form, the Spark showed itself in red, black and green but when he created the arch, the order of the colours in the space between the arch and his back became green, black and red, which only affirmed the way the colours of the 'parts of being' should be displayed is unknown.

Seh looked at the arch over the back of the form and wondered if the Glorified was attempting to make himself bigger, to develop a new posture—to show the others he should be set apart. The extension to the backbone on the form, although similar to the extension Seh had created, had more functionality. The Glorified used it to follow the silvery path on the back of the form of the 'other'. He gently ran the extension along her back, wondering about the interplay of the glow of the Spark and the silver streak. Such sharing, he thought, as the glow of his Spark brightened and shimmered with the silvery streak on her back.

The extension was gentle in its touch but strong and firm in its grip. He held to Hu's form only with the tail. He swung back and forth, slowly at first and then faster and faster. As he swung forward, he released the hold and he leapt from one stem to another. Then, without swinging, he jumped to yet another. The speed and agility of the tiny form surprised the others, and it caused Hu's form to sway like trees being blown by the wind as he jumped from shoot to shoot.

Hu maintained her form. Two other Glorified, losing control of their forms, drifted back into the forms of their creation. The Glorified whose place in the circular assembly is two positions on the left of Hu and five positions on her right did not recreate her form. She picked up a *ndo* and started to play. The other Glorified who lost control of his form is the Glorified whose place in the circular assembly is one position on the left of Seh and six positions on his right. The form he had created, although similar to the others, was the second largest of the five. He too did not recreate his form, choosing instead to be of service to the others by sharing food and drink. He knew not how to share with Hu. Her form with its various shoots and the vines spread around her did not have a face. There were no identifiable parts, no hands or feet, no ears or eyes, and no nose or mouth. The first shoot was shaped differently from the other shoots she made. On the top of the stem sat a circular bulb-like part. At the centre of it was a nucleus wrapped by many individual pieces, but the pieces loosened as they fell away from the centre. Hu used that part of the form to speak and used the vines to partake in ale. Seeing Hu partake in ale in such a manner, the whole gathering brightened with the glow of the Sparks and that section of the Realm filled with the many different voices that their forms made. The Glorified playing the *ndo* underscored their sounds by beating a quick tempo, adding to the merriment at the gathering.

She played the first *ndo* that Hu had made. She played it in the way the Glorified treated the *ndo*, as an instrument with its own tongue, which always has something to share. The Glorified whose place in the circular assembly is one position on the left side of Hu started jumping around. She did not lose control of her form when she saw the small form jumping from shoot to shoot. Her form was nearly identical to the one created by the Glorified whose place is two positions on the left side of Hu. These two Glorified, whose places are side by side in the circular assembly, had created forms that were nearly the same. Those forms looked so similar that humans would think they were from the same family. Unlike the small form, this form had no extension to the backbone. Its arms were longer than its legs and it shared the concern of using the vessels of the Sparks as feet. It too rolled its fingers into balls and used the bony part as feet. She walked in and out of Hu's form, touching the shoots as they sprouted in various places. After the Glorified in the small form jumped from shoot to shoot, this Glorified climbed up into a shoot. Using all four of her limbs, she climbed up and down the shoot, then, hung from it holding on only with her hands. She swung back and forth similarly to the small form, but her form lacked a tail, so she held on with the long arms and pushed back and forth with her legs. As she swung forward she let go, but instead of jumping to another shoot, she landed beside the Glorified playing the *ndo*, reverted to her form of creation, and began to dance. Then all the Glorified drifted back to their forms of creation except Seh, who maintained his chosen shape throughout the gathering.

That was the first gathering where each Glorified created a contribution by him or herself. There had been gatherings before where the Glorified contributed things they had created during the *while of quiet*. Those things were all part of 'collective creativity'. The Glorified added to the collective outcomes by including suggestions he or she had made which were not part of the final outcome. The outcomes would be similar but not the same. The Glorified would bring them to the gathering to share 'know-how'. Those contributions had a common beginning, but the contributions at this gathering were different. They were a departure from a common beginning and a drifting away from the *harambe* of 'collective creativity'. Transformation opened a door to an unknown, and the Glorified did not seem to realise it. More and more creativity would follow that method. By the while human beings came into existence, the Glorified would be exploring the unknown alone.

In uncovering the unknown, the Glorified always had a common experience, which they called 'in the beginning'. The beginning had always been collective, thought of together, explored together, and uncovered together. Although the truth was a secret, the Glorified thought that their beginning was collective. They were certain that the First, the Self-Generator, created them together with one thought, word, or act. The fact that they were not all exactly the same—neither in form nor in Spark—demonstrated *Its* will. It showed the First, the Self-Generator, could create many outcomes with one thought, word, or act, while the Glorified could only achieve one outcome with many thoughts, many words, and many actions.

The Glorified considered that to be a limitation. They tried to overcome it by adding to the outcomes they gained together. These additions were considered part of 'collective creativity'. That was how the others were able to see the *ndo* as an outcome of what they had done together. There was a common beginning for the *ndo*, while the knowledge of form only had a common outcome. They tried to expand transformation in similar ways, except they did not know which thoughts had been part of its beginning that were not included in its final outcome. They waited for Seh to open a circular assembly. While they waited, they added to the number of different forms. Transformation marked a departure from a collective beginning, from a common place of start, and although the outcomes were the same, there were seven individual experiences represented by the forms at the gathering. There were seven beginnings towards the same outcome, with each Glorified gaining the knowledge in his or her way.

The Glorified began with the same endowment. They added to it through 'collective creativity' and '*sharing of know-how*'. 'The path to the unknown is a mystery but uncovering it is a shared journey', is what the Glorified would say when the endowment was silent. The Glorified did not know the path to transformation. The endowment was silent and Seh had denied them the opportunity to uncover it in a shared journey. After the revealing of transformation, it was no longer an unknown. The Glorified knew they could recreate the outcome since whatever one has done, the others can do.

Recreating the outcome was the point where the others started. They began not with knowledge of the beginning, but with the vision of the outcome. They gained the shape slowly, transforming each part until the full shape came into being. Each Glorified began with the part he or she had gained at the gathering. They thought of the part they had gained as an outcome of 'collective creativity'. Their partial outcome was added to, just as they had done with collective outcomes. They added the remaining parts of the shape Seh created. They each gained the same outcome as Hu—a shape exactly like Seh's, except smaller. At the gathering, Hu did not slowly transform one part of her form and then another. Her whole form transformed together. The process for the five others and Seh took a different path. The knowledge of forms was simple, but it had many peculiarities. Seh began with the unknown, the five others began with an outcome in search of its beginning, but where Hu began was known only to the First, the Self-Generator.

Hu's whole form transformed together when she gained the 'know-how'. The Glorified were focused on the outcome and no one—not even Seh, noticed that Hu transformed all of her parts at once. No other Glorified had that experience. It should have been the subject of a circular assembly. There were other peculiarities which should have been pursued. Why all the others began with a smaller version of the form than Seh, for example. The others were waiting to bring their experience to a circular assembly. They waited, but Seh did not explore transformation any further, not even to understand the mysteries along the way. His purpose was to be set apart. He knew some changes occurred in him. He did not know if those changes also occurred for the others. Seh did not share his experience and he did not explore transformation, not even after Hu started exploring the path to the Rapture. He only wanted to fulfil his purpose. With each new form, he said to himself, 'This is the one.' This is the form that will cause the others to call him names.

CHAPTER 11

MEANING IN THE JOURNEY

None of the Glorified considered exploring transformation in the manner Hu explored the path to the Rapture. She began to follow the Spark after wondering whether there was any meaning in the path to the Rapture. She uncovered that there were things along the path not seen by the Glorified. She shared with the others that there was more to the Rapture than just the 'simultaneousness of being'. Seh listened to her in the way the Glorified listen, with all of their being. He thought that even though things about the Rapture had been missed, the Glorified had all gained the outcome. When Hu had wondered if there was meaning to be found along the path to the Rapture, Seh questioned if the journey could be of more value than the destination. He realised, as Hu shared her insights, that even though the outcome appeared to be the same, the others might have missed features along the way to transformation. Seh thought his experience the only true path to follow. He did not share with the others the things he had experienced since uncovering transformation. He thought his path not only led to the outcome, but also included the value in the journey. He did not know whether the journey ought to be of more value than the destination, yet he assumed the features of transformation the others missed were of more value than the outcome.

There were many whiles after transformation was revealed before the Glorified uncovered the Rapture. There were many more whiles before Hu began following the Spark. So, it was a while before Seh concluded the others did not have the same experience with transformation. This was further proof to him that they could only gain the knowledge by following his path. He examined the shapes the others contributed, looking for signs that they had uncovered his path. The others gained the outcome, but no one pushed their chest out or held their head high to appear bigger. He did not observe any Glorified standing apart with feet firmly planted, with hands rolled into tight balls. Those were the features Seh thought would indicate the others had the same knowledge as he. Those were the signs of the true way to him. The Spirits of the others did not manifest those behaviours. They gained the outcome, but Seh was certain they needed guiding into the new way, to be shown the value in the journey.

The Glorified journeyed alone yet arrived at the same destination. There were no indications that they had not followed the same path. That let a *false truth* to grow among them: the assumption that they, all, added the same value to the endowment. Even without the beginning, without the collective start, they thought they had gained the same outcome and acquired the same knowledge. They saw no difference between the outcome from their use of transformation and Seh's. Their senses were not expanded as Hu's senses were during the announcement. They could not see that Seh had an unfulfilled purpose. They did not notice Seh standing apart with his feet firmly planted and his hands rolled into tight balls. They saw no difference in him or in the Spark within him. It was only Seh who knew he uncovered features unknown to the others, which made him certain that the others did not follow the true path.

He, too, created a *false truth*, assuming his way was the only true path to the destination. He assumed his thoughts, the sensations he felt, and the manifestation of his Spirit represented truth. He assumed only in his footsteps could the others find the way. Humans, too, lived that *false truth*, trying to follow in the footsteps of prophets and messiahs. Assuming their thoughts, their words, their feelings, the outcomes of their Spirits was the only true way. That is not the way of creation. Humans have *nia*. Their purpose is the same as the purpose of creation but for many humans—the believers—that *false truth* is the only way. Human beings are form, Spark, and Spirit, and no human—whether preacher, prophet nor messiah—is able to lead them into the way of creation. In both the Glorified and humans, the Spark is the only indicator of the way.

Seh saw no changes in the Spirit of the others. There were no signs the others had travelled his path. He knew that, for the first, there was a difference in the knowledge of the Glorified. Sharing the journey and uncovering the unknown together added the same value to the endowment. The Glorified added to and expanded the endowment with their activities. However, transformation, unlike their other outcomes, had no natural place nor purpose in creation. It differed from contributions which were made from the Mystery of Creation or other things found in the Realm. New foods had a place and purpose among the foods and drinks, which the Realm brought forth. There was no question of a place or purpose for the *ndo*. Unlike the *ndos*, a place and purpose for the forms created with transformation could not be found. Seh had uncovered a path to a true unknown. There were no references to it in the endowment. There were no likenesses of it in creation. Seh was the only Glorified who recalled the passing mention of it at a circular assembly. The Glorified gained the same outcome but they did not have a shared common experience. Like the human journey from the marketplace to home, some travelled the path quickly and others slowly, but unlike the human journey, transformation appeared to be without purpose.

Transformation existed only as 'know-how', as knowledge to know for the sake of knowing. Seh thought the knowledge should set him apart, above the others. However, there was no place in creation for knowledge that lifts one above another. It is only the First, the Self-Generator, who has no equal and everyone and everything is dependent on *It*. The tenth truth of creation says, 'There are no hierarchies in creation, no greater than or lesser than, no consciousness above another; but none that is independent of the First, the Self-Generator.' There is nothing in creation that could elevate one of the First, the Self-generator's creation above another. Seh's purpose with transformation had no place among the Glorified nor in creation.

Seh thought the others did not travel the true path because his actions did not cause them to put aside a truth of creation. Five of the Glorified travelled a path similar to Seh, but they did not uncover any mysteries along the way. The others began their journey with the vision of the destination, not with the purpose of setting themselves apart, not with the assumption that greater than or lesser than could be created among the First, the Self-Generator's creations. Seh began his journey with a purpose. He assumed Hu had been set apart and that started him on a journey to create a hierarchy among them. That was the first difference among the Glorified. It was a first they had not shared the path to an unknown. It was a first their purpose was not the same. Seh had uncovered a path to knowledge without a place and purpose in creation because it was the first a Glorified had not chosen from among the indications of the Spark. That was the only difference among them, until Hu began to follow the Spark and she was given the task in the announcement. Until the moment the others referred to

Hu as 'a master of sound', there were no differences among the Glorified other than being shaped like males and females, as humans define those. Hearing the others refer to Hu as 'the master of sound' started Seh on his journey. It created a difference between him and the others, though only he knew it.

Seh was the only Glorified whose Spirit gave meaning and substance to the mysteries found along the way. He did not discuss them with the others, nor did he attempt to understand them, to find where along the path they had arisen and for what purpose. The path he thought should lead to him being heralded 'the master of transformation'. Beyond that outcome, he assumed transformation had no other purpose. The others longed for the shared journey but Seh coveted something that was not in the way of creation. That prevented him from opening a discussion in a circular assembly. He could not explain transformation or why he pursued it by himself. He had his planned responses to the questions. He looked for opportunities to smooth over his choosing, but he chose not to share his purpose or to say more about how he reverted to the idea. He did not share those parts of his journey or mention the mysteries he found. The birth of the idea that a Glorified could be set apart and above the others created within Seh a space—one he felt could only be filled by him being acclaimed 'the master of transformation'. Humans called that manifestation a desire, but the Glorified had no symbols for it.

In the Realm the Glorified need not and want not. Yet there grew within Seh a space that creation could not fill even though he was in the Realm, a place of everlasting plenty. The Realm—a paradise like the human universe would be—is a place, space, or time of the First, the Self-Generator, where the vessel is forever full. Seh had hidden himself away from the others and, for a while, the Spark within him did not have an opportunity to brighten. During that while, he did not choose the indications of the Spark. His choosing, his purpose, and his actions caused him to fall out of harmony with creation. For a first in the Realm, a Glorified did not choose the way of creation, and the Spark within him reflected it.

That was what Hu noticed during the announcement. The Spark within Seh appeared to be different. It was dim compared to the Spark in the others. It was like the Spark had a haze over it, dampening its glow. She did not know the glow of a Spark could be as low as the glow of the Spark within Seh during the announcement. The Sparks were always alight in the presence of others. At the gathering where Seh revealed the knowledge of transformation, there were no differences in the Sparks. Hu looked for the Spark and slowly ran her fingers along the part of his form where the Spark located itself. The Sparks were bright, and as the vessel of her Spark passed over the Spark in him it twinkled, becoming even brighter. After that, she knew she could rec-reate the shape Seh had created. She looked at the form and without fully understanding how, she recreated it, except for one detail. Then, the glow of the Sparks brightened. The Sparks displayed in the three colours of the 'parts of being' and the whole section of the Realm gleamed with a warm radiance.

The Spark in both the Glorified and in human beings indicates the way. Choosing the indications of the Spark is choosing the way of creation. Seh did not choose 'sharing of know-how'. He did not bring his purpose into the glow of the Sparks, and he questioned the know-ledge of the First, the Self-Generator. It could have been those actions, or some other thought that caused him to fall from the way of cre-ation. It could have been his attempt to create greater than and lesser than among creations of the First, the Self-Generator, that caused the slight tinge upon the Spark. The Glorified knew not that Seh had fallen from the path indicated by the Spark. They did not know that his choosing was driven by compulsion. There were no hints in the Spark at the gatherings. They did not notice his Spirit as he stood apart, and there were no signs that, in some whiles or moments, Seh could not hear, feel, or see the oneness within creation.

CHAPTER 12

TRUTH IN PERFECTION

With each new form, Seh told himself, 'This is it! This is the one.' This form would cause the others to call him names, to set him apart and above them. He would say there should be no other master but him. He repeated it several times, like a human being making an affirmation. He spent the quiet thinking about the shapes the others presented, assessing whether they were more or less creative than his. During the announcement, Hu witnessed Seh thinking about the form she presented and heard him resolve to be more creative at the next gathering. He was concerned that the form she presented was more creative than his. At that gathering, the Sparks were alight with the outpouring of creativity. The gathering was full of mirth, and there was much eating and drinking. Seh thought that would be the gathering— the gathering where he would be set apart, where he would be made 'the master of transformation'. He wondered what he should say when the others acknowledged him as the master. He considered whether it would be appropriate to reveal the mysteries he had found. Seh was in deep thought, anticipating being set apart. The sounds of the others around him seemed distant as they admired the many unusual features of his form. He wondered which Glorified would be the first to name him 'the master of transformation'. The form with the oversized ears and the elongated nose made Seh the focus of the gathering. He was certain that he would be set apart, but, as with many other gatherings, Seh, instead of being set apart, was asked why—why he pursued transformation by himself?

A Glorified was lamenting the loss of the beginning. It was not what Seh was expecting. He felt the mysteries growing in him. As the mysteries rose in him, he pointed the elongated nose upwards, raised his form so it stood on its hind legs, and made a sound as the heat of the mysteries flowed through him. The Spark within him relocated itself by sliding down the back of the form as he rose up on the hind legs. Seh exhaled slowly through the elongated nose, which caused the form to make a trumpet sound the others thought had musical elements. As the heat from the mysteries flowed through him, the others sampled the ale he had prepared for the gathering. They did not notice his Spark had relocated itself. They were expecting the same explanation Seh had provided over the whiles. His responses never met the needs of their queries. The Glorified no longer listened to his explanations. The others did not know what Seh had done to travel the path to transformation or that he coveted something that was not the way of creation. He did not respond, and the Glorified moved on from lamenting the loss of the shared journey to enjoying the ale he had prepared. It added to their merriment, allowing them to put aside the loss of the common beginning.

Seh did not participate in the ale. He stood apart, silently yearning. His desire to be set apart was known only to him and to the First, the Self-Generator. There are no purposes that can be hidden from *It*. *It* is a knowing being, but Seh's purpose and the reason he journeyed alone were unknown to the others. They had not noticed any changes. They wondered about his physical appearance when he revealed transformation, but no longer seemed to recognise Seh's posture. The

Glorified are one within the First, the Self-Generator. Their physical appearance has no value or purpose. That is also true for human beings, but humans pour much into physical appearance. They see purpose where there is none. Their *false truths* about physical appearance caused humans to lose the strength to see the Spark within each other.

In pursuit of appearance, they sacrificed the knowledge that each human being is a child of creation. Even though the ninth truth said the First, the Self-Generator, has no shape or form, humans preach that they are created in *Its* image. That *false truth* blinded them to the purpose of creation. Ritual societies preach that physical appearances are blessings or curses. That preaching, like many other human beliefs, is not a truth. There is no value in the physical appearance of the Glorified or humans. The Glorified recognise each other not by their appearance but by the Spark. Over the whiles, even as the Glorified focused on each new shape, they saw no difference in each other. When Seh was in his form of creation and the mysteries arose in him, they saw only his Spark, not his hands rolled into tight balls, or his feet firmly planted. They knew that Seh did not choose *'sharing of know-how'*, but they did not know it caused a difference within him.

The Glorified had only ever witnessed the Spark brightening its glow. Hu had noticed a twinkle in the glow of the Spark within Seh. It caused her to wonder if the glow of the Spark was the Spark's way of communicating. In the Rapture, the Glorified would see the Spark brightening its glow. The Spark in the physical form can recognise the Spark in the Rapture even though the Glorified in the physical form cannot see another in the Rapture. Hu brought her thought to a circular assembly, suggesting that the glow of the Spark might be how the Sparks communicate. They searched the endowment. There were no references to the glow of the Spark or whether the Sparks communicate with each other. Neither she nor the others had any indication that the Spark could lower its glow. It was only during the announcement that she witnessed a change in the Spirit of the Spark. She was able to look upon the Sparks of the others without the glow brightening. She knew the Spark within each Glorified was not the same. There were small differences in each Spark, which the Glorified use to recognise each other—but she expected the glow to be the same. In the announcement, expanding outwards, she recalled the fifth truth of creation: 'All of creation is one within the First, the Self-Generator.' She acknowledged, as they did after the Rapture that there were two parts to the Spark: The Spark and the Presence within the Spark.

In the announcement, she was the Presence within the Spark. She expanded outwards, filling the place, space, or time opened for her. She heard Seh, as her expanded *'self'* flowed in all directions, and felt his resolve to be more creative at the next gathering. She listened and looked at his Spark. She saw the Spark lower its glow and reveal a slight tinge on it. She had not known a Spark to lower its glow. She did not know a Spark could have a mark. The Spark is the First, the Self-Generator; it is part of the *'gift of being'*. It leads the Spirit, and it indicates the path towards *nia*. She looked at the others to see if their Sparks would lower their glows, but the Sparks in the others were unchanged. She tried to focus on Seh as she heard him declare, 'There can be no other', but the glow of his Spark brightened again; the slight tinge on it was gone. 'No other what?' she thought, drifting out-wards, listening with all of her being. Although the glow of his Spark was again the same as the others, she wanted a while more to linger with him. Seh needed—she had never known any such thing. She sensed the need within him. It was due to something he lacked; he was being drawn by it like a moth to a flame. As she expanded outwards, filling in the place, space, or time the 'nothing' had opened, she heard his thoughts no more, but she wondered: what could a Glorified need that has not been provided by creation?

Hu did not know what Seh lacked. She was certain, even though he awaited it, that it were empty. It was a need that had no place or purpose. The Spark lowering its glow caused her again to wonder whether the glow of the Spark was its way of communicating. The Glorified had not explore her suggestion that the glow might be the Spark's way of communicating. They searched the endowment and then the circular assembly moved on to explore whether there was any rhyme or rhythm to where the Spark chooses to locate itself in transformation.

The Spark has its vessels. In the form of creation, especially during the *whiles of quiet*, it could be found reclining in its vessel, with its parts flowing towards the fingers. However, the Spark could locate itself anywhere in the form. At whiles, the Spark would locate itself in the tight curls of their hair. It would loosen the curls so the hair stood tall, causing the hair to appear as a dome on their heads. In other whiles, the Spark would spread itself throughout the form so it could be seen in the whole form. The Glorified could not look upon the Spark within themselves. They had to be told where the Spark had located itself. This was especially true when the form of creation was transformed into a different shape. At the gathering before the announcement, the Spark within Seh had located itself in the oversized ears and between the ears it formed an arch, which was displayed in the 'three colours of being'. The Spark, then, relocated itself to the small tail of the form when the mysteries found along the way arose in Seh.

Locating the Spark in the form became part of the merriment at the gatherings. Each Glorified, after changing into the shape he or she created, would be asked to guess where the Spark chose to locate itself. Before guessing, the Glorified would listen—there would be a quiet—and then all of the Realm would erupt with the sound of laughter. The Glorified did not know where the Spark would choose to locate itself. They had not been able to determine whether there is any rhythm to its choice. It was as if the Spark itself participated in their merriment, choosing its location as if it knew the answer the Glorified would give. The Glorified's suppositions about the location of the Spark had never known truth. They had not been able to guess where the Spark would locate itself in the form they created. The Spark's choice, they thought, was like the acts of the First, the Self-Generator, known only to *It*. It appeared not only was the choice known solely to the Spark, but also once the Spark had chosen, it did not change its location. That was a certainty to the Glorified, but it was a *false truth*, as a Spark relocated itself when the mysteries found along the way arose in Seh. That was the first a Spark changed its location in a form, but no one noticed. It passed without being heralded, like the oneness in creation among human beings.

Focusing on the ale, the Glorified did not notice the change in the Spark's location. They thought the Spark did not change its location once it had chosen. That was not a truth—it was a certainty. If it were a truth, it would be a truth forever and a more. The Spark is the First, the Self-Generator, and the last truth of creation says: 'The First, the Self-Generator's truths are eternal; they are truths forever and a more.' That certainty was a *false truth* and at the gathering it was revealed for all to see. Yet the Glorified, discussing the ale, did not see it, and the certainty remained true among them.

The Spark chooses its location in transformation, but no two Sparks have ever chosen the same part of a form. When a Glorified acknowledges the creativity of another by recreating his or her form, the Spark would locate itself in a different part of the form, as if it knew which part of the form had known a Spark. That was not what the Glorified expected. They expected the Spark to have its vessels in transformation similar to the form of creation. They had not witnessed two Sparks choosing the same location in a form. When the Glorified created the form that Hu had described, the Sparks located themselves in different parts of the form, even though each Glorified created the same form. The Glorified reasoned that the slight variation in the Sparks and the truth that the Spark is the First, the Self-Generator, caused the Spark not only to choose a different location in each shape but also to remain in that location forever and a more. That *false truth* was revealed to be false, but it passed without being acknowledged.

They could find no rhyme or rhythm in the locations the Sparks chose. The endowment says the Spark's proper place is in its vessels. In the circular assemblies with each Glorified in his or her place, the Spark would always be in its vessels, as if it too had a place in the circular assembly. In the beginning of their existence, the Glorified awoke searching the endowment as they sat in their places. Unlike humans, who do not know whether they were standing or sitting, kneeling or lying down, when their existence began, the Glorified know when their existence began they were sitting in a circular assembly, searching the endowment. The Glorified awoke at the same while and beheld the presence of each other as they came to know existence. That was what caused them to assume they were created at the same while. The endowment is silent, but each Glorified thinks of his or her place in the circular assembly as the place chosen for him or her by the First, the Self-Generator. In the circular assembly, the Glorified always knew the location of his or her Spark. If the Spark's choice in transformation had rhyme or rhythm, it was known only to the First, the Self-Generator. The Glorified did not know the reasons the Spark kept its choices out of their reach. They were certain the Spark knew their choice and was participating in their merriment.

'There is *truth in perfection* and the Spark, like the First, the Self-Generator, is perfect in its truths', said the Glorified whose place in the circular assembly is one position on the right of Hu and six positions on her left. She, like the others, had not been able to locate the Spark in transformation. After the laughter that followed her guess, she added, as her face revealed the purity of a smile; 'The truth in this perfection is that no one knows the will of the First, the Self-Generator.' The Glorified in their exploration of the Spark's choice affirmed the sixth truth of creation—only the First, the Self-Generator, knows what *It* might or might not do. That knowledge was out of reach not only to the Glorified but also to the rest of creation. The Glorified acknowledged that they had not been able to locate the Spark in transformation, yet they continued to ask each other to guess the location of the Spark because they were certain the Sparks were participating in their merriment and, in so doing, affirming a truth of creation.

The Glorified did not explore the glow of the Spark like they explored where in the form the Spark might locate itself. Similar to how they were certain the Spark would position itself forever and a more, it was also a certainty that the glow of the Spark always brightened. That was because over the whiles, in the presence of each other, the glow of the Sparks always brightened. If the Glorified had been the Presence in all things as Hu had been during the announcement, they would have seen—as Seh's Spark tumbled down the back of his form—a slight lowering in the glow of the Spark. The others' senses had not been expanded, and their thoughts and minds were upon the ale Seh had contributed. So, they did not witness the movement of the Spark or the lowering of its glow. As they discussed the ale and how deep the *while of quiet* will be, the glow of Seh's Spark brightened again. The Spark within him moved back to the position it had chosen before the mysteries rose in him.

Witnessing a Spark lowering its glow added to Hu's confusion during the announcement. She had looked upon her Rapture particles and her physical form at the same while. She saw, for the first, the Spark within her. These, along with not having insight into the glow of the Spark, added to the rambling of her thoughts. She recalled how Seh's Spark brightened slightly when he revealed transformation. Then, her thoughts drifted away from the glow of the Spark as the question of why Seh pursued transformation by himself arose in her. She had never asked Seh that question. The other Glorified questioned Seh but Hu accepted transformation as a contribution to the gathering. Her thoughts swirled and swung around to a *true gift* and briefly stumbled unto the difference between truths and certainties. Then, she recalled spending a part of the quiet in thought, contemplating the reasons for their being before her thoughts ambled towards the idea that creation is sharing.

She thought about the sharing at the gatherings—about how, over the whiles, the Glorified shared with each other—and how the glow of the Spark brightened with giving and receiving. She had not considered it before but in her confusion, she wondered if the Sparks also shared 'know-how'. Her thoughts then returned to the gathering with the *ndos* and the revealing of transformation. The Spark within Seh twinkled. Was that how she gained transformation, she wondered? She tried to explore the thought that the Sparks shared 'know-how' as she listened to the 'nothing' in the announcement. As the Presence in all things, it was not the sounds of creation that caused her thoughts to drift but rather the silence that surrounded her. It was different from the quiet in the Realm and listening caused her thoughts to become unclear and unfocused. She recalled wandering throughout the Realm. She would walk aimlessly, without direction or purpose but deep in thought. She wondered about the Spark and the 'three parts of being'. She would clear her mind to let her thoughts flow freely. She always arrived at the same place—standing beside the Mystery of Creation as it began, wondering about the reasons for their being.

She looked upon her Spark and then on the Sparks of the others. The Sparks did not brighten, so she wondered if the Sparks were at rest. She was trying to understand what she was witnessing. A Spark had revealed a slight tinge upon its golden form. There was a mark the colour of Seh's Rapture upon the Spark within him. That caused her thoughts to stumble from one idea to another. She compared Seh's Spark to the Spark within the others. She tried to focus on Seh, wondering what could have led the Spark within him to lowering its glow and what could have placed a mark upon it. The tinge upon Seh's Spark was as fleeting as the twinkle in the glow. It was there, and then the Spark regained its glow and the mark could no longer be seen, but, like the knowledge of forms—it had been revealed.

After the Rapture, Seh had been asked if he had let the Spark lead to uncover transformation. They thought the knowledge of forms was part of the *perfection in creation*. They did not know that Seh had put aside a truth of creation and wanted to elevate himself above them. Seh's purpose, although kept out of sight of the others, became part of him. It was in the way he held his head. It could be seen in the way he pushed out his chest. His hidden purpose showed itself in the mysteries found along the way. When Seh's chosen purpose became part of him, the Spark and he were no longer in harmony. They were no longer moving along the same path or flowing in the same direction. There was the path that led to the uncovering of the unknown, and then there was the way Seh planned to go. As Seh travelled along the path he chose, he no longer followed the indications of the Spark. His Spark no longer led, but it could not follow either, and the farther he travelled, the more he distanced himself from the Spark. That was what Hu witnessed in the announcement. Seh had distanced himself from the indications of the Spark.

The mark on the Spark indicated that there was something different about Seh, and in the announcement, Hu could feel it. If she lessened the randomness of her thoughts, like clearing her mind during her aimless wandering, she could be everything in creation. She felt the contentment of the others as they rested in a *while of quiet*. They appeared to be whole. The parts of their being were content as the quiet replenished their form of creation. If she turned her thoughts to Seh, she felt the parts of his being did not have the same peace. That was due to something Seh lacked, and she wondered if he allowed the Spark to lead, would it lead to the outcome? She did not know what caused the space within him. She tried to consider what in the Realm could have given rise to the faint tinge upon his Spark. Had they not all travelled the path together and uncovered the unknown together? Her thoughts were fleeting, but she concluded that if what he was waiting for was part of the *perfection in creation*, then choosing the way of creation should gain him the outcome. As her expanded '*self*' flowed outwards, she put it aside and gave it no further thought until Seh found her and the Creature as they journeyed towards the seal.

CHAPTER 13

SHAKEN

Hu's eyes widened—her lips fell apart—as she looked upon the Spark within Seh. She had not expected to see a mark on it, even though she had seen it in the announcement. Her first thought was of the emptiness. She tried to speak, to ask him what outcome he awaited. Before she could ask him about the Spark, Seh stepped closer to her and asked if she had uncovered the path to the *duality of being*. He was shaken back into his form of creation. His words stumbled over each other. He too had seen something unexpected as the Creature leapt from her shoulder to her arm and back again. He did not look for a Spark within the Creature, nor did he search the endowment. His first thought was that Hu had found another way to set herself apart. He thought she had uncovered the path to the *duality of being*. The *duality of being* is the idea of existing in both the physical form and the Rapture at the same while. Seh applied that idea to transformation. Seeing the Creature, he assumed Hu had found a way to create a shape and maintain her form of creation. He thought she had found a way to divide herself into fractions, so she could be in a transformed shape and in her form of creation simultaneously.

He considered what in creation could have opened the path to such knowing. The Creature continued leaping, reminding Hu that they should not delay. She turned towards her destiny and started walking again. Seh did not know how she created the shape, but he was certain it would cause the others to call her names. He felt the mysteries found along the way boiling within him. He took a deep breath; the vessels of his Spark opened, and his fingers became less tense and rigid as his shoulders fell slightly. He put aside all thoughts about the shape he had created, the form with the long neck, the one he thought was it. He drew another deep breath before setting off to join Hu and the Creature. The Creature was still jumping on her when Seh joined them, heading towards the seal. As he walked beside her, matching his pace to hers, he asked again: how—how did she uncover the path to this *duality of being*?

Hu did not respond to Seh's inquiry straightaway. She waited before answering, assessing how to respond, trying to find the right symbols to begin the tale. After a while, she began her explanation with the words, 'These are the creations of the First, the Self-Generator. *It* has created these *gifts*.' Seh, listening while walking beside her, recognised the rightful use of the symbol '*gift*' for only the First, the Self-Generator, could create *gifts*. "This Creature", Hu said, "like all of creation, is one within the First, the Self-Generator. It is not a form. It was not created with the knowledge of forms. It was created from 'nothing'." Seh stepped in front of her, causing her to stop walking. He looked directly at her Spark. He noticed the Spark within her looked as if it had been polished or newly recreated. Those were not the words he had expected. He had expected her to say that the Creature is her contribution to the gathering, that she found a way to expand upon transformation to gain a kind of *duality of being*; he had expected her to say that the form was just an extension of herself. Instead, she began her explanation with a reference to the First, the Self-Generator, that caused Seh to search the endowment.

The Glorified almost never referenced the First, the Self-Generator. They did not speak of *It* in vain. They searched the endowment whenever *It* was referenced. Truths concerning *It* are found in the endowment. Seh searched the endowment, pausing after the first truth of creation, but focused on finding any reference that might hint the Creature existed. He listed each of the First, the Self-Generator's creations as they appeared in the endowment. *It* created *Itself.* He started at the beginning, stating the truth that is known to all of creation. *It* brought forth the Realm and everything in it. Then, *It* waited a while before *It* created the Glorified Seven. Beyond those, the endowment is silent. There were no other creations of the First, the Self-Generator, and he looked at Hu and asked her, 'How? How is it a truth?'

Again, Hu paused before answering. She looked upon his Spark, and how each part of it sat in its vessel, before she said, 'It has been announced.' 'Announced!' Seh repeated the term as if to verify what was said. 'By whom? Who announced it?' '*It* announced it', Hu said. '*It* has spoken?' Seh asked. '*It* speaks? If *It* speaks, should not all hear?' As he asked the questions, Seh searched the endowment once more. He had listed the creations of the First, the Self-Generator, as they were known to the Glorified. They had no knowledge of any other creatures and the endowment did not indicate that *It* speaks.

Hu, attempting to get on her way, said, 'The First, the Self-Generator, does not speak', as she stepped around Seh, who stood in her path. 'At least not in the way of the Glorified', she added. 'With the First, the Self-Generator...' she paused again to choose the appropriate symbols before saying that she heard because she was *It*; she knew because she became *It*. '*It*?' Seh interrupted her explanation as he kept pace with her, asking how she could become *It*. 'Creation is one within the First, the Self-Generator', replied Hu. In the announcement, she knew because she was one with *It* and she was *It*. Seh heard the symbols but did not grasp the meaning of the words. He recalled the second truth of creation: 'There is only one First, the Self-Generator', as he pondered the meaning of 'to be one with *It* and to be *It*.' He knew what she meant when she said creation is one within *It*—the fifth truth of creation: 'All of creation is one within the First, the Self-Generator.' However, he did not understand what she meant by 'she was *It*.' The Glorified cannot be *It*. Again, he thought of the second truth as he tried to understand the meaning of such symbols.

Seh, not comprehending the words Hu had spoken, wondered if Hu had a hidden purpose behind the form he was certain she had created. Her explanation was just a truth of creation and he fell on the idea that she was attempting to distinguish herself once more. His certainty that Hu had uncovered the path to a kind of *duality of being* prevented him from fully hearing her explanation. Many *false truths* begin in that manner: the answer to the question is assumed, and certainty prevents the acceptance of the explanation. They walked on as the sound of Hu's voice drifted away and the Creature continued to remind her not to delay.

She thought of the journey ahead and the task to be done. Seh was thinking that the shape—or Creature—was her contribution to the gathering. In a voice that filled the void and chased silence away, he asked her, where is she going? Again, she waited, weighting what her next words should be. She then said in a low voice, 'There is a task to be done.' 'What task? Where?' Seh asked. 'Beyond the Realm', Hu said. They both walked on for a few more steps before she added, 'There have been many gatherings and many journeys, but this journey to the seal may be the last within the Realm. The announcement provided the directions to a task. This Creature and these objects', she held up the container, 'were created for that purpose. They are part of a task. The destination of this journey', she said in almost a whisper, 'is beyond the Realm to a place, space, or time *It* has prepared. But first, the seal must be broken.'

She continued walking. The Creature jumped onto the top of the container as she held it up for him. It positioned itself so one eye looked at Seh, who was walking on the left side of Hu, and the other eye looked towards the journey ahead. The Creature spread its limbs as if to cover the opening of the container. There was silence again, but not the kind of silence in which the First, the Self-Generator, could be heard; rather, it was the kind of silence brimming with anticipation, waiting for the next sound. In that kind of silence, there is a void which could be filled with either sounds or actions. Seh, trying to comprehend, filled it with the symbols Hu had mentioned. In the void, the sound of his voice lingered as if standing still and Hu was uncertain whether Seh was simply repeating what he had heard or was asking questions. Seh reached out to touch the container, but the Creature flapped its limbs as if to maintain its balance, causing Hu to move the container to the right, just out of Seh's reach.

After trying to reach the container, he searched the endowment once more for references to an announcement, a seal, or a place, space, or time beyond the Realm. His thoughts were no longer clear, but he clung to his certainty that Hu had found a path to a type of *duality of being* like an anchor. His assumption seemed a better explanation than her words. They walked on and the silence deepened. He continued to search for references to the things she mentioned. The sound of the others at the gathering was in the background. They seemed more distant with every step. Hu looked at Seh's Spark again; it was alight. It was brighter than she had ever seen it. Yet she knew its glow had dimmed and it bore a mark. She disturbed the silence, intruding upon

Seh's thoughts, by asking him, 'What is it that he lacked? What is it that has caused the Spark within him to lower its glow?'

Seh was focused on searching the endowment. He seemed as distant as the others at the gathering. It was as if he had not heard what she asked. She explained that she saw it in the announcement and again when he *'remade'* his form of creation. 'What is it', she asked, looking at him, 'that creation has not provided?' Holding his hands out in front of him, looking at the vessels of the Spark, he said, 'The Spark always brightens its glow. It has brightened its glow from the awakening.' His voice trailed off as he spoke. He was trying to understand what she meant by the Spark having lowered its glow. 'Could a Spark lower its glow?' he asked. 'That was unknown until the announcement, but it has been witnessed', Hu replied. 'The glow of the Spark was the same as the others until it lowered its glow to reveal a mark.'

Seh, still looking at the vessels, fell into silence. He kept up the pace with Hu, matching his footsteps to hers. As she continued towards her destiny, she explained that the mark on his Spark is due to something he wanted. He was focused on the vessels of the Spark and it seemed as if he was not listening to her words. Looking at him, raising her voice slightly, she asked him again, 'What is it the Realm has not provided, that the First, the Self-Generator, has not prepared?' Seh, still trying to understand, asked, 'What is a mark?' 'A mark', Hu said, 'is a sign, a slight tinge on the Spark. It is a thing that shows on the Spark', she said, 'and it is not upon the Spark of the others.' 'Sparks are not all the same; they were marked differently by the First, the Self-Generator', Seh responded. 'It is not the same, nor is it similar. The mark is the colour of the Rapture; it is not just a slight variation in the Spark', she replied.

Seh slowed his pace as the weight of her comments washed over him. He wanted to distinguish himself from the others, to set himself apart—but not in that way. He did not want to be the Glorified whose Spark lowered its glow and bore a mark upon it. He had never seen any difference in the glow of the Spark within any Glorified, not even a twinkle. He slowed his pace. Hu continued walking towards the seal. The Creature settled down on top of the container. Seh, falling behind, looked at his hands—the seats of the Spark—and thought about the questions Hu asked. 'What is it the Realm has not provided? That the First, the Self-Generator, has not prepared?' Seh had no answers to those questions. What could he say the Realm has not provided? There is perpetual plenty in the Realm. Everything that is needed in creation has been prepared. He knew that within the *perfection in creation*, whatever is needed is forever 'becoming'. He continued to look at the seats of the Spark even though he could not see the Spark within them. Seh was no longer walking; he was just standing and thinking about how to answer the questions, what he should say to Hu; as he stood in silence, he considered what he knew about the Spark.

Seh did not understand how a Spark could have a mark on it. He was certain he could not have affected the Spark. He knew a Glorified could not cause the Spark to change, to alight, or to be set asunder. The Glorified did not have the will to command the Spark. Yet he wondered if the answers to her questions could lie in the way transformation was gained. Seh, breathing slowly but deeply, searched the endowment to find the first reference to the Spark. There were no indications in the endowment that the Spark could be marked. 'The Spark', he said in a low voice, as if it were a secret, 'is the First, the Self-Generator. It indicates the way towards *nia*: purpose and destiny.' As he looked at the vessels of the Spark, he thought, he did not know whether or not the Spark had changed, or even if the Spark was in its vessels. Each Glorified had been created with a Spark. He knew a Spark was within him. The others affirmed the existence of the Spark within him, but he did not need their confirmation. Seh and the others knew they had Sparks because that knowledge is in the endowment. He found all the references to the Spark, and none indicated a Spark could lower its glow or have a mark upon it.

Seh stood looking at the seats of the Spark, wondering if the most appropriate answer to the questions was that he did not know. He did not know the Spark had lowered its glow. He did not know what the Realm had not provided. He considered the notion that there might be things the Realm has not provided, but everything they require has been bestowed upon them. There is everlasting plenty in the Realm. If there are things not provided, those things are known only to the First, the Self-Generator. Since transformation, Seh had asked and answered many questions of himself. Once again, he stood, wondering about the Spark, trying to comprehend the meaning of a mark upon it. He was questioning and answering himself.

In silence, he assured himself that he did not know. He returned to her comment that it was due to an outcome he lacks. He paused, like the space between a question and an answer, and said, 'an outcome'. He was not certain if he had spoken the words out loud or if they were only in his thoughts. Seh searched the endowment once more. He pushed aside the thought that the answer to her questions might be in his purpose with transformation. He set aside the idea to once again choose a path that is not in the way of creation. As he had done before, he planned what he would do. He would put aside all thoughts about the glow of his Spark or the mark upon it. He would focus on Hu and the Creature. The glow of his Spark, whether it was alight or dimmed, in its vessels or in some other part of the form, mattered not. He reaffirmed for himself that the Glorified could not command the Spark to alight or dim, which made him certain that whatever it was Hu had witnessed was not an outcome of his Spirit.

He quickly rejoined Hu and the Creature walking towards the seal. He noticed again that the glow of the Spark within her looked as though it was renewed. He matched his pace to hers and the Creature repositioned itself, looking at him and spreading its limbs over the opening of the container. The red piece on the top of its head stood up, firm and rigid. Neither Hu nor Seh knew why the Creature had repositioned itself. The Creature had a role in the task; it carried a golden sphere like the glow in the midst of the design in the announcement. Hu was certain it held knowledge that was not known to her. Seh noticed the Creature's eyes were different from those of the Glorified. They were round with two different-coloured circles. He wondered what the Creature could see. Could it see the Spark? He walked alongside Hu, trying to look inside the container. He could find no symbols of the First, the Self-Generator, that would explain what he was seeing. He heard the words Hu had spoken but did not recognise the value the symbols were meant to share.

He did not speak when he rejoined her, and Hu did not ask about the Spark again. He walked as if he had decided to accompany her. As they walked, he tried to direct his thoughts by focusing on the Creature and the container. The container was plain and the colour of ripened wheat. The Creature's limbs prevented him from fully seeing inside. He could only glimpse parts of the orbs as they hung, and he wondered why Hu had created them. Unlike all the other Glorified, he knew a Glorified could hold his purpose out of sight of the others. He wondered again how Hu had created the Creature. He thought that if the Creature was one within the First, the Self-Generator, it would have a Spark. He was certain Hu, too, was trying to set herself apart. She had been made 'the master of sound' and at whiles was called 'the master of forms'. He reasoned, as he matched his steps to hers, she was again trying to set herself apart with a tale about an announcement. As

Seh thought about the name-calling, he struggled to control the sensations in his form of creation. He had to set aside the mysteries found along the way, as he recalled her being called 'the master of forms'. He thought her reference to the First, the Self-Generator, and knowing it because 'she was *It*', was meant to prevent the others from requesting the '*sharing of know-how*.' He assumed she was trying to prevent the others from asking why—why she pursued this 'know-how' by herself. He was certain she spoke of the First, the Self-Generator, in vain. He quieted his thoughts, pushing the mysteries aside and, as he walked with her, he asked in a low voice, as if he did not want to disturb the silence or intrude upon her thoughts: 'What is in the announcement?'

Hu was not certain he had asked a question. She looked at him; his Spark glowed bright, and there were no signs there was a difference in him. As she looked at him, he asked again, 'What is in the announcement? How was the path uncovered?' Hu walked on for a few steps. She did not know how to answer his question. She did not know how she had gained an expanded '*self*'. If there were a path that could lead a Glorified to be both one with the Presence in all things and also be the Presence, she did not know how to enter it. The announcement was beyond all of her experiences. It was unknown to her.

"In the announcement", she said, answering his question directly, "is to be one with creation, to hear the voices and stories of all things, and to stand at the end of everything and look upon the beginning of 'nothing'." Then she quietly walked on. She wanted him to consider her words without interruption. After a while, she concluded her answer, saying, "If there is a path to the announcement, it has not been uncovered. If there is a path a Glorified could follow that would lead to the end of everything and the beginning of 'nothing', it is unknown."

Silence fell upon them again. She did not know if a Glorified could enter the announcement by his or her will, or if he or she had to be carried. If a path was travelled, she did not know it, but in the silence, she heard Seh whisper, 'Yet she travelled a path that led to an announcement.' 'If there is a path, it is unknown', she replied in a gentle and soothing voice—that humans would recognise as speaking truth rather than certainty. The announcement, she told Seh, was confusing. It was too much for her to comprehend at once. In her confusion, it was not clear to her whether her thoughts were truly her own. Seh too, appeared to have been given more information than he could comprehend. He did not understand the description of being in the announcement, so he grounded himself with certainties.

Seh drifted into quiet thoughts as the Creature continued to keep an eye on him. Silence wrapped around them like a bubble, and Hu's thoughts returned to the journey ahead and the seal to be broken. As they walked, Seh wondered again—if there was an announcement, should not all of creation hear? The sound of his voice filled the void and lingered there after he said, "All of creation is one within the First, the Self-Generator. *Its* Presence is in all things. How is it a truth", he asked, "that in the announcement a Glorified could be the Presence or could be at the end of everything and at the beginning of 'nothing'? Creation is the First, the Self-Generator. *It* has no end", he added. They took a few more steps together before Hu said, 'The announcement started with the *duality of being*.' She chose not to answer the question he asked, but to begin the telling of the tale from the beginning. 'The *duality of being* is beyond the will of the Glorified', she explained as Seh listened. During the *while of quiet*, she found herself in the Realm and yet not in the Realm. Her physical form and her Rapture form were within reach of each other, allowing her to look upon herself from herself. 'In the announcement', he asked, creating a space to add his thoughts, 'the *duality of being* means there were two ways of being?' 'There were two forms in the shape of the form of creation.

One was created with the particles from the Rapture', she replied. Seh, knowing what was known to be a certainty among them, could not comprehend how the physical form and the Rapture particles could exist at the same while. 'When the Glorified is in the Rapture, the physical form is not to be found in existence', he said. 'How could the form of creation look upon the Rapture?'

The Glorified had uncovered that the physical form could not be found while a Glorified was in the Rapture. She agreed with Seh, saying the form of creation could not be found within the Realm. 'The *duality of being* is not within the will of the Glorified', she added. 'In the announcement, the *duality of being* exists. How, is not known', she said. Seh recognised a slight difference between her thoughts and his but continued to listen. She explained that she thought she had uncovered a new way of being. But, knowing the *duality of being* was beyond the Glorified, she tried to dismiss the experience. Before she could create a *false truth*, she saw the Creature standing on her physical form, and a 'nothing' was upon her.

He continued to keep pace with her as silence enveloped them again. The sounds of the others at the gathering were growing fainter. She might not be able to hear them once she entered the section with the seal. She listened to the Mystery as it travelled its path and thought the Mystery of Creation provided a steady foundation for the sounds in the Realm. Seh slipped into deeper confusion as he walked with her. He thought about what he saw and what she said. The Creature still sat on top of the container with its limbs spread, the red piece on its head standing upright, and one eye looking in Seh's direction. Seh put aside all thoughts of the gathering and the form he had created. He too could hear the sounds of the others, but his focus was on Hu and the Creature. He did not understand what she had said. He noticed she did not explain what she meant by "the end of everything and the beginning of 'nothing'." A void of silence waited to be filled. As they took each step, Hu could hear their footsteps like drummers playing *ndos* together. Seh opened his voice. The sound was true to its purpose, intruding upon the silence and moving it away. In the void, his voice seemed louder than he intended. He wanted her to say more. She had said this might be the last journey. He asked her, 'How is it a truth that there might be no more journeys in the Realm?'

She had carefully considered the symbols to use in telling the tale. She was not certain that Seh understood. She expected him to search the endowment for the things she mentioned. She referenced the First, the Self-Generator, without acknowledging that the endowment said so. She wondered whether he thought she had spoken of *It* in vain. She did not know how to share what she had received, how to show Seh the truth of the announcement. She heard his question but set it aside, letting silence have its place. She was listening to the sounds of the Realm. The *ndos* were playing, the others were singing, and beneath it, she heard the sound of the Mystery of Creation.

Silence once again washed over them, but it was Hu who intruded upon it—not to respond to Seh's inquiry, but to say, in a voice more distant than present, she would long for the sounds of the Realm. She matched her footsteps to the beat of the *ndos*. Seh too heard the sounds and asked her, 'Should this tale not be shared with the others?' Seh's question was about '*sharing of know-how*', but Hu said, 'The task should not be put aside. The journey to the seal must not be delayed.' The *ndos* ceased their conversation and silence found its place at the gathering. The Creature raised its head slightly as though it too was listening to the *ndos*. They must be partaking in ale, Hu thought, but then there was an eruption of laughter, and she knew a Glorified did not know where the Spark had located itself. 'The *truth in perfection*', she said, brightening her face as the *ndos* found their voices again. She had not answered Seh's question about the last of the journeys. She was considering how to answer, knowing that, to him, the truth of the announcement had no foundation.

She was thinking about the gathering even as the laughter drifted away. With each step, she distanced herself from the sounds of the *ndos*. She slowed her pace not because she wanted to linger with the sounds but because she had entered the part of the Realm the Glorified considered to be the section of fragrances. This was the section where the Glorified whose place in the circular assembly was two positions on her left side had stationed herself during the Rapture. Many of the smells and tastes of the Glorified were created by that Glorified and shared at the gatherings. Seh matched Hu's pace as she absorbed the aromas. He too knew this section. He had added many of these scents and flavours to his ales. He took a deep breath and mentioned the fragrances of the Realm, asking whether she would long for them as well, attempting to move her back to the telling of the tale. She did not respond. Her thoughts were drifting. Seh wanted her to continue with the tale, so he asked her again in a formal manner, 'How is it a truth? What did she mean when she said she would long for the sounds of the Realm?' She had not answered his questions because she was trying to choose the appropriate symbols to distinguish between truth and certainty. Truth is known. It has a foundation and it is true forever and a more. But a certainty could be without a foundation—and might lead to a *false truth*.

The seal to be broken was a truth. It had a foundation. The last journey in the Realm might be a certainty. She was not certain whose thought it was during the announcement. She considered how to answer his question—how to distinguish between truth and certainty. She then said—she believed that this was the last of her journeys in the Realm. After breaking the seal, after doing the task, she would be entombed as in the Rapture. She would have neither strength nor will to move about creation. Seh heard her in the way she intended. He said, as if to affirm her statement, 'Believe, but know not?' She agreed; she believed her place would be in the centre of the design, raising the container for Seh to see. 'That would make this the last journey in the Realm, but it would also be a beginning,' she said. "If that were to be the outcome…", Seh paused, as if to consider the possibility it could be the outcome, before he said, in a voice shaded with the thought of not knowing, "This Seven would long for the *'other'*."

The glow of the Sparks brightened as if in agreement. The Creature had not changed position since Seh rejoined them but had settled down, as if it were content with the sounds, colours, and fragrances of the Realm. They were approaching the section with the seal. Hu reminded herself to enter the Rapture before breaking the seal. She knew the section well. It was the section where she had stationed herself when they were exploring the Rapture. It was the section where the Mystery of Creation falls into the abyss to start its journey throughout the Realm. She had made herself one with everything in it. It was the place where her aimless wandering always ended. There is *perfection in creation*, she thought, looking at the Creature. Everything that is required has been created, whether it is known or unknown to the Glorified. The seal could have been there since the creation of the Realm. Without the announcement, without knowing what story the Realm would tell, the seal would have remained unknown to the Glorified. She thought about the sixth truth of creation. She knew she would be able to see the seal with the Spirit's eye, but that would not indicate whether it was newly created or had been there since the beginning. Still, she wanted to enter the Rapture before breaking the seal. Entering the Rapture would allow her to be everywhere and to see the Presence in all things once more. She tried to stretch her ears to catch the last of the sounds from the gathering. The sounds of the Glo-rified were distant and drifting farther away. She did not brighten her face; she quickened her steps, saying to herself, 'The circular assembly will have only six—even though, there will always be places for seven.'

What Seh heard and saw boiled and bubbled within him. He noticed how the container sat lightly on her palms. The Creature allowed only a glimpse inside. He saw small, round spheres, hanging without support. They were touching neither the sides nor the bottom of the container. His thoughts drifted, but it was the idea that Hu would again be set apart that surfaced to the top. As they walked, he noticed she had quickened her pace. He continued to think about what she had said. He did not know the meaning of the 'end of every-thing' or the 'beginning of nothing'. The Realm is not sealed; all is one within the First, the Self-Generator. His thoughts, bumping from one idea to another, wove themselves into a knot. He did not understand, so he tried to hold to what he thought was truth.

He reminded himself creation would hear an announcement. Shared journeys, collective outcomes, he thought, started with cir-cular assemblies. He wondered how the journey to the seal could become a shared journey. Seh wanted her to share 'know-how', but in a way that would not set her apart. Seh was again planning an outcome as he had with the knowledge of transformation. He slowed his pace. It had been a while since he said he would long for her, and the silence was heavy with anticipation. There was only a faint sound of the *ndos* at the distant gathering. The Creature noticed Seh falling behind and leaned forward as if it were wondering why he slowed his pace. 'If this is to be the last journey...' Seh's voice was loud in the emptiness, and could be heard repeating itself, drifting through the Realm. He has-tened to match her pace once again.

He then repeated himself. 'If this is the last journey in the Realm, should that knowledge not be shared with the others?' He was not certain the others should be gathered, but he wanted Hu to share 'know-how' before she entered the section where she said a seal was to be found.

Hu slowed her pace as she once again considered sharing with the others. 'How could it be said the Seven is no longer in the Realm? What knowledge could serve as the foundation for such a truth?' Seh asked. Hu did not look at Seh as she acknowledged the tale should be shared before adding the task must not be delayed. She picked up her pace again, but Seh continued, 'The journey need not be delayed. If the outcome is that neither the form of creation nor the Rapture particles would be found in the Realm, who should tell such a tale? What symbols could be used? How should certainty be distinguished from truth?' he asked. Again, Hu slowed her pace, and they walked on for a few more steps as Seh waited for her to consider his questions. 'The task must not be put aside', she said. They both walked on for a while before Seh asked once more, "How? How could the story of 'in the announcement' be told by a witness who has not travelled the path? How could the telling of such a tale fall to the one who has not seen, nor heard, and knows not how to separate truth from certainty? The task needs not be delayed nor the path set aside, the others could share in this journey." Hu looked at Seh as his voice lingered. She appeared to be considering his comments. She stopped walking and then, in a clear but uncertain voice, she said, 'If the task will not be delayed, then, perhaps the tale of being in the announcement could be ...' Seh did not wait for her to finish her statement before he set off to gather the others. He chose not to enter the Rapture and appear at the gathering. Instead, he left as he had arrived, using the speed the Glorified used when they were attempting to be in seven places, spaces, or times at the same while.

CHAPTER 14

ALL THAT IS GOLDEN

The Creature flopped its limbs and landed on her shoulder. It positioned itself so that one eye looked ahead and the other looked at the road travelled. Its touch was light and gentle, not the unfamiliar sensation from the announcement. Hu noticed no difference in the weight of the container. Without Seh's company, she focused on her last Rapture. She had not uncovered how the particles were created. As she thought about the Rapture, she stopped walking, thinking she knew the reason. She wondered what other knowledge had been shared with her. She knew where the seal would be found and how it should be broken. She tried to quiet her thoughts. She listened, reaching for the reason she had not witnessed the particles being created. The reason sat at the edge of her being, but she could not quite bring it to light. She continued in silence, hearing the Mystery and the faint sound of the *ndos* in the distance. She wondered why Seh had slowed his pace. Then, she tried to put aside all thoughts so she could focus on the edge of her being. She sensed the knowledge she sought had been found. As she walked, she thought again about entering the Rapture before breaking the seal. It might bring to light the reason she has not observed the creation of the particles.

She let the Mystery of Creation intrude upon her thoughts. She listened to its melody, wondering if anyone would ever hear its full tale. She said in a hushed but certain tone, 'Like the First, the Self-Generator, the full tale of the Mystery might never be wholly known.' As she spoke, she heard the *ndos* cease their conversation. She thought it had taken Seh a while to reach the others. The sound of the *ndos* ceased and a void, as heavy as the human burden, seemed to cover the Realm. She listened with all of her being. The silence unsettled the Creature. It rose and the red piece on its head stood upright in a firm and rigid manner. As the Creature surveyed overhead, the other Glorified, including Seh, 'remade' themselves.

They 'remade' themselves on both sides of Hu, taking their places as in the circular assembly. There were two lines of Glorified, one behind the other, three Glorified on her right side and three on her left. Seh was in his proper place on her left side. There were two Glorified in the front and two, including Seh, at her back. The other two were on either side of her. This would be the circular assembly position for each Glorified if Hu were to lead the procession. As the Glorified 'remade' themselves, there was no sound, and they matched their pace to hers. The Creature looked at each of the Glorified but remained standing. The Glorified looked ahead and walked with confidence, as if they knew the destination of the journey. They walked for a while. A while could be a long time, a short time or no time at all. It was a solemn procession. The others had come not to gaze upon the *duality of being*, nor to know if its path had been uncovered. They had come for Hu. They came so that she would not journey alone. If this were to be the last of her journeys in the Realm, if this were to be her last path travelled, then it must be as it was in their beginning. It must be travelled together. They came to accompany her to wherever her destination might be. For a while, nothing was said; no sound was made by any of the Glorified. The glows of the Sparks enhanced the colours and fragrances of the Realm and as Silence occupied its place, they could hear a beat—and they knew that they were hearing the harmony in creation.

They walked on for a while before Silence was chased from among them and their thoughts intruded upon by the voice of Seh. In a clear voice, full of certainty, he declared, it is as he said: 'She has uncovered the path to the *duality of being*.' When Seh returned to the gathering, he was unsure of the tale to tell. The others asked about Hu, for she never missed a gathering. He was not sure what his eyes had seen and his ears had heard. Before answering their questions, he asked, 'Did anyone hear an announcement?' They did not know what he meant by an announcement. Seeing their expressions, he explained, 'Hu had uncovered a kind of *duality of being*, and she will not be attending the gathering because she is on the last of her journeys in the Realm.' Seh began to explain how Hu might have used the knowledge of transformation, but he was interrupted by the others inquiring about the meaning of 'the last of her journeys in the Realm.' Seh told them there was an announcement of a task. 'She believes', he said, pausing after the word 'believes' to ensure the others understood that his words did not have a foundation in truth. 'She believes', he said again, 'that the task requires her to journey beyond the Realm.' Seh was still talking when the others vanished. The Rapture allowed the others to locate Hu and '*remake*' themselves as she walked towards the seal. It was not that Seh did not hear what Hu said, rather that he had heard it in his way. He could not put aside the idea that she had uncovered another way to distinguish herself. He was certain if the First, the Self-Generator, spoke, everything in creation would hear. With Seh clinging to the idea that she had found a path to the *duality of being*, Hu knew the tale of the announcement was her tale to tell. The story had to be told so the others would not have the burden of accepting a certainty without knowing, without witnessing, without seeing and hearing with all of their being.

Seh chased Silence from among them because he wanted to guide the discussion. He wanted the others to see and hear her tale in the way he did. He tried to lead the discussion towards affirming his conclusions, but the others waited for Hu. They came to be with her in silence, if she chose. Hu did not want to put the task aside, but Seh's comments convinced her that her experience had to be shared. His comments made her wonder if she had chosen the appropriate symbols to explain the announcement. Seh did not understand what she said, so with the others, she began by focusing on the Creature. She reasoned the others would look for its Spark and searched the endowment. She reasoned that even without knowing the announcement, the Creature existed. They could see it; they would have seen the Presence within it. She wanted to choose symbols so that the others would hear the truth in her words. She wanted to share the experience before they, like Seh, made any assumptions about the Creature. As they continued looking ahead and walking towards the seal, she said, 'This Creature is without a Spark, yet it has a *true gift.*'

Hu neither affirm nor refute Seh's comments, yet she did not want them to become certainties for the others. Any tale could become a certainty for those who do not know but are willing to bear the burden of not knowing. Seh's comments reflected his interpretation of what he saw with his eyes and heard with his ears. She told the others that, following the last gathering, she found herself inside the Realm and yet outside of it. The others, listening as Hu began, were taken aback by the idea that the Creature lacked a Spark. They interrupted, 'It has a golden sphere!' They expected the Creature to have a Spark. They had noticed the golden sphere while they were in the Rapture. The sphere had the same colour as a Spark. It seemed to be part of the Creature in the same way the Spark is part of the Glorified. It also had the same Presence within it.

Unlike the others, Seh did not expect the Creature to have a Spark. He did not see a Spark while he was with Hu, and thought that it was because a Glorified cannot create a Spark. The Creature, not having a Spark, affirmed for him that it was created using transformation. Seh, like the others, had noticed the golden sphere. He reasoned that if the golden sphere were a Spark, it could not be kept out of sight. Though it shared the Spark's colour, he reminded himself, 'all that is golden is not a Spark.' He assumed that the golden sphere was Hu's attempt at creating a Spark. She was not only trying to set herself apart, he thought, as he took his place among them, but also trying to emulate the First, the Self-Generator. Hu did not tell Seh the Creature was without a Spark nor refute his comments about the *duality of being*. Seh wondered if her silence indicated agreement. He listened as she continued to tell the tale, expecting she would soon affirm his assumption that the Creature was some type of *duality*.

The Glorified whose place in the circular assembly is three positions on the left side of Hu, asked, 'How is it a truth that the golden sphere is not a Spark?' He asked in the way the Glorified questioned each other. 'How is it a truth?', they would ask to began a conversation about a certainty. The question, 'How is it a truth?' is a request to bring to light and make obvious the assumptions upon which a certainty rests. That question allows each Glorified to assess whether a certainty could be a truth. The answer to, 'How is it a truth?' does not include any reference to the endowment. The Glorified had the same endowment. The endowment included all the truths of creation. It required no interpretation and the Glorified did not question the knowledge found in it. Over the whiles, the *'sharing of know-how'* ensured the endowment and their knowledge remained the same. Hearing the question, Hu knew her comments about the Creature were considered to be no more than certainties.

The question, 'How is it a truth?' was a request to share 'know-how', to share the thoughts or actions which made a truth out of a certainty. The others, like Hu before the announcement, did not know a creature could be without a Spark. They saw the golden sphere in the Creature, in the same way they saw the Spark in the Glorified. They wanted to explore it, to see, to hear, and to come to know with all of their beings, 'How is it a truth the golden sphere is not a Spark?' Before the question could be answered, before Hu could share how it is a truth, the Glorified in front, whose place in the circular assembly is one position on Hu's left and six positions on her right, said, 'It is a truth that only the First, the Self-Generator, could create a *true gift*. A *true gift*', she said, 'means this Creature is *Its* creation.'

They were silent again as they searched the endowment for the creations of the First, the Self-Generator. They were doing what Seh had done. Listing *Its* creations, starting with, *It* created *Itself* and the Realm. The Creature, which had been standing on Hu's shoulder since the *'remaking'*, jumped onto the top of the container and back again. As the Glorified in the front spoke, she and the other Glorified in front transformed into the shape of the Creature. They were followed by the two Glorified on either side of Hu, and then both of the Glorified in the back. They perfectly recreated the form of the Creature. Even the Spark within them formed a golden sphere and was located in the same position as the sphere in the Creature. Hu, with the Creature on her shoulder and the container in her hands, looked upon each form and saw that each reflected the Creature in every way. She too wanted to transform into the shape of the Creature. She wondered why she had not done so before starting the journey.

The Glorified were honouring the presence of the Creature in the same way they acknowledged the creativity of each other. They recreated the form of the Creature, including its feetless toes, the individual pieces that covered it, and the red piece on top of its head. When the Glorified recreated the shape contributed by another, the Spark would locate itself in a different part of the form. That had been the way of the Spark since Hu recreated Seh's form when he first revealed transformation. Her form reflected Seh's original form except it was smaller. There was one other difference between Seh's original form and Hu's version of it. The Spark located itself differently. Both halves of the Spark within Seh had lodged themselves at the tip of the tail, almost out of sight of the others. The others had difficulty recognising the form as Seh because the Spark had positioned itself as if it did not want to be seen. It was as if Seh's form was without a Spark. In Hu's recreation of Seh's form, her Spark remained in its vessels and spread itself into the three fingers, then, up the arms, along the shoulders, and down into the chest. Her Spark positioned itself as if it wanted to be seen. The other Glorified recreated Seh's form in the quiet that followed the gathering. The others achieved the outcome alone, and there were no witnesses to the positioning of the Sparks. Thus, no Glorified knew whether the Spark chose the same position as it did in either Hu or Seh's form, but the History of Creation says no two Sparks have ever chosen the same position in transformation.

The Glorified had never witnessed two Sparks taking the same position in transformation. When the others created the form that Hu described, the Sparks were positioned in different parts of the form, even though each form was in every way the same. In their form of creation, the Spark has its vessels, similar to their positions in the circular assembly; the vessels are the Spark's place. With transformation, the Spark chooses its position, but this was the first that all the Sparks chose the same position. In that way, the form the Glorified created to acknowledge the presence of the Creature truly reflected the Creature. There was a perfection in that outcome which was unknown to them. In honouring the creativity of each other, the difference had always been the position of the Spark. The Spark not only would choose to locate itself in different positions, but at whiles, it would also display itself in the colours of the 'three parts of being'. No form had ever been perfectly recreated. There was always a difference because of the Spark.

With the Creature, there was no difference. The Sparks all took the same shape and located themselves in the same position. A Glorified whom humans would consider male, and whose place in the circular assembly is two positions on Hu's right and five positions on her left uttered what they were all wondering: 'What could it mean that the Sparks have chosen the same position in this transformation? It is a perfection', he said, 'but what truth is there in it?' They were silent as they searched the endowment, looking for a truth that might be the reason for such an outcome. There were no references other than the sixth truth: 'No one knows what the First, the Self-Generator, might or might not do.'

The Spark recreating the golden sphere added to their knowledge of the Spark. It joined the Glorified in honouring the presence of the Creature in a similar way to how it participated in their merriment. Although the Spark could be seen, the form that the Glorified created was still a perfect reflection of the Creature. The only form that the Glorified ever recreated that was a perfect reflection of the other was their form of creation.

Human beings, from their perspective would consider the Glorified either male or female. The idea of being male or female was unknown to the Glorified. The endowment provided no symbols to distin-guish among them. Being male or female is an earthly and a wholly human ideal. The Glorified simply refer to the male or the female to use the human idea as '*the other*'. There were four '*others*', who would be considered females by humans, and three '*others*', who would be described as males. The female-other or the male-other can only be distinguished from other females or males by the Spark. The symbol '*other*' refers to the other form of creation the First, the Self-Generator, created. They did not know the reason *It* chose the other form or the *nia* of the '*other*'. The Glorified, from their beginning, knew they were the same. They were both the '*chosen form*' and '*the other*'. They were created together and both '*other*' entered existence at the same while. Human beings do not see the sameness the Glorified see in the '*other*'. Their storytellers teach that the male was created first and then a piece of the male was used to create the female. Before the storytellers it was known among them that the First, the Self-Generator, creates things from 'nothing'. *It* would not need the male to create a female; they would be created together, if one needed the other, and they would be created from 'nothing'.

The only difference between the '*other*' and the '*other*' was a slight vari-ation in the Spark. There was no outcome in transforming an '*other*' into the same kind of '*other*'. There would be no change. The Spark would remain the same and the Glorified would appear to have trans-formed into him or herself. The Spark could not be commanded to change to the slight difference in the Spark of the '*other*'. For a while, when transformation was new, transforming into the '*other*' was part of their merriment. The Glorified would switch places. There would be four males and three females, but the Spark would remain unchanged in its vessels. It was as easy to identify Hu among the male-other as it was to identify Seh among the female-other. The Spark always revealed truth. That was the reason Hu tried to locate a Spark in the Creature during the announcement. Humans refer to that feature of the Spark as 'seeing is believing'. The Glorified could transform into the 'other', but the Spark remained in its vessels unchanged, revealing its truth for all to see.

Honouring the Creature was the only occasion where the Spark had assumed the same position in a form of transformation. The male-other, whose place was two positions on the right side of Hu, added, 'The truth in this perfection shows not that the Creature is without a Spark, but rather the Creature is not a form created with transformation.' He assumed that the reason the Spark located itself in the same position in honouring the Creature was the same for the Creature as for the Glorified when the Glorified transformed into the 'other'. Both the Creature and the Glorified are the creations of the First, the Self-Generator. Hu had told Seh the Creature and the objects were the creations of the First, the Self-Generator, but Seh clung to his thought that she had found the path to a type of *duality of being*. In describing her experience again, she chose to focus on the Creature, and the unusual outcome with the Spark allowed the others, both male-other and female-other, to uncover that the Creature is indeed the creation of the First, the Self-Generator.

While the others transformed, the Creature jumped onto the top of the container. It turned to look at each Glorified as they honoured its presence by taking its form. This seemed to put the Creature at ease, and it opened its limbs, flapped them three times, and made a loud cock-cock-a-doo sound before launching itself from the top of the container to the front of the procession. The Creature joined the Glorified and began to lead the procession towards the seal. It landed, tucked in its limbs, and held up its head as if it had taken its rightful place. The others noticed and brightened their faces at how it tucked in its limbs, and held up its head as if it always had a place among them. Hu noticed and thought: the Creature knows that creation is sharing. It is giving and receiving, sharing with the others. Hu was in the middle with three Glorified on her right, three Glorified on her left, and the Creature directly in front of her leading.

She told the others she thought the announcement was an effect of ale until she saw the Creature. She described how both the Rapture form and the physical form were present. How she waited to see if another Glorified would enter the Rapture without crumbling the physical form. She knew that to look upon the particles from the form of creation is beyond the Glorified. The particles had the colour of her Rapture, but they did not flow and she could not spread them. The others listened, trying to understand being without will or strength to move their form of creation or spread the particles. After a while, the Creature appeared, standing on her form of creation as if it had 'remade' itself. Seh had not heard this part of the tale but thought he knew what the outcome would be. He noted she did not say that the announcement began with the *duality of being*; he thought that would be the outcome. So, he turned his thoughts to the Creature.

He noticed how the Creature held its head up, looking forward and walking as if its role was to lead and theirs was to follow. While the others smiled at the Creature setting itself at the head of the procession, Seh thought, even the Creature was trying to distinguish itself. Seh knew the tenth truth of creation, but where the others saw sameness, he observed difference. He saw a Creature that wants to set itself apart and above the others. He saw no symbols of sameness in its gesture, as Hu told them that after the Creature appeared, it spread its limbs as it had when joining the company, and jumped off her form.

In calling the others 'the company', she acknowledged the journey is no longer just hers; it had become a shared journey. The others had 'remade' themselves around her, and in their silence, she felt as if she was being carried to her destination. They were her company, on her right side and on her left side, accompanying her on her last journey in the Realm. The task was hers, but the journey to the seal was no longer her journey; it had become their journey. There are, in the fragments of lost human tales, many stories with reference to the company. This was the first company. The company numbered seven, and the Creature made eight.

After the Creature jumped off her form, she no longer wondered if the particles were from her Rapture. The particles began to move, flowing into the vessels of the Spark. She paused as she again stumbled on the thought that the reason she had not uncovered how the particles are formed sat at the edge of her being. She had not been able to quiet her thoughts enough to take hold of it. The answer to the question was there; putting it aside, she described the feeling in the vessels of the Spark as the particles flowed into them. 'It began as a slight tingle in each vessel', she said, 'but grew until the palms were pulsing'. It was a feeling she had not experienced before. It was a feeling of expecting, a 'becoming' that was long awaited, and the Spark anticipated it as if it knew the announcement.

They were listening as the procession made its way towards the seal. Her voice was gentle and sure of the tale as it kept chasing Silence away. The Glorified whose place is three positions on her left and four positions on her right asked if the announcement was a reduction in self? 'In the opening, the announcement was limiting, with the Rapture and the form of creation within reach of each other. There was no place, space, or time to stand, there was no will, or strength to spread the particles, and the distance was too far for the eyes to see.' She explained that before the Creature appeared standing on her form, before the particles of the Rapture began flowing, she thought she would be restricted. The male-other, as if he was trying to know with certainty what he heard, asked if in the announcement, the Rapture particles waited in the form of creation rather than in the four-sided structure. 'If the announcement was a Rapture, that might be true, but the announcement was not a Rapture', she said. At first, she thought that she had found a new way to exist, and then she was certain it was an effect of ale. 'That is quite an experience', the male-other three positions on her left said. His face brightened as he repeated what he heard, trying to understand what it would be like. He paused to search the endowment before concluding ale would have been his first thought as well.

They all turned to look at him with knowing smiles; even the Creature clucked, as if it understood the symbols. The Creature spread its limbs, flapped them, and hopped three paces ahead. The others did the same, as if they were playing a game of follow-the-leader. They then waited for Hu to take her place in the middle of the procession before the Creature signalled, *begin again*. The light-heartedness of the male-other told Hu that she was not alone. It lifted the burden on the procession. It was a while before they were settled and quiet enough for Hu to continue. She was still smiling when she said the Creature had positioned itself, so one eye looked at her and the other looked off into the distance. She repeated herself, as if trying to find her place in the telling of the tale. She did not know what had caused the feeling in the vessels of her Spark. It became more intense, and the Creature started jumping around. It was as if the Spark stood at an entrance, knocking, expecting it to open. The Spark and the Creature were expecting. They were waiting for a '*becoming*', but she did not know what was happening.

Seh examined the Creature as he had examined the forms the Glorified had contributed to the gatherings. He noticed how the Creature had changed since he was the only member of the company. The red piece on its head was no longer standing upright and rigid, but his evaluation was interrupted when he heard the mention of new feelings. He wondered if the feelings were similar to the mysteries found along the way. Before she mentioned the vessels pulsing, Seh was considering what had caused the change in the Creature. He thought it was because it had distinguished itself from the others. Seh was only partially listening to Hu, listening for the outcome he expected. He heard her explain how she wanted to explore that part of the Realm because it was unfamiliar to her and how after the particles had found their place again, her Spark started to grow in contented anticipation. As the vessels of her Spark pulsed, the Creature spread its limbs and started jumping around as if dancing to the sound of a *ndo*. That was the moment, to use an earthly reference to time, that she had a thought— fleeting though it was—that had never occurred to her before. She fell into silence for a while and then, exhaling, she added, 'If there were not a task to be done, the thought could be explored in a circular assembly.' She said no more. The procession walked on with each Glorified in quiet contemplation of what he or she had seen and heard, and Silence, once again, claimed its place among the company.

CHAPTER 15

TRUTHS AND CERTAINTIES

The Creature led the procession as if it were a kind of merriment. The procession would take a few steps, then the Creature would spread its limbs and hop three paces ahead. The Glorified followed, then the company would wait for Hu to take her place before the Creature swung its head, first to the left, and then to the right, to indicate: *begin again*. That made the journey—like the container in Hu's hands—seem burdenless. A feeling of merriment, almost like a gathering, came over the company. There were no signs that this could be the last of Hu's journeys in the Realm. The Creature's contentment could be seen in the way the red piece on its head swung lightly from one side to the other. The Sparks looked as if they were polished. If this were a gathering, the *ndo* would be playing and the Glorified would be singing. Hu did not answer the question: 'How is it a truth the Creature is without a Spark?' She thought, like Seh, if the golden sphere were a Spark, it could not be held out of sight. The others might have had the same thought. The Creature hopped three paces ahead, and the others followed, with Silence in its place. Seh wanted Hu to continue with the tale, but it was the Glorified whose place was one position on Hu's left side who disturbed the quiet, asking if the announcement was a *'becoming'*.

The Glorified referred to entering the Rapture as *'becoming'*. They thought of the Rapture as a way of being with the First, the Self-Generator, of *'becoming'* one with everything in creation. Hu did not respond to the question right away. She had spent many whiles following the Spark along its path to the Rapture. Yet she had not uncovered how the particles of the Rapture were created. The Glorified assumed the form of creation had been crumbled to create the particles. As the question was asked, she again knew something had been added to her knowledge. The question about *'becoming'* helped her to bring it to light. 'It is the seventh truth of creation', she said in a voice that was more distant than present. The others started to search the endowment. She interrupted them, saying that as the Creature jumped around and the Spark anticipated, the 'nothing' came upon her. It was that which the Spark and the Creature awaited. It was the reason she could not spread the particles or raise her form to its feet. It mattered not, she said, whether she was sitting, kneeling, or standing. "In the presence of the 'nothing', all else is impotent." 'That is because there are no equals to the First, the Self-Generator', added the Glorified whose place is two positions on her left and five positions on her right. Human beings once understood creation in such a way. They knew that for existence to be, the First, the Self-Generator, created a place, space, or time for it—similar to how silence makes a space for sound and darkness creates a place for light. They used to know that everything in creation is one and it is only the First, the Self-Generator, who has a value other than one.

Hu told the company that her form was on its knees and entombed in a glow, but she did not *'become'*. The Glorified listened; the merriment that had come upon the procession seemed to have drained away as Hu described being in the presence of the 'nothing'. The whole company was focused on the first tale about the 'nothing' not found in the endowment. The Creature had not hopped ahead since the tale arrived at the part about the 'nothing'. The others had done the same as Seh: they had searched the endowment for references to the things Hu mentioned, but none searched the endowment for references to the 'nothing'. They knew that a truth among many truths in creation is, "To know the First, the Self-Generator, is to know 'nothing'." That is the eighth truth of creation and it needed no further explanation. She told them that as the 'nothing' came upon her, it was not the physical form that '*became*'; it was the Presence within her.

The Presence in her—the same Presence that is in all things—'*became*' more than it was. It '*became*' one with the Presence in creation. Even though she did not know the path she had travelled nor how she came to be in the announcement, her '*self*' was everywhere in creation. She paused for a while, then said, trying to ensure the others understood her experience, in the Rapture, the Presence in all things could be seen. In the announcement, she '*became*' that Presence and for a while, she was everything; she was everywhere; she was creation. The company walked on and she lingered in thoughts before continuing. She told the company as the 'nothing' came upon her, she felt her '*self*' expanding outwards. As she expanded, the Creature jumped onto the top of her form. The Creature, as if to acknowledge the truth, flapped its limbs and bounced up and down as the company meandered towards the seal. She was herself, yet also the Presence in all things. The 'nothing' drifted outwards and her expanded '*self*' followed, filling the place, space, or time the 'nothing' opened for her. As she spoke, she heard the male-other whose place was two positions on her right side, say, 'Creation is sharing and that shows how existence is shared.' She looked at him in agreement, adding, 'There is so much more to creation than is known, but its purpose is sharing.'

She told the company she could hear the thoughts and voices of all of creation. She paused to listen to the Mystery of Creation before saying, 'The Mystery tells a tale of the beginning. It starts its telling of the History of Creation with the symbols: Creation began with the First, the Self-Generator, creating *Itself* ... All of creation has a tale', she said. She walked on for a while. A while—the endowment's only reference to time—could be a long time, short time, or no time at all. She waited a while as she considered the symbols to use. That while was pregnant with anticipation, but the others waited. She then said, '*It* does not speak', as if she were answering Seh's question again. 'At least not in the way the Glorified speak.' In the announcement, she knew because she was one with *It*, not because she heard *It*.

After she spoke, Silence tried to take its place, and she tried to turn her thoughts to the form to use to break the seal, but Seh chased Silence from among them. His voice, full of certainty, said, 'That is the reason all of creation did not hear the announcement.' Seh was part of the conversation again. He had not heard the part about the 'nothing' and being the Presence in all things. He looked at her in the middle of the company and thought he should have been the one positioned above all and the Creature. As he coveted her place and role, she said her '*self*' followed the 'nothing' until she stood at the end of everything and at the beginning of 'nothing'. She came to the edge of everything she knew, looked beyond, and there was 'nothing'. There was no before or after, there was no has been or to be; everything she knew, all of creation, all existence, just was, and for no other reason than sharing. She paused as if she had stated a truth of creation, and the Glorified whose place was one position on her right, added, 'The fourth truth of creation is that there is no before the First, the Self-Generator.' Hu brightened her face in agreement, then she said she tried to reach beyond the edge, and even though the 'nothing' was upon her, *It* was too far to reach. She took a deep breath and exhaled slowly, longing to be the Presence in all things again. For a while, she stood at the end of everything; the Creature without a Spark stood on top of her entombed form, and the design of the task surrounded her. At the end of everything, the 'nothing' resembled the '*crossing*', and she wanted to enter it like the particles to see if she would come forth on another side.

Silence rested among them for a while. It was as if the others were assessing what questions to ask. They seemed overwhelmed by the information and knew not where to begin. She was uncertain whether the tale should have been shared. She had first chosen not to join the gathering because she did not want to delay the breaking of the seal. As the company continued and Silence laid its burden down among them, she looked at each Glorified as if it would be the last. The story of being in the announcement had been shared, and the task had not been delayed. She expected the others to question. She waited, deciding on the form to use to break the seal. She was reviewing the steps in breaking the seal when the Glorified whose place was two positions on her left, asked, as if she wanted the telling of the tale to *begin again*, 'How is it a truth that the Creature is without a Spark?' The male-other whose place was two positions on Hu's right side added to her query, further clarifying the question. 'How is it', he asked, 'that the golden sphere appeared not to be a Spark in the announcement?' They thought that she too would have assumed that the golden sphere was a Spark. She had not mentioned the sphere, nor explained how it was a truth that the Creature is without a Spark.

Instead of telling the others that the sphere was not part of the Creature until after the announcement, she said that as she stood at the end of everything and at the beginning of 'nothing', she knew the announcement had arrived at the *beginning again*. The Creature was still standing on top of her form, looking at the design, and the 'nothing' gently started moving her back towards her form. She was almost back into her form—still part of creation, one with the First, the Self-Generator, but the Presence in all things no more—when the Creature started knocking. It started to knock its mouth against her entombed form, breaking the glow into pieces. She saw the Creature jump from the form and pick up a piece. That was the last thing she witnessed in the announcement. She paused, and Silence tried to take its place. Then she added, that the Creature did not have the golden sphere, or any parts that resembled a Spark in the announcement. After the announcement, she was again in the Realm, rising as if awakening from a *while of quiet*. She entered the Rapture and, in *'becoming'*, she noticed the golden sphere. She did not know when the sphere became part of the Creature. Beyond that is the Creature's tale to tell, but as the announcement closed, the glow that entombed her form crumbled as the Creature pecked at it. All she could affirm was that she saw the Creature pick up a piece, and after that, she was again herself in the Realm.

The Glorified whose place is one position on Hu's left and six positions on her right asked if the announcement was the awakening of the Creature. 'It is not known when the Creature was awoken into existence', said another Glorified. "It could be the *'remaking'* in the announcement was a *'becoming'*. The Creature's form of creation is unknown." The others kept Silence from its place and Hu listened as they questioned and answered each other, sharing their thoughts about the Creature. They were considering when in the History of Creation the Creature was created. 'Everything begins with the First, the Self-Generator, creating a place, space, or time for it.' Before the others could create a *false truth*, Hu said, 'The Creature was created after the Glorified.' 'How is that a truth?' asked another. 'It is a truth because nothing existed before the Glorified other than the First, the Self-Generator, and the Realm. How and when the Creature was created are secrets. The Glorified should not assume, since *false truths* are certainties that rest upon assumptions.'

As they were reminded that there were no witnesses to creation, Silence again tried to find its place among them. It was sent on its way by the Glorified whose place is one position on the right of Hu. 'That is the reason', she said, 'this journey had to be witnessed by each Glorified. The only way for the announcement to become truth is to bear witness to the existence of the Creature, to know that it is a creation of the First, the Self-Generator.' She looked at Hu as if she knew Hu had wondered if the tale should be shared. 'This knowledge', she said, 'had to be shared so each Glorified could know the First, the Self-Generator, waited a while before creating again. The existence of the Creature affirmed a truth of creation in the same way the outcome of this journey will bear witness to the announcement. It will turn the certainty that there is a seal in the Realm into a truth.' They walked on, and each Glorified thought about the uncovering of truths. 'Truths are found in the endowment', she continued, 'and those truths are true forever and a more. If the others had not joined the company, the existence of the Creature would not have been witnessed, and the endowment would be silent. When the endowment is silent, the only way for the Seven to know truth is to see with their eyes, hear with their ears, and reason with all of their being. The existence of the Creature is a truth only because the Glorified have witnessed it', she said.

The Creature had no reaction to the Glorified discussing when it came to be. It continued leading the procession. The male-other whose place is three positions on the left of Hu asked if the glow of the Sparks could be broken. 'There is the seventh truth of creation', he added. As the Glorified searched for references to the seventh truth, they were interrupted by a Glorified who asked if the glow in the announcement was broken, or was it transformed? 'Things in creation', she said, 'could change and transform.' 'That might also be true for the glow that entombed the Seven', said the Glorified whose place is one position on Hu's left side. 'The form of creation crumbles into the particles of the Rapture. The Mystery of Creation becomes solid or formless and, in the Realm, there is everlasting plenty. The First, the Self-Generator, created them, and they are perpetually 'becoming' and 'remaking'. They reflect the seventh truth. The glow that entombed the Seven may have broken into pieces in the same way the form of creation breaks into particles in the Rapture. Both the glow and the form of creation transformed. Transforming is not the same as uncreating. Things created by the First, the Self-Generator, last forever and a more, according to the seventh truth of creation. They cannot be uncreated; no Glorified, form nor creature has the will to undo what the First, the Self-Generator, created, but things created by *It* could transform and renew. Only *It* can undo *Its* creations, like closing the place, space, or time *It* opened for existence.'

They all agreed with the Glorified whose place is one position on Hu's left side, before Hu continued sharing her experience. The Creature, Hu said, might have transformed the glow into the golden sphere. She explained that the outcome for the Creature is unknown. The Creature has a role and a place in the task. The purpose of the sphere might be to extend the glow of the Spark. The others were quiet, as if trying to understand how the Creature transformed the glow or how it could use it to add to the Spark's glow. 'The Creature', Hu said, 'has strengths that are beyond the Glorified. It can see and feel the particles of the Rapture, even though the particles are burdenless.' 'The physical form cannot see the Rapture particles', Seh reminded the others. They were tempted to enter the Rapture to explore the certainty, to experiment with the Creature and the particles, to see if a certainty might become a truth. 'It is true', Hu said, 'that a Glorified in the physical form lacks the strength to see or feel the particles of the Rapture. The Creature is not a Glorified. It has strength and knowledge unknown to the Glorified.' She knew they would try to uncover whether the certainty was a truth. She waited to see if any Glorified would enter the Rapture, but the procession continued with each member of the company in their place.

Silence once more thought it had a place among them to rest. They knew the golden sphere was not a Spark, and this caused a Glorified to send Silence on its way, asking if the Realm was also without a Spark. They had witnessed a golden sphere in the Realm, and they were certain it was a Spark. They uncovered it in their exploration, but had not explored it further. They first saw it with the Spirit's eye and the certainty that it was a Spark prevented them from exploring it. They could recall no difference between the spheres in the Realm and the golden spheres in the Creature. Unlike the Spark within the Glorified, the golden sphere in the Creature and in the Realm were exactly the same. The Glorified would not be able to tell the Creature from the Realm by looking only at the golden sphere. They would see the Presence within them. They would know they are one with the First, the Self-Generator, but they would not know one from the other.

The question, 'How it is a truth that the Creature is without a Spark?' led to a question about the Realm. Whether it is a *false truth* that the Realm has a Spark. If there were not a seal to be broken and a task to be done, said the Glorified whose place is one position on the left of Hu, one certainty might be shown to be a truth and a truth might be shown to be a *false truth*. 'The task must not be set aside', she said, echoing Hu's words, 'and if this is', she looked up at Hu, 'the last of her journeys in the Realm, then this is a while for sharing.' The Creature seemed to agree, spreading its limbs and hopping three paces ahead. The Glorified followed and then waited for Hu to take her place before the Creature signalled: *begin again.*

CHAPTER 16

KEEPER OF SOUND

'*False truths*', said a Glorified, 'build their own foundations.' Every Glorified seemed to have a thought to share about the Spark within the Realm—except Seh. Seh wanted Hu to reveal more about the task. He had heard there was an unknown that might be explored in a circular assembly. He wondered whether there were mysteries in the announcement. The company was nearing the seal and he wanted to guide the conversation back to the task. Seh looked at each of the Glorified in the procession, and it reminded him of a form he created. The form symbolising the way the circular assembly could be restructured to set him above the others. Once more, he thought, Hu was being set apart in the way he ought to have been. He exhaled slowly and deeply, as if to let the mysteries flow through him. He could feel truth of the tale Hu shared. Before he could sink deeper into loss, he asked her whether she still felt her Spark knocking. He was not leading the company; he was not in the place he thought he should be, but Seh was again trying to guide the conversation. Seh had grown in his certainty that a Glorified could be set apart—raised above the others. That *false truth* had built its own foundation. As Hu responded to his question, he thought, they almost created a *false truth*, assuming she found a path to a kind of *duality of being*. The announcement appeared to have been far more. The company was listening to Hu while Seh was reasoning with himself. He was creating another *false truth*. He knew there was neither greater than nor lesser than among the creations of the First, the Self-Generator. Yet he reverted to the idea that Hu had not shared her true purpose. That started him along a path to ensure Hu would not become 'the master' of another outcome among them again.

After replying to Seh's question, Hu opened the way so that Silence might again claim its place among them. Seh was only partially listening; he did not hear what he was listening for, so he wanted her to continue. He asked, 'What mysteries have been uncovered that could be explored in a circular assembly?' He asked a question of her the others could not ask of him. They did not know Seh had found mysteries along the way of transformation. Hu responded, saying she had a thought which she had never had before. She said, 'It was fleeting, but clear. It is the kind of thought that should be explored.' Hu looked at Seh, affirming she was responding to his query. 'It may be a secret, but it should be explored to uncover whether the Glorified could gain any insight into its outcome.' As the Spark knocked, she thought an entrance would open, and the Spark would leave its vessels in the form of creation. 'What would a Glorified become', she asked, 'if the Spark is no longer in the form of creation?' 'They would be as the Creature without a Spark', Seh responded. He was certain, but the others hesitated and a hush fell upon the company like drizzle on a chilly day. It was not the kind of quiet where Silence came to rest nor the silence where the first truth of creation could be uncovered. It was the kind of silence that begged for either sound or action to warm the chill.

The others did not know what she meant by 'the Spark leaving the form of creation.' They contemplated the thought, while Seh, with his knowledge of certainty, jumped to a conclusion. 'There would be a difference', said another, putting aside Seh's certainty. "The Creature does not have a Spark and as far as it is known, it has never had one. That means a Spark does not lead its Spirit. It is a truth that each Glorified has a Spark. It is part of the *true gift*. The Glorified awoke into existence looking upon the Spark of each other. It must be at least a certainty that there would be a difference. If the Spark were to vacate the form of creation, then that would be a reduction in 'self'," she said.

She did not have the certainty of Seh. She hesitated before adding, "There would be a difference; there would no longer be three 'parts to being'. There might only be one. If the Spark were no longer in the form of creation, could there be a Rapture?" 'The Spark cannot leave the form of creation', Seh said, his voice firm, clear, and certain. He was trying to put an end to the discussion, to prevent the conversation from drifting away from how the task should be done. Yet the discussion continued. The male-other whose place was two positions on Hu's right looked up at Hu and asked, 'What in the announcement led to such a thought?'

Hu took a few steps, then said, before flowing towards the end of everything, she thought the Spark had been on a journey, and it was at a *beginning again*. She reminded the others that in the announcement, the thoughts were both her thoughts and not her own. There was something in the way the Spark's vessels felt. She could feel its contentment. It was as if it had completed a journey, as if it had followed the path and arrived at its destination. The Spark felt as if it knew it could rest after a while of giving and receiving. The others looked upon the Spark within her. It looked as though it had been made again. They did not intrude upon her sharing even as she hesitated before adding—'The announcement is the Spark's place of being.' She paused, giving the others an opportunity to consider her words. The Creature continued to lead the company, still holding its head up, the red crown on its head bobbing lightly from side to side.

The Glorified whose place was one position on the left side of Hu, asked, "Could it be the third 'part of being'?" Her voice was uncertain. She knew the question had not been explored. "There are three 'parts to being', she said. They are part of the *perfection in creation*; known to be there even though all have not yet been uncovered. The first 'part of being' is physical existence, and in it, the Glorified are the speakers. The second 'part of being' opened the Spirit's eye for the Glorified to be everywhere, to be one with creation. It could be", she said, "in the Rapture, in the second 'part of being', the Seven are the seers."

Before the Rapture, they did not know the answer to the question, "What is the second 'part of being'?" The answer to that question was revealed when they were exploring being everywhere. So, they thought the third 'part of being' would also be revealed. It had been many whiles since the Rapture and the third 'part of being' has not yet been uncovered. The Glorified one position on Hu's left side wondered if the third 'part of being' could be found when the Spark *begins again*. The Spark would vacate its vessels, they would become the Presence within all things and would be the 'listeners'. They would have their thoughts—and not their thoughts.

The others searched the endowment. They did not know if the Spark was on a journey or could have a place outside the form of creation. 'The Spark's place', said the female-other, two positions on the left side of Hu, 'is in its vessels', as if she needed to affirm what was known to creation. Hu agreed that the vessels were the Spark's place in the form of creation. She repeated that in the announcement, the vessels of the Spark felt as they never had before. 'It felt as though the Spark was returning to its beginning', she said, 'where an entrance

179

would open, and the Spark would position itself in a way that would leave the form of creation behind.'

'The Spark and Spirit did not leave the form of creation behind', Seh interjected. "It '*became*'. It entered into another way of being." Seh spoke with certainty, as though he had already entered the third 'part of being'. He was trying to direct the discussion. He tried to dismiss the comments about the 'parts of being' by asking Hu, 'What does it mean when she says the thoughts were her thoughts and not hers.' The others heard his certainty but chose not to assume he knew the answer. They did not know what a Glorified would be if the Spark was not within them, nor did Seh. Seh wanted Hu to reveal more about the task and, without waiting for her to respond, he added, 'Was there a conversation in the announcement?'

'If the Spark vacates its vessels there would be a difference', the female-other whose place was two positions on the left side of Hu said, before Hu could respond to Seh's inquiry. "It might lead to the third 'part of being'. The Spark indicates the way and without it, the paths towards *nia* cannot be known. Even though, it has been said on this journey that the Seven have uncovered a path to a kind of *duality*, the *duality of being* is beyond the Glorified. If the Glorified cannot be in the Rapture and in the form of creation at the same while, how could the Spark leave the form of creation and continue to indicate the paths towards *nia*? The Glorified are not the creator of beginnings. They cannot '*become*' and '*remake*' at the same while. They are '*becoming*' or they are '*remaking*', not both together. In entering the second 'part of being', in '*becoming*', the Glorified exist in a way that is unknown to the physical form, but the Spark is still there. It still indicates the way." Seh intruded again, still trying to move the discussion back to the task. 'The form of creation is not left behind by the Rapture', he said. "The physical form is not to be found in creation when the Glorified is in the Rapture. The outcome of '*becoming*' is that the form of creation crumbles into the particles of the Rapture. The '*other*'," he looked at Hu, "has not uncovered how the Rapture particles are created, but the form of creation is part of the Rapture. The Spark vacating its vessels would be similar'," he said, "in that the physical would not be left behind. It would '*become*' *as* in the Rapture, transformed into some other way of existing. What does it mean", he asked Hu, raising his voice slightly, "that the thoughts were her thoughts and not hers."

Hu took a while to collect her thoughts. She was thinking that there was 'know-how' to share about the particles of the Rapture. She put it aside and said, in the announcement, her thoughts were unclear and there were also thoughts in creation. In the silence, as she expanded outwards, the thoughts were at whiles her thoughts. She was questioning and being smiled upon. She did not know the right questions to ask. Even in this while, she paused to show she meant this moment with the company, it is unclear whether she asked about the size of creation. The question she said should have been about the purpose of creation. The others brightened their faces, as if they knew that, in the presence of the 'nothing', any question to which an answer is sought is the right question. Before she could long to ask the right question, the male-other three positions on her left and four positions on her right, asked, 'What is the size of creation?' Their smiles turned to laughter. 'It is not known', she said with a big smile and a slight giggle. The thought or the question was smiled upon. She paused to reflect upon the symbols to choose. Then, she said, she felt or saw through her expanded '*self*' the Seven—or she was the Seven—playing seven *ndos*, in the seven places, spaces, or times of the Realm. She hesitated before adding, she did not know the size of creation. The male-other three positions on her left said to her, as if his words would unravel the greatest mystery in creation, 'The answer to what is the purpose of creation is the same as it has been from the beginning.' She smiled again, looking at him, hearing his contentment with existence in his laughter.

Then she continued, saying she did not know the symbols to describe the sharing of thoughts in the announcement other than to call it 'being smiled upon'. Her expanded 'self' was pushed and pulled outwards in ever-widening circles. There were thoughts, which were not her thoughts. As Presence in all things, she 'became' those thoughts. She knew it because she was it. She spoke in a voice that was sure of the telling, yet she paused, wondering how she could provide a clearer explanation. In the announcement, her thoughts were unclear and before fully considering any thought, she would leap to another. The announcement was silent, but her thoughts were not and, she said, lowering her voice as though revealing a secret, she felt all of her thoughts and sounds since awakening into existence were there.

She took a few more steps before saying, 'The Silence in the announcement is not like the silence known to creation. It is not the silence that could be chased from its place by sound. It is much more. In the announcement, there is a place for it to rest and it can be heard. It is loud with all the thoughts and sounds in creation.' There was a deafening quiet, as she assessed whether to share her next thought. Then she said, she was certain Silence in the announcement kept every thought and sound made in creation since the beginning. "It might be that Silence is not chased from its place by sound. It might be that sound is led to a place, space, or time, where Silence is the 'keeper of sound.'" Those thoughts and sounds could be heard in the announcement', she said. Those were some of the thoughts that were not hers. She could hear them or feel them or see them; she could be one with them as they rested with Silence, but all of creation is not heard in that way. Again she paused, before saying the thoughts were hers and not hers.

A Silence that is the 'keeper of sound' was new knowledge. She did not know if it was her thought. She walked on, looking ahead, before adding, "The Silence in the announcement is where voices and sounds go, not to chase Silence from its place, but to be among its company. It is a Silence that is always there. It is immutable. It cannot be chased from its place. It gathers thoughts and sounds like the Spark gathering the particles. It may be that the 'nothing' uses Silence to hear all of creation." Her words bumped up against each other as she quickly said, 'That is not known.' She did not want to speak of the First, the Self-Generator in vain. The announcement was voiceless. Her questions were answered not with sound but with being. She felt the answer to her questions as if she were being smiled upon and the smiling caused her to be in the answer. 'It was sharing', she said. She did not have the will to create the Silence. It was shared with her so she could hear all the voices and sounds in creation, and for a while, like Silence, she was the keeper of them.

The Glorified whose place was one position to her left asked if the Silence in the announcement was similar to the silence in the Rapture. 'The silence in the Rapture is different', she said. 'It would only qualify to be the surface of the Silence in the announcement.' Adding, as she flowed outwards, the design of the task appeared. She was the Presence in all things, but she did not witness the creation of the design. It appeared as if it 'remade' itself. Like in the Rapture she could see, hear, and feel, but unlike the Rapture, she felt a Presence that was not hers, almost like having a second 'self' or like hearing an inner voice. It was not like the voice of the Glorified, yet no other symbols can describe it. It was in the place where Silence—the 'keeper of sound'—rested, but Silence was not chased away from its place by the sound. Her thoughts seemed jumbled and she rambled for a while as she tried to describe sound inside Silence. It was voiceless and loud, she said, but in it there was sharing. She could see, hear, and feel what needs to be done. 'Sharing', she said, repeating it in a low and distant voice, longing for that Presence again. She then said as if to answer Seh's inquiry, 'It was not a conversation. It was a sharing of creation.' The others listened, but they were confused by her descriptions. They knew silence could be forced from its place like light chasing darkness. They did not understand how silence could be 'the keeper of sound'. They searched the endowment for any truth that might further explain her comments. 'Everything is possible for the First, the Self-Generator, is the eleventh truth', said a Glorified, 'and it is known that creation is sharing'. Hu agreed, looking at the male-other whose place was three positions on her left. He was smiling because the purpose of creation had been affirmed. They knew the answer to the question, 'What is the purpose of creation?' but they did not know the size of creation. Seh, too, affirmed the purpose of creation, adding, 'The purpose of this company is to share in the task.' She was not sure she had responded to Seh's query with the appropriate symbols. After he spoke, a quiet washed over the company, and they let Silence rest among them for a while.

CHAPTER 17

TRUE GIFT

Silence rested, waiting to lead sound along a secret path towards the 'keeper of sound', as they considered what they heard. The male-other whose place was two positions on the right side of Hu said, "So many unexpected outcomes. The endowment has been expanded. It is known anew", he said, looking at the Creature, "that the First, the Self-Generator, continues to create things. The announcement shows the mysterious ways in which *It* works. The path to the announcement remains a secret, even though the '*other*' travelled it all the way to the end of everything and back from the beginning of 'nothing'. She knows neither the entrance nor the exit. She has been everything in creation yet has not witnessed how things are created. The works of the First, the Self-Generator, are forever '*becoming*'; they bear witness for *It*. They are the heralds of the first truth of creation and they last forever and a more", he said without hesitation.

"There is so much to explore", he continued, "from what has been shared. The Creature without a Spark, whether the announcement is the third 'part of being', and the 'keeper of sound'. Silence is the keeper of sound! Is there any aspect of creation that is without a purpose? These will be explored, but the most interesting question—the one that will be explored for many whiles—is the fleeting thought. It might be a question that cannot be answered. There might be no foundation on which any certainties about the Spark leaving its vessels could rest, but the exploration of it might provide more insight into being." The others agreed that the exploration of the fleeting thought had not come to a close.

The journey to the seal revealed many certainties, but the announcement was not like anything the Glorified uncovered. The Rapture had a shared beginning and a path that led to an outcome. The knowledge of forms had an outcome, and each Glorified was able to uncover its path. The path to the announcement could not be uncovered in the same way. Other beings, creatures, or consciousnesses cannot do as the First, the Self-Generator, has done. The Glorified could not make themselves the creator of beginnings because they knew existence. The announcement was an outcome to an unknown. It was not found because the Glorified sought. A door was opened, but not because the Glorified knocked. If it were an answer, the Glorified did not know the question.

Hu did not know why the announcement and the task were shared with her. She could not think of anything that would distinguish her from the others and she offered no explanation. She could only describe her experience. The Glorified saw the Creature and heard the tale, but unlike the knowledge of forms, they could not uncover the path to the announcement. They wanted the journey to continue so they might hear more and further explore the announcement, but they had come to accompany Hu as she journeyed towards her destiny. As they neared the entrance, the Seven whose place is one position on her right, said to her as though attempting to comfort her, 'The last journey in the Realm might lead to a *beginning again*. Similar to the Mystery of Creation, where the last of it is the first of it.'

The others nodded. Hu, recalling the omnipresence of the announcement, said, 'It may not be a *beginning again*, for all things come to an end; the last shall...' 'That is not a truth', the female-other on her right interjected. 'There is no end to creation; there is no end to the First, the Self-Generator, or to the perpetual plenty in the Realm. There are no ends to the things created from 'nothing' because the First, the Self-Generator, creates things forever and a more. There are only beginnings, journeys, and *beginning again*, like the elements in the Realm, which are forever '*becoming*.'

The others did not understand the symbol 'end'. Hu thought of it because the announcement came to a close, and she did not know how to *begin again*. She knew there were things which were forever '*becoming*', but she longed to be the Presence in all things again. Accepting that she did not know how to *begin again*, she let her '*self*' be at peace with the thought, 'all things come to an end.'

'The task', she said, 'is more of a beginning than a *beginning again* for the path has yet to be travelled. The last shall be the first', she said, 'but not in the same way.' She held up the container and said to them that she 'believes' that her role is to be the centre of the design. There would be no more journeys; only the glow of the Spark would travel throughout the place, space, or time. There was a pause, as if they were all holding their breath, before the male-other whose place was three positions on her left, whose contentment is heard in laughter, said, 'Believed but know not?' He heard her comment in the same way Seh did. 'Belief', the Seven said, with brightened face and sparkling eyes, 'is not required.' Seh wondered if she had chosen the symbol 'believe' not because she did not know but because she did not want to share the task. The Glorified three positions on her left, added, 'If the task means no more beginnings in the Realm, the Seven would long for the '*other*' three positions on the right and four positions on the left.' He called her by her place, and they all looked at her, affirming that he had spoken for them. The glow of the Sparks brightened. The Creature, for the first in a while, flapped its limbs and hopped three paces ahead. The Glorified followed and then waited for her to take her place before the Creature signalled: *begin again.*

As they hopped, Seh thought it was not belief; it was not uncertainty; it was her hidden purpose. Refusing to let Silence rest, he asked her, 'How would the task be shared with the others? Would she command the others to do a part of the task, similar to how the First, the Self-Generator, commanded the task to be done?' Seh's question was as confusing as Hu's comment about the end. They did not understand because no Glorified had ever commanded the others to do or to do not. The Glorified always shared 'know-how' and participated in the uncovering of the unknown. Being part of the company was sharing in the journey. They came to accompany Hu and to witness the outcome of the journey. They wondered if Seh thought that one Glorified could command the others. Or was he saying that one Glorified should lead the others as the Spark leads the Spirit? They did not understand his request. There was nothing in the endowment that would clarified his comments.

The male-other three positions on the left side of Hu said, 'A Glorified cannot command the others to do or to do not.' He thought the task would be shared when the others add the outcome to the endowment. Seh's thoughts drifted back to the knowledge of transformation before he said, "The *'other'* has been commanded to do a task." The male-other who hears the *true gift* in songs and laughter, said, with a smile as bright as the rising sun, 'If the task was commanded, it would be done. The Seven', he continued, 'are not the creator of beginnings. They are not the giver of the *true gift*; the one without equal, who has no need to command', he said. "The '*other*', three positions on the right and four positions on the left", again identifying Hu by her place, "did not say a task has been commanded. She said only there is a task to be done and what her role might be." Seh listened as the Glorified, who seemed to have a perpetual smile on his face, shared his thoughts. 'It is a truth, found among many truths in creation, that they are no greater than or lesser than in creation. A Glorified cannot command another', he said again. 'The Glorified, like the First, the Self-Generator, command no other to do or to do not. The creator of beginnings gave the Glorified the *true gift* with a Spark and *nia*. They are all the Glorified need.' He searched the endowment, once more, before saying, 'There are no commands, for to command it is to make it a truth.'

'The outcome of the task is known,' said the Glorified one position on Hu's right. She spoke with confidence, saying there is but one uncertainty: How the glow for the task would be provided. If the glow is to be provided by the Spark within the Seven, then this may be the last of her journeys. The others had not heard the tale in the same way as Seh. The male-other, two positions on Hu's right side, said, 'The tale of the announcement has been shared. There will be many circular assemblies, many whiles to explore the truths, the certainties, and the outcomes of the announcement.' As the company neared the entrance to the section with the seal, he put aside the discussion of Seh's question and said, 'The fleeting thought might be about the *true gift*.'

He was again referring to the idea that the Spark could vacate its vessels. The others had put aside that conversation without any insight into its meaning. This male-other, whose place in the circular assembly is two positions on Hu's right side, had continued to consider it. He had searched the endowment and reaffirmed what the Glorified knew: creatures with a Spark had a *true gift*. He quietly listened and considered how that truth would apply to the Creature. As he listened to Hu telling the tale, his thoughts were mostly focused on the Spark and the *true gift*. 'Creatures with a Spark have a *true gift*', he said, repeating the truth from the endowment. The Glorified thought that meant only creatures with a Spark had a *true gift*. He searched the endowment again, pausing at that truth, seeing it in a new way as he applied it to the Creature. Then, he considered the Realm and its ever-coming elements. He recalled the Rapture and the Presence in all things. Creation, he thought, has a *true gift*; it is not just creatures with a Spark.

'Creation is sharing, and the first thing shared was the *true gift*. The *true gift* was only shared with creatures with a Spark after it was shared with the Realm and everything in it. It is the *true gift* which brings forth the everlasting plenty. It is the *true gift* that caused the Mystery of Creation to fall from the mount and to spring forth from the abyss.' He was quietly considering the *true gift* as the others discussed the meaning of not knowing how to *begin again*. He thought the Glorified did not know how to *begin again*, but he was certain the Realm, with its forever-coming elements, knows nought but beginnings.

The *true gift* —*the gift of existence*—was created from 'nothing', he thought, as the others considered the meaning of 'the end'. He paused to acknowledge the thirteenth truth: 'Things created from 'nothing' are the creations of the First, the Self-Generator.' The endowment says creatures with a Spark have a *true gift*. That is a truth. It is also a truth that this Creature did not have a Spark, and yet it has a *true gift*, which broadens the meaning of the truth in the endowment. Why the endowment did not include the knowledge that there might be a creature with a *true gift* but without a Spark is unknown. Again, he looked at the Creature. He wondered if there would be other creatures with a *true gift* but without a Spark. He knew that no beings, creatures or consciousnesses know what the First, the Self-Generator, might or might not do. He thought that there could be many creatures without Sparks, but he was certain that there could be no Realm, no place, space, or time, no Glorified or any creature without the *true gift*. The *true gift* was what the First, the Self-Generator, created when *It* was begotten of *Its* own '*becoming*'. That truth surrounds creation, and without it, existence would not be.

The *true gift* is found in all of creation, but the Spark is known only to the Glorified, he thought. The Spark had been at the centre of their being since they awoke into existence. The Spark, too, has its purpose. It guides the Spirit and indicates the directions to follow to fulfill *nia*. As the male-other two positions on the right side of Hu thought about the *true gift*, he wondered whether the Creature, like the Realm, knew how to *begin again*. He could see the Creature had *nia*, but wondered why it had no need to know which direction to travel. He was considering the role of the Spark when Seh asked how the task would be shared. He was trying to understand how a creature without a Spark could start towards its purpose, as the Glorified three positions on Hu's left shared his thoughts.

The Glorified uncovered not only that the Spark commands the Spirit, but also that the Spirit might roam. They thought it meant they could connect their Spirits across sections of the Realm. That was not the outcome, and since then, they had not considered the meaning of the 'Spirit could roam'. He thought about the many ways in which the Glorified tried to uncover the path to the Rapture before allowing the Spark to lead. Choosing the way of creation leads to the uncovering of the unknown. But the Creature did not have that choice. Why would the Creature not need the indications of a Spark? Could it be that without a Spark, the Spirit did not roam, and the Creature needed no guiding? It could be that all of its directions lead to the same outcome. The Creature could be *anointed*, he said to himself.

The Glorified considered anything in creation that always travels the same path as *anointed*—knowing only the way. For them, to be *anointed* means to follow the same straight and narrow path and to always gain the same outcome—like the Spark travelling the same path towards the Rapture or the Realm bringing forth its plenty. As he compared the Creature to other aspects of creation, he thought the Creature and the Realm have a similar golden sphere, but the Creature's *true gift* is more like the *true gift* of the Glorified. He understood why Seh would think if the Spark vacated its vessels, they would be like the Creature with a *true gift* but without a Spark. He let his thoughts rest for a moment on the idea that the Spark could vacate its vessels. The Spark is the First, the Self-Generator, and for *It*, everything is possible. The Spark could vacate its vessels, he thought, if that is part of the *perfection in creation*, but it is not known what the Glorified would become.

He then began to consider what he knew about the Spark. The Glorified awoke into existence looking upon the Spark, and their first thought before Silence was intruded upon was: the Spark is the First, the Self-Generator. They all affirmed that to be true. They thought it witnessed that they were created at the same while and began their journeys in existence together. He wondered what the first thought of the Creature was when it awoke into existence. Did it know it had *nia* but not a Spark? He thought again about why the Creature would not need the guidance of a Spark. The Creature's similarity to the Glorified should mean the Creature needed a Spark. The Spark indicates the way. How is it that it is the Creature that could start towards its purpose and destiny without a Spark to indicate the way?

The Glorified had explored the Realm and witnessed sharing everywhere. The Realm shares its plenty, renews, and *'remakes'* its elements so the Glorified have no symbols to describe lack or not having. Through sharing, the path to another way of being was uncovered, and they learnt everything in creation shared the same Presence. Sharing is the only symbol in the endowment that could explain all of the acts of the First, the Self-Generator. Sharing is the way of creation and the purpose of everything in creation. Without sharing, existence would not be and having a Spark means that creation has been shared differently with the Glorified than with the Creature.

Both the Glorified and the Creature had *nia*. Their purpose, as well as the purpose of every creature and thing, is sharing, but destiny they did not know, and no Glorified other than Hu wondered about the reasons for their being. That was until the Creature caused this male-other to wonder about the Spark and *nia*. The Creature's purpose ought to be the same as the purpose of creation. It is similar to the Glorified, but not the same; it is similar to the Realm, yet not the same. Could it have the same destiny as the Glorified or the Realm?

Hu had shared with the others that during the *while of quiet*, she wandered throughout the Realm. She explained that she wandered without direction, drifting slowly. The journey, she said, always leads to the Mystery of Creation. The male-other two positions on the right side of her had suggested she might be journeying towards her destiny. That notion had not been explored. Over the whiles, the idea that a destiny is something that is journeyed towards slowly settled among them. At whiles, the term 'journeying towards destiny' would be heard, yet no further explanation of it was developed.

As the male-other considered the Creature relative to the Spark, purpose, and destiny, he recalled Hu's sharing and his suggestion that she might be journeying towards her destiny. He wondered whether he was thinking of a truth when he suggested it or if he had created a *false truth*. He did not know what a destiny might be. The endowment said creatures with a Spark had *nia*: purpose and destiny. Was it a way of being, or was it an outcome, as he thought? There were no other thoughts or suggestions among them about destiny. The others had accepted his certainty, but as the company neared the seal, he wondered if his certainty had hidden a truth. He did not know how to consider destiny. It may not be the same as an outcome. Whatever destiny is, it could only be gained as part of the *perfection in creation*, he thought; then, he tried to put his ramblings about destiny aside.

His thoughts were almost as jumbled as the thoughts of Hu during the announcement. He listened to the tale like Hu listened in the announcement. Nestled in the thicket of his thoughts was the idea that the fleeting thought might be about the *true gift*. While he considered what he knew about the role of the Spark, his jumbled thoughts about destiny would intrude upon him like sound upon silence. He would start again by reminding himself that the Spark is the First, the Self-Generator. It provides guidance for the Spirit. As Hu told her tale, he considered the Spark's role in the *'gift of being'*. After the Glorified, whose thought was that there is no unknown to uncover, had allowed Silence to take its place. He said, "The question may not be whether the 'parts of being' *'became'* or were left behind. The question might be about the *true gift*. The Creature has a *true gift* without a Spark, and it is a truth that the Spark indicates the way." The *'other'* whose place is one position on the right side of Hu, added, 'Towards purpose and destiny, it provides guidance for the Spirit.' 'That is a truth', he agreed, 'but the Creature is without a Spark.' He paused before asking the others, 'Why would the Creature not require the guidance of a Spark?'

The company walked on, nearing the section with the seal. 'Could it be,' he asked, 'that the Creature is *anointed*? There might be a straight and narrow way for it to travel, so it may gain the outcome of *nia* even without a Spark.' 'It is not known whether that is true', Hu said. 'The Creature is like no other in creation. All that is known of it is that it has a role in the task, and although it has the same Presence within it as everything in creation, it could stand apart from the rest of creation.' 'How is that a truth?' Seh asked. He looked at the Creature again, thinking that Hu had affirmed that the Creature had distinguished itself from the rest of creation.

'The Creature is part of creation', Hu said. 'It is a creation of the First, the Self-Generator.' In the announcement, it was positioned atop the entombed form, but its presence was not found among the things in creation. Even as she stood at the end of everything and at the beginning of 'nothing', the Creature remained an unknown. Its presence was not among the things that she knew, and it was not felt at the beginning of 'nothing'. She knew creation and everything in it, but she did not know the Creature. In that way, the Creature stood apart from the rest of creation, but it has the same Presence. It has purpose and destiny. 'Being *anointed*', she said, agreeing with the '*other*' whose place was two positions on her right, 'might be the way it travels its path.'

CHAPTER 18

LAST GATHERING

'The paths to *nia* are many', said Seh. 'The Spark in its vessels indicates the way. Each part points in a slightly different direction, but it is the Glorified who chooses the path.' He paused for a while, then said, 'It is not known, for the endowment is silent, whether it is within the will of the Glorified to choose a path not indicated by the Spark. The Glorified are not *anointed*. The Spark shows there are many paths. It leads the Spirit, but it is only a guide for the Glorified.' Seh's sharing dampened the mood of the company like frost on a spring morning. There was a crisp certainty to his words, speaking without hesitation, as though he had knowledge. He did not wait to be asked, 'How is it a truth?' He continued to share, saying, 'The truth may be seen in this journey. If the '*other*' were *anointed*, there would be no need to travel through the Realm—The 'nothing' would have chosen the way, like the Spark leading the Spirit. That is a certainty', he added, trying not to speak for the First, the Self-Generator, nor to speak of *It* in vain. 'Choosing', he looked up at Hu, 'may be a part of the task. The '*other*' has chosen the path towards the seal, but she could also choose to share the task and who should break the seal. She could choose to have the task done by another. This may not be known to her, but she could choose to do or to do not. In choosing, she would not know the outcome. The Glorified chooses without knowing how that choice would shape their Spirit or act upon creation.'

Hu, listening to Seh, looked at him to see if the slight tinge on his Spark could be seen. His Spark, in the shape of the golden sphere, was bright; it seemed polished, like the others. 'There are many paths, and the Spark indicates the direction to travel', said Seh. 'If the Glorified were led by the Spark, there would be one path towards *nia*. Each Glorified would follow the path as in entering the Rapture. It is a secret what the Glorified would be with only one path. It might be similar to the Rapture. The Glorified might not be able to act upon creation. Choosing among the indications of the Spark is choosing the way the Spirit should be and how it acts upon creation. The Spirit could roam', he said, referring to the truth from the endowment, 'but it may not know which paths are in the way of creation. That might be the reason it needs guiding.'

'The Glorified have *nia*: purpose and destiny. Purpose is known but it is not known how destiny should be considered', Seh continued, as if he was having the same thoughts as the male-other whose place was two positions on the right side of Hu. 'Over the whiles, the Glorified have had many outcomes, but destiny is not just the gaining of an outcome. It is how the Spirit acts upon creation. When the Glorified choose, they do not know what the outcome might be. The Seven did not know that gaining the Rapture would mean their Spirit could not affect creation. The endowment offers no reference. It is not known if destiny is similar to the seal, in place, waiting to be uncovered, waiting for the path to be chosen.' Seh shared his thoughts, while the others searched the endowment. "It is true that following the indications of the Spark leads to *nia*. That truth existed, even before it was known that the Spark leads the Spirit. The purpose of the Glorified is the same as creation, but the destiny of the Glorified is unknown.

It may be", he said, "that the reason destiny is unknown is that each Glorified is the maker of his or her destiny. Destiny might be a *'becoming'*. The Glorified make their destinies by choosing the paths to travel." After Seh spoke, Silence rained down on the company. He spoke as if he had knowledge and a foundation for his certainties. In pursuing transformation, Seh had chosen. He chose a path that was not among the indications of the Spark. That was his first hint that the Glorified are not *anointed*. It allowed him to speak of choosing without hesitation. He believed, but he knew not, that choosing was choosing how the Spirit should be or how it should act upon creation. He thought about how his Spirit had changed since uncovering the path to transformation. He was certain that if he had chosen another path, if he had waited for a circular assembly, he might not have known the mysteries found along the way.

The others agreed they do not know their destinies or how destiny should be considered. The idea that Hu could choose to do not, and the Seven were the makers of their destinies, were new ideas for the others. 'It is true', Hu said, raising her voice slightly with a warm tone, trying to comfort the company, 'that choosing the path indicated by the Spark leads to *nia*, but the Glorified are not the makers of their destinies. It is the First, the Self-Generator, who reveals the path, and *It* is the maker of destinies.' The male-other whose place was two positions on the right side of Hu had similar thoughts about destiny as Seh. But Seh's comments about choosing a path not indicated by the Spark seemed strange to him. He agreed the paths are many, but he thought the many paths are all indicated by the Spark. In a sure and steady voice, which bore no witness to his jumbled thoughts, this male-other agreed with Hu, saying, 'The First, the Self-Generator, is the first and the last maker of destiny, but like the fleeting thought of the *'other'*, choosing is part of the *true gift*. The Glorified are the only creatures with a Spark. Existence has been shared differently with them than with other parts of creation. It could be that choosing the indications of the Spark is choosing to act in the way of creation. All the indications of the Spark, all of its directions, lead to purpose and destiny, which suggest the paths are many, but the destinies are few. The *true gift* without the many paths to choose from would be similar to the *true gift* in other aspects of creation. The Realm did not choose its path; its path is part of the *perfection in creation*. It can only follow its path and bring forth its plenty. Like the Creature, it is *anointed*. The way has been chosen for it. The *true gift* and the many paths indicated by the Spark mean the Glorified could choose the path to follow. In so doing, choosing not the way to act upon creation—but to act in the way of creation.'

'If the outcome of this journey is a destiny, then the '*other*' has chosen the path towards that destiny. She has chosen from among the indications of the Spark. Another Glorified might have travelled along a different path. Their Spark would have indicated a slightly different way. Choosing the way of creation might cause the Spark to lead the Spirit to act in the way of creation. Even though each Spark would indicate a different direction, the journey would lead to the same outcome.'

Seh heard a slight difference in the male-other's comments and intruded upon his sharing, saying, "Choosing is how the Spirit '*becomes*'. The Spark leads the Spirit, but after the journey, the Spirit is not the same!" Seh knew the others were searching the endowment. The idea that the Spirit '*becomes*' was a first. He had not shared that thought with the others before. As the company journeyed towards the seal, exploring the role of purpose and destiny, he thought the Spirit of the Glorified reflected their choosing. 'It might be similar', he added, 'to how the *true gift*, or the *gift* of existence, reflects the First, the

Self-Generator. Choosing causes the Spirit to *'become'*, and whether the Spirit acts in the way of creation or acts upon creation, it reflects the choosing of the Glorified.'

'That is not a truth; there is no reference to the Spirit *'becoming'* in the endowment', said the male-other two positions on the right side of Hu. 'It c-could … it m-may be a certainty', Seh added, his words stumbling over each other as if he had said too much. 'There are no differences among the Spirits of the Glorified', added the male-other. 'That is not known', Seh said, 'for the Spirit is not the Spark, nor the physical form, there for all to look upon. The Spirit can only be seen in its outcomes, in the contributions to the gatherings, in the works of the Glorified. It could be said that all Glorified have a Spirit of giving and receiving, and that is because of their purpose.' 'If only there were not a task to be done', intruded the male-other. He set aside Seh's certainties about the Spirit to conclude that, 'Choosing must be one of the reasons for the *true gift* with a Spark, since the paths are many.'

'The purpose of the Glorified and their destinies are part of the *true gift*', he added. 'They are part of the *perfection in creation*. Purpose is known, but destiny—for both the Glorified and creation—is unknown. For the Glorified, the paths are many, but for the Creature, who is *anointed*, there is one path that leads to purpose and destiny.' Humans in the village would ask if that indicated the First, the Self-Generator, has a chosen plan for everyone in creation. The Glorified would say there is only the *perfection in creation*. They would remind humans of the sixth truth of creation, but among human beings, much could change between the telling and the hearing. After humans spread themselves about the Earth. After the stories of the village were changed to meet the needs of the storytellers, humans would speak of destiny by saying, 'There is a plan.' The First, the Self-Generator, has no plan that is known to humans. In creation, creatures with a *true gift* but without a Spark are *anointed.* They have only one path towards purpose and destiny. The Glorified and humans are not *anointed.* Their *'gift of being'* included a Spark, and their way is neither straight nor narrow, for the Spark indicates that there are many paths. Creatures with a Spark do not need the First, the Self-Generator, to have a plan. They do not need the way to be chosen for them. The Spark indicates the paths to *nia* and guides the Spirit in the way of creation.

The company continued towards the seal as if they had no more to say, as if there were no further thoughts about destiny, before Hu forced Silence from its place, saying, 'The knocking in the vessels, and the fleeting thought have provided such insights and questions about being, but they were not the most unfamiliar feeling in the announcement.' Seh heard the symbols 'unfamiliar feeling' and thought of the mysteries found along the way. He expected the others would eventually uncover the path to the mysteries he had found, so he looked, and listened for signs. He listened as Hu began telling the part about the strange sensation of touch. She did not know what it was. It occurred only in the announcement, where the form of creation and the Rapture form were within reach of each other. Like the *'other'*— and she looked at Seh—she thought of the *duality of being.* Seh did not intrude upon her sharing, even though he thought she might reveal what she knew about his Spark. Hu, looking at Seh, said that she knew the ale was strong. She had expected the *while of quiet* to be long and deep. Knowing that she had drunk much, she started to dismiss the announcement. She was about to create a *false truth* when the Creature appeared, standing on her form of creation. It stood on her form, and she felt its weight. Its feetless toes sent an 'unfamiliar sensation of touch' along the side of her form. The feeling was as if a piece of her form was being removed. She held the container with one hand so she could point to the spot on her side where the Creature stood. She did not know the symbols to describe it. It was not like the touch of the Glorified. It lasted only for as long as the Creature remained on her form. 'That', Seh said, as if he were expecting to hear some other tale, 'is the most unfamiliar feeling in the announcement?' The company took a few more steps before Hu said she had not felt any sensation like it in all the whiles of being. She was looking ahead at the path that led into the section with the seal. 'Is that a *ndo*?' she asked, putting aside her thoughts about the unfamiliar sensation of touch.

'It is everything that is required for a gathering', Seh said. 'If this is the last of the journeys in the Realm, then there should be one last gathering of the Seven. The task would be put aside for only a while of sharing, and to partake of the plenty from the Realm.' That was the reason Seh had taken so long to reach the others at the gathering. Seh had left to gather the others so Hu could share the tale of the announcement. She agreed to share the story after Seh said the task would not be put aside. After Hu agreed, Seh left with such haste she wondered if he had heard her complete her statement. He did not enter the Rapture; instead, he used the speed the Glorified used to explore being everywhere.

Before rejoining the others, Seh collected things to be used for a gathering. He collected Hu's favourite foods from the plenty of Realm. He gathered the Mystery of Creation as it fell from the mount, but before he collected it, he searched that section to see if he could uncover the seal. He even entered the Rapture to see if it could be seen with the Spirit's eye. He did not know what the seal looked like, but he saw no difference in that section of the Realm. The section appeared as it had from the beginning; nothing was added or taken away. If there were an announcement, he thought, as he took one more look around the section, should not all of creation know it? He found nothing indicating the existence of a seal, and before gathering the others, he was certain Hu had uncovered a type of *duality of being* and that she had a hidden purpose.

He then travelled to the section where he was stationed during the Rapture. In that section, the Mystery of Creation did not fall from the mount; it came forth from the abyss. There were lakes and creeks, which flowed into a river that meandered through the section and into the other sections of the Realm. Among the lakes and creeks Seh passed many whiles, adding to and expanding upon the knowledge of ale. Ale was an outcome of 'collective creativity'. The Glorified uncovered it together. Seh created many different types of ale. He first added sweetness to the ale the Glorified created together. He had suggested the ale should be sweet, but the outcome did not have a sweet taste; rather, it had what humans described as a 'bland, sour taste'. He then created ales which he called *wet* and *dry*, which the others did not fully understand. They thought of *wet* and *dry* as a way to distinguish between the tastes of the ales. Seh shared 'know-how' with the others to create those particular types of ale. Even though the others had the same knowledge of ale as Seh, they did not have the same interest. The Glorified all partook of ale, but none pursue the knowledge of ale like Seh. Seh's favourite types of ales which he created were the *hot* and *cold* ales. Those ales are strong and mysterious; the *hotter* the ale, the stronger the ale. The *cold* ales are unpredictable. *Cold* ale was only drunk in small amounts because the effects of *cold* ale on the Glorified varied. That was why Hu had thought the announcement could be an effect of ale. She knew the drink at the gathering was not only strong, but it also had a trace of *cold* ale.

Seh collected ale in equal portions with the Mystery of Creation from the ponds and lakes of ale that he created over the whiles.

Although not the plenty that was usually found at the gathering, he placed the things he collected where the path Hu chose crossed with the path that led into the section with the seal. Humans called such places *crossroads*. Among humans, *crossroads* are places of mystery—where fortunes are made and lost, where the lost could be found and the unknown discovered. Humans have lost much because, in their beginning, those were places where one could become two, where the purpose of creation could be affirmed, and the first truth of creation could be witnessed.

As they approached the *crossroads*, Hu considered whether she should delay the task. She thought that both she and the Creature had already chosen not to put aside the task. She had shared her experience of the announcement. What other reasons could there be for delaying the doing of the task? As she tried to decide whether to delay the task, Seh said, that after they partook of the plenty, she could enter the Rapture once more to see if she could uncover how the particles were created. The others did not know Seh had prepared a gathering. They did not think there could be a delay in the journey. Seh's comments reminded Hu of the reason she had not witnessed the creation of the particles. She then thought she could quickly put aside the task, break bread with the others, and share with them the reason the creation of the particles has not been witnessed.

There were all manner of foods at the *crossroads*, to use the human symbol. There were the foods the Realm brought forth and the foods the Glorified created, including different types of bread, many of which would also be found among humans. Here too was the food Hu created as her contribution to the gathering when she chose not to contribute a form. In the middle of it all was the Mystery of Creation. The gathering at the *crossroads* had something for each of the Glorified. As the company approached the *crossroads*, the Creature hopped three paces ahead and the others followed, but the Creature did not signal, *begin again*; instead, it stood at the *crossroads*, looking upon the plenty which the Realm had to offer. The Creature waited for Hu as the Glorified at the front of the company transformed back into their forms of creation, and took their places as in the circular assembly. Then it was Hu. She stood beside the Creature as the '*other*' on her left and the Glorified on her right transformed and took their places. Finally, it was Seh and the male-other completing the circular assembly.

Seh positioned a *ndo* that each Glorified had made by his or her place. The Glorified sat down with their legs crossed and the vessels of their Spark resting on their knees as they had been when they awakened into existence. The circle was complete with a *ndo* on the right-hand side of each Glorified. Seh did not create a *ndo* or any other instrument. He spent the whiles since the introduction of the *ndo* creating forms and deepening his 'know-how' of ale. In arranging the things at the *crossroads*, he did not have a *ndo* to put by his place, so his place remained plain, without a marker. It was not known why Seh marked the positions in the circular assembly in such a manner. Their positions needed no marking, for each Glorified had had the same position since they awakened. Their places in the circular assembly were chosen for them by the First, the Self-Generator. At every gathering with all seven Glorified, they would each position themselves as in their beginning. As Hu sat down, she placed the container beside her and offered the Creature her hand, thinking the Creature would want to stand on her shoulder as it did before. The Creature instead flapped its limbs and landed on the top of the container. Seeing the Creature choose to be on the top of the container, instead of with Hu, Seh said that 'She would be able to enter the Rapture. She may uncover how the particles are created before completing the task.'

'How the particles are created is a question that is worth asking', said the female-other whose place in the circular assembly was one position on the left side of Hu. She spoke before entering the Rapture, saying the delay in the journey was an opportunity to turn certainties into truths. She vanished; she wanted to explore whether the Creature could truly see the particles. As her physical form disappeared from the sight of the others, she gathered the particles and allowed them to rain down on the Creature. The Creature jumped off the container, flapped its limbs, and shook its form to free itself of the particles. The Glorified 'remade' herself, not in her place—but just behind Hu and the Creature. She was making the most precious sound in creation. She had affirmed what Hu said with her eyes, her ears, and her being. The Creature had strengths that were beyond the Glorified. She was laughing, for she thought the Creature was a testimony to the eleventh truth, the mysterious ways in which the First, the Self-Generator, works. The other Glorified got up from their places. They entered the Rapture for they, too, wanted to turn certainty into truth.

As the others experimented with the particles and the Creature, Seh moved closer to Hu. He wanted to take a closer look at the container. The others used the particles to recreate the shape of the Creature. They were certain the Creature could see their Rapture, as the Creature joined them as they imitated the Creature's walk. Hu did not join the others; she remained sitting, thinking the task should not be delayed too long. The others were starting to share and make merriment. Seh looked at the container as the Creature joined the others.

Seh still could not see the design on the outside of the container. He looked at each of the orb and its place in the container. He reminded himself that he had not found a seal. There were things about the task that were unknown to him. Hu was to be the centre of the design, he thought, with the glow of her Spark flowing throughout the place, space, or time. As he considered Hu's role, he recalled the discussion about the Realm; he entered the Rapture to look upon the Spark of the Realm, to see whether it was truly a Spark or merely a golden sphere. He saw that neither the Creature's golden sphere nor the golden sphere in the Realm brightened their glow. He looked at both spheres, trying to distinguish one from the other as he might with the Sparks in the Glorified. After examining the golden sphere, Seh 'remade' himself next to Hu and said to her, 'The Realm is without a Spark. The golden sphere in the Creature is the same as the golden sphere in the Realm; one cannot be distinguished from the other.' 'With one thought, sound, or act the First, the Self-Generator, can do many things', Hu said, 'for it is a certainty the Realm and the Creature do not have the same destiny.' She spoke in a voice that seemed distant, as though still pondering whether the task should be delayed. As she spoke, Seh looked at the orbs in the container, studying them as if studying a plan, while the others were 'remaking' themselves all around the crossroads.

The Glorified who wanted to turn certainty into truth offered her hand to the Creature. The Creature jumped up onto her shoulder. The others formed themselves in a row so the Creature could jump from one Glorified to the other. As the Creature jumped onto the male-other, whose contentment in being flows out in sound, he said to Hu, 'The touch of the Creature is no different than the touch of the Glorified. What was the strange sensation of touch in the announcement?' Hu once again said she did not know. It was unlike anything she had ever felt. Seh began to listen. After pursuing transformation, he too could have said that the mysteries found along the way were unlike anything he had ever felt. It was a feeling of 'physical non-content-ment', she said. She struggled to find the appropriate symbols, as the Glorified had no symbols to describe what humans called 'pain'. 'Physical non-contentment', the male-other slowly repeated her words as though he was trying to comprehend what such symbols could mean. She looked at him, and for the first on the journey, his face was not brightened. In place of a smile, he wore a look of confused thought. He was trying to unravel the meaning of 'physical non-contentment'. As he struggled with the meaning of the words, he left the others to their merriment and sat beside Hu. Then, he said with a smile, 'Contentment is not physical—it is to be.'

Only Hu and Seh were listening to his thoughts. 'The announcement was being part of creation in a way no other Glorified had been. Being outside the Realm might cause the feelings of a Glorified to deepen', he said. "The Creature has strengths that are beyond the Glorified. It can look upon the particles. Its feelings are sensitive enough to sense them if they fall upon it. The particles might give the Creature 'a strange sensation'. That does not mean the Creature is non-contented in being. Contentment", he said, raising his voice slightly, speaking in a way to ensure his words were understood, "is not the same as a passing touch. To be contented is to accept being, to accept the 'gift of being' for what it is, a gift. It is not known if the feel of the particles is the same strange sensation to the Creature. What could be said is that it is not the same pleasant and gentle feeling that the Creature is experiencing." He gestured with his head towards the Creature. "The particles to the Creature could be as being outside the Realm is to a Glorified. The Creature may not be able to enter the Rapture, so to be covered in the particles may give the Creature a strange sensation. The Realm was prepared for the Glorified; to be outside the Realm might have heightened the feelings of the Glorified. That should not cause the 'other'—three positions on the right and four positions on the left, once again, calling her by place—to be non-contented in being." Again, Hu said she did not know what the sensation was, yet she agreed with the '*other*' that contentment was not the same as a passing touch.

As the male-other shared his thoughts about contentment, a Glorified began beating a *ndo*. She was playing the rhythm the Glorified used to announce the beginning of a gathering. Seh picked up the *ndo* Hu had created and joined the conversation. Hearing the sounds of the *ndo*, Hu was more settled, knowing, again, she would long for the sounds of the Realm. One by one, each of the Glorified picked up a *ndo* and added its voice to the conversation. The Creature stood upon Hu, looking at the Glorified, and listening to the conversation of the *ndos*. Seh gave the *ndo* to Hu so she might participate in the conversation. She put it aside, choosing to listen to the others instead. As the others played, Seh shared a portion of ale for each of the Glorified, then took his place. He waited until after the *ndos* had spoken, until Silence was searching for its place among them, before raising his ale, saying so all could hear, 'To beginnings and *beginning again*.'

They drank, then the Glorified one position on Hu's right said, 'The Creature's touch is the touch of being. It may be', she said, looking at Hu, 'that the strange sensation was the Creature's way of announcing its '*becoming*'. Once more, Hu said she did not know the reason for the strange sensation; she added the '*other*' three positions on the left thought it might be because she was outside the Realm. 'The effects of being outside the Realm are unknown; the strange sensation of touch, like all things in creation, has a purpose.' 'The truth may be a secret, but it could be that the strange sensation was to make the Seven aware that she is in the presence of the creator of beginnings', said the Glorified on Hu's right. 'There have been more thoughts of the First, the Self-Generator, on this journey than there have been over the whiles since the Glorified awoke into existence. The Glorified', she said, still looking at Hu, 'thought not of the First, the Self-Generator, when the announcement opened. She thought of her will and strength. She thought she had uncovered a new way of being', then, before considering the creator of existence, she considered ale. If not for the Creature, if not for the strange sensation of touch—she might have created a *false truth*. She may not have had any thoughts of the First, the Self-Generator. The purpose of the strange sensation of touch may have been to enliven.' She paused, trying to ensure she had chosen the appropriate symbol, 'To make her aware that she is in the presence of the only thing greater than herself.'

The Glorified agreed it was unusual for them to speak of the 'nothing', since they did not know *It*. What they knew was the First, the Self-Generator, was everything—and *It* was 'nothing'. 'No Glorified would have thought of the First, the Self-Generator', she said, still looking at Hu. "Ale is more likely to be thought of than *It*. They would not have thought this was an act of the 'nothing'; or that they are in the presence of the maker of beginnings. A Glorified would have to be enlivened to consider the creator of existence. That may be the reason for the *duality of being* and for the strange sensation. There is no reason any Glorified would have thought of the First, the Self-Generator." She paused and Silence rushed to join the company, and even though it was pregnant, the others chose not to chase it from among them. They waited for her to continue. 'The endowment', she said, 'is silent; it gives no reason, it provides no need, and it indicates no purpose requiring a Glorified to think of the First, the Self-Generator. The First, the Self-Generator, does not need the Glorified to think of *It*. *It* has provided everything creation needs. *It* even prepared a meal for the Glorified when they awoke into existence.' She picked up part of the meal dripping with its golden nectar, and broke it into seven pieces.

She gave one piece to each Glorified, saying, 'This is a *true gift*; it was brought forth by the Realm to share with creation.'

The '*other*' two positions on the right side of Hu picked up a container with another part of the meal and poured seven portions, one for each of the Glorified. That part of the meal the Glorified uncovered came from what humans would call a fruit. It had a green outer layer, which was pimpled with harmless prickles. The Realm brought it forth in one section only. Inside were black seeds in white, individual pockets. It could be eaten as it was found in the Realm. They uncovered that if they squeezed it, it would produce a white, milky liquid. That liquid was part of the meal which was prepared for them. They called it the 'essence of the meal'. These foods are the reason humans think of the Realm as a land of milk and honey. But together, the Glorified referred to them as the meal. The meal was the first foods the Glorified shared in the Realm.

When the Glorified awoke into existence, in front of each Glorified was the complete meal. It included a combed wafer, which had six sides, dripping with nectar. The essence of the meal sat beside it and next to that was the Mystery of Creation. The Glorified always wondered at the reason a meal awaited their awakening. They thought it was a part of the *true gift* but also a symbol—meaning, everything the Glorified needed had been prepared. In their beginning, the Glorified partook of the meal before starting their exploration of the Realm. At the *crossroads*, the Glorified each had combed wafers and the essence, but they did not partake, for the meal was not yet complete. The '*other*' three positions on the left side of Hu poured the Mystery for each Glorified. In front of each Glorified, in a straight line, were the combed wafer, the essence, and the Mystery of Creation. That was the way the Glorified always partook of the meal, for it was that way in their beginning. Even though the Glorified do not have rituals, they always prepared the meal as it was when they awoke.

They ate the wafer and drank the essence as they did in their beginning. The combed wafers were sweet. They put their fingers in their mouths to eat the last of its nectar. They drank the essence, which differed from the wafer in that it was sour, not sweet. This fruit when it appeared on Earth was in part called 'sour'. They partook of the Mystery of Creation after the wafer and the essence. After the human beginning, food and the Mystery of Creation would be considered two of the three goods of creation. There were no symbols among the Glorified that would allow them to represent food or anything else as good or bad. They knew that everything they needed was part of the *perfection in creation*. As they ate, a male-other said, 'Creation is sharing; the meal is best when it is shared.'

After the meal, Seh poured more ale for each of the Glorified. The ale was neither *hot* nor *cold* and Seh said if there were not a task to be done, he would have shared 'know-how'. The Glorified drank it, commenting it was not as strong as the ale at the last gathering. Then, they shared the fruit that Hu created and gave her the brown core to offer to the Realm so it could bring forth another. Seh transformed into the form with the small head perched on top of the long neck. The others, too, transformed into the forms they had created. Seh asked if they had already uncovered where the Spark had chosen to locate itself. Before Seh could guess where his Spark located itself, Hu stood up as if to remind the others that the journey must not be delayed too long. Seh was trying again to lead the company, so, he asked Hu if she was going to enter the Rapture. 'How the particles are created could be uncovered', he said with a smile. 'It is known', she said, 'why the creation of the particles has not been witnessed. The First, the Self-Generator has answers to all questions.' The Glorified who had said that there were more thoughts of the First, the Self-Generator, during this journey than there have been in all the whiles, acknowledged another reference to *It*. Hu said she did not know if she asked a question or just wondered about it. She recalled hearing, feeling or being the answer during the announcement. The answer had sat on the distant edge of her being since she began the journey towards the seal. As she spoke, the others transformed back into their forms of creation and took their places in the circular assembly. Hu sat down again, knowing the others were requesting *'sharing of know-how'*.

CHAPTER 19

PASS OVER

Seh was the first to transform back into his form of creation, but he was the last to take his place in the circular assembly. 'It is known', Seh repeated the words, sounding confused, and looking down. Again, he was shaken by an outcome. If the others had an expanded '*self*' like Hu during the announcement, they would have seen a slight change in the Spark within him. 'It is known', Hu said, confirming her words for Seh. 'There is no need to enter the Rapture. The reason the creation of the particles has not been witnessed is the seventh truth', she said.

'Things created by the First, the Self-Generator, last forever and a more', the '*other*' three positions on her left side added. The others waited for Hu to share her knowledge. Over the whiles that she followed the Spark, she always shared what she uncovered. She even asked the others to join her in following the Spark. As they waited for Seh to take his place, he asked, 'How is it known?' He was surprised to hear she knew the reason. That, there was an explanation for her failure. He thought, as he sat down, that if she had uncovered that knowledge, she would again be set apart and above the others. Over the whiles, Seh had reminded her that she had not been able to follow the Spark without losing her way. 'That is true', Hu would say, agreeing she had not been able to witness the creation of the particles. She would then add, 'All has not been lost, for there will always be another while to try again.' The Seven, whose voice betrayed his contentment in being, would interject and say, 'The truth is, she has forever and a more.' He would always follow that comment with laughter as though he had shared some deep secret of contentment.

'The creation of the particles will not be witnessed', she said. 'In the beginning, there were no witnesses to creation, and it remains true that there are no witnesses to the acts of the First, the Self-Generator. The Rapture begins with the Spark entombing the Glorified, and it has always been a certainty that it leads to the physical form being transformed into the particles. Inside the entombed glow, there is a dark inner layer. It is separated from the golden glow of the Spark by a bright silvery lining.' As Hu shared her knowledge of the path to the Rapture, Seh seemed to have regained himself. As the others listened, he was again being of service to the company. He broke bread into seven portions. The bread was flat and plain in taste, it was the first bread the Glorified had created. He gave each Glorified a portion and refilled their drinks: one with the Mystery of Creation and another with ale.

'Inside the entombed glow', Hu said, 'the form of creation is there. The Glorified could see, hear, and feel. The glow of the Spark flows through the silvery lining and is taken in by the dark inner layer. Inside the dark inner layer, there are particles.' She had told the others this part at many circular assemblies. She slowed the telling of the tale as though she was considering a new thought before saying, 'The announcement was not the first the particles of the Rapture and the physical form were within reach of each other. Before the sight is darkened, the form of creation and the particles are together. The particles in the dark inner layer are the Rapture particles. They could be felt brushing the physical form as the glow of the Spark flows into the dark inner layer.

'After the last of the glow is absorbed, the sight is darkened, and the Rapture is at the place where the Glorified is and is not. This is the point where focus and concentration are always lost.' She had not spoken this knowledge aloud, and she was uncertain of the appropriate symbols to use. She wondered whether focus and concentration were the symbols or whether there was another way to describe a sudden loss of awareness. The others did not interrupt her sharing, even as she paused and seemed unsure of the directions to the tale.

'As the last of the glow flows through the silvery lining, the silvery lining brightens and the sight is darkened', she continued. 'It is at this point where the Glorified loses the way, for they have not the will nor the strength to pass over into a new way of being. At the point where the Glorified loses the way, at the point where the Glorified is and is not, the Glorified is picked up and carried so she could come forth on the other side; similar to the particles entering the *crossing*. The next step along the path, which is known to the Glorified, is the four-sided mound, resting in the midst of the combined Spark. This is where the Glorified come forth after being carried over the bright silvery lining. There is a part before coming forth, which is not known to the Glorified. It is where being passes from the physical form into the particles of the Rapture.'

Once more, she slowed the telling of the tale as though searching for the path to take. The Glorified had assumed the form of creation was crumbled to create the particles because it could not be found in the Realm. That was a certainty based on their exploration. 'The form of creation passes over', she said. 'It has not been crumbled. At that point, the Glorified cannot see, hear, or feel, but the Glorified has not ceased to be. The passing over of the physical form cannot be witnessed—but not because the sight of the Glorified is darkened. The passing over cannot be witnessed—because there are no witnesses to the acts of the First, the Self-Generator', she said.

'As the form of creation is carried through the dark inner layer and over the bright silvery lining, being passes from the form of creation to the particles in the dark inner layer. The Glorified does not see, hear, nor feel as being flows from one part to another. Yet the Glorified still is; she has not ceased to be.' She was trying to address the question the others had asked when she first spoke of a place where the Glorified was and was not. The others wondered if the Glorified ceased to be. 'The form of creation passes over the bright silvery lining. The being of the Glorified remains within the dark inner layer and becomes part of the particles. That is why, at the *crossing,* the Glorified always appeared in the form in which they entered the Rapture.' She knew the others were searching the endowment as these truths were only certainties to them. They had not been able to follow the Spark along its path as she had done. The dark inner layer had not caressed their form of creation. They had not seen the particles within it. She knew the others would ask 'how it is a truth?' 'In the announcement', she said, trying to provide the others a place to rest the certainties, 'the thought was smiled upon'.

As she began towards the seal, she felt the reason she had not witnessed the creation of the particles sat at the edge of her being. She looked upon each of the others and she said to them, 'The form of creation rests at the *crossing* while the being of the Glorified becomes part of the particles, which allows for the opening of the Spirit's eye. The particles of the Rapture are made whole as being flows into the dark inner layer.' She chose not to use the symbol created as the dark inner layer appear like the Mystery falling upon the mount. "As the last of being flows into the last of the particles, the Glorified regains focus and concentration in the form of the four-sided structure. The four-sided mound is the Glorified coming forth in a new form. It is the outcome of the form of creation being picked up and carried over the silvery lining. It causes the Glorified to pass over into a new 'part of being.'" She then waited, and as she waited ate the bread and drank the Mystery of Creation that Seh had shared.

The Glorified, one position on the right side of Hu, tried to follow the Spark, but she had not yet overcome the hurdles. She had not experienced the inside of the glow of the Spark. She always questioned Hu concerning what Hu had uncovered. Like the others, she was certain the form of creation was crumbled to create the particles. 'The physical form', she said, 'is not crumbled. It passes over a silvery lining.' She was trying to understand. She did not know there was a dark inner layer or a silvery lining. She was exploring how it could be a *false truth* that the form of creation was crumbled to create the particles. 'It is a certainty uncovered by exploration', she said, 'that the form of creation is not found in the Realm. How is it not a truth that it has been crumbled to create the particles?'

Her comments had no clear direction, and the *'other'*, whose place was beside her and two positions on Hu's right side, said, 'Certainties which are based upon exploration could hide *false truths* even as they are looked upon.' He too had followed the Spark, and for the first before this journey, witnessed the dark inner layer. He had tried to follow the Spark since Hu had said there might be things along the path to the Rapture which were unseen and unknown. He had asked Hu how to follow the Spark along its path. She told him to focus on the vessels of the Spark. He changed the way he entered the Rapture so he might know where the vessels of the Spark were located. He told the others he could affirm the dark inner layer, but he had not yet witnessed the particles within it, nor the silvery lining. In a low voice, as if trying to soothe the thoughts of the *'other'* on his left, he said, 'There are many things in creation, which are not known to the Glorified. Even with exploration, the Glorified could still create *false truths*. In fact', he added, 'every certainty of the Glorified could be a *false truth*. Truths are found only in the endowment. Certainties are assumptions about the unknown. Any certainty could be a *false truth*.'

'Then', intruded Seh, 'it could be a *false truth* that being transitions into the dark inner layer.' 'It is not a *false truth*', Hu said, acknowledging that for others who have not witnessed the dark inner layer and do not know the announcement, it can only be a certainty. Again, she said, she did not know whether she had asked a question or simply wondered why she had not witnessed the creation of the particles. Yet she knew with all of her being her knowledge of the Rapture has been expanded.

'There are no references in the endowment which indicate the truth of the tale', said the Glorified two positions on Hu's right. 'This Seven,' he said, 'knows it to be truth. This Seven has looked upon the dark inner layer.' 'It could be a *false truth*', injected Seh, looking at the Glorified one position on his left. 'The Glorified uncover truth at the same while. Only certainties could cause a difference in the endowment.' 'The endowment has not changed and knowledge from following the Spark has been shared', replied the Glorified, looking at Hu. 'There is a difference, but it is not a difference in the endowment. The difference is two Glorified know the knowledge to be truth because they have seen it with their eyes and felt it with all of their being. The others', he said, looking at Seh on his right, 'have not witnessed it for they have not yet overcome the hurdles to following the Spark. The certainties could be made truth for the Glorified similar to how the certainties about the Creature were made truths. They only need to follow the Spark along its path to the Rapture. To look upon the dark inner layer would be to hear the truth of it when spoken, to feel the truth of it with all of their being, but to know that truth, the path must be travelled.' He paused, then said, 'There were no references to the Rapture in the endowment. It was part of the *perfection in creation*, to be uncovered by the Seven. The dark inner layer, the particles, and the silvery lining are also part of the *perfection in creation*. The truth in that perfection is that along the path to any outcome, there might be as much knowledge in the journey as there is in gaining the outcome.' He looked at Seh again before saying, 'It is true that how the particles are created is still an unknown. That will be a truth forever and a more. What could be known is how the particles are made whole and where the form of creation could be found when the Glorified is in the Rapture.'

The Glorified whose place was two positions on the left side of Hu, said, 'The tale has turned a certainty into a truth. It is a truth', she said, 'that to be in the Rapture is to be with the First, the Self-Generator.' The others, including Hu, looked at her, for they were taken aback by the implication. Over the many whiles, the Glorified referred to entering the Rapture as '*becoming*'. They thought of the Rapture as a way to be with the First, the Self-Generator, '*becoming*' one with everything in creation. In '*becoming*', the Glorified was certain the physical form was crumbled to create the particles. What happened to the form of creation in the Rapture was a secret—knowledge known only to the First, the Self-Generator. That secret has been revealed, and it gives meaning to the idea of being with the First, the Self-Generator. There is no other truth like that among the Glorified. Once a secret—then revealed to a Glorified. It, too, affirmed the sixth truth of creation. She admitted she had not yet arrived at the place to look upon the dark inner layer, nor to have her sight darkened. 'This Seven', she said, 'knows the tale has expanded her knowledge and understanding of the Rapture. The physical form is not crumbled. It flows through the dark inner layer and passes over to be with the First, the Self-Generator.' She repeated Hu's comments as if affirming the truth for the others. "In the Rapture", she said, brightening her face, "the Glorified is one with all of creation and rests in full contentment with the 'nothing'." She let Silence take its place and waited for it to be chased away by one of the others, but no one spoke. They were all considering her thoughts as they sat at the *crossroads*, around the plenty provided by the Realm.

For many whiles, the Glorified searched the Realm, looking for the form of creation. One Glorified would enter the Rapture and the others would search everywhere—in both their physical form and their Rapture—looking for their form of creation. The form of creation has never been found, which the Glorified thought affirmed their certainty that it had been crumbled to create the particles. After many whiles of searching the Realm, the Glorified added to their merriment a form of amusement, which humans called a game. One Glorified would enter the Rapture and after a while would 'remake' themselves somewhere in the Realm. The others would try to find where the Glorified had hidden. There were no rules as to where they could hide, but they were to hide themselves in the form of creation. A similar form of amusement is found among humans. Humans called their version 'hide and seek'. What humans do not remember is that this form of amusement was first played in the Realm.

After no one spoke, the Glorified two positions on Hu's left, continued: 'It is also a truth that the form of creation has been left behind.' The Glorified had wondered if the Spark and the Spirit left the form of creation behind. "It has been left behind, yet not the way in which the Glorified would have thought. It is kept by the 'nothing' so long as the Glorified remains in the Rapture." Humans would practise more from this part of the History than just the child's game of hide and seek. Humans still reference this part of the History, where it was revealed that the form of creation rested with the 'nothing'. There is a lamentation among humans of giving their soul to keep while they lay their forms to rest. This lamentation is based on the History of Creation. It is a reference to the form of creation passing over to be with the First, the Self-Generator.

As the Glorified rested her thoughts, Silence descended upon them, as though it was demanding to have its place. They were searching the endowment to see whether they had a foundation for their certainty that to be in the Rapture is to dwell with the First, the Self-Generator. The Seven whose place was two positions on the left of Hu looked at her and said, 'The tale of the announcement has been shared. New knowledge of the Rapture has been gained, but the journey has been delayed for longer than expected.' She rose to her feet as though she were signalling, *begin again*—saying to the others to let the task be done. Hu rose to her feet as well, then all the others stood up to resume the journey towards the seal. Seh picked up the ale he had shared and said in a clear and confident voice, 'To beginnings'. The others picked up their ale and drank, 'To beginnings!' while Hu drank a portion and paused. She intended to say, 'And to *beginning again*', when the Creature leapt from her shoulder unto her arm and back to her shoulder as though to say they have delayed long enough, knocking the ale from her hand. Seh offered another, but Hu said, 'It is strong'. The male-other, three positions on the left side of Hu said, 'It has an undertaste. It is not the finest choice for this sharing.' Then Hu picked up the container and turned towards her destiny.

CHAPTER 20

LAST JOURNEY

The company began the journey towards the seal again with each of the Glorified taking their place. Silence, too, found its place among them as they left the last gathering behind. There were no more tales to tell, no more questions to ask, and no more requests for *'sharing of know-how'*. The company knew this was the last part of the journey. They knew not the outcome—only that they journeyed towards a beginning for Hu. They put aside all thoughts of the gatherings, of journeys and explorations through the Realm, recalling only that they had come to accompany Hu. If this were the last of her journeys, it should be a shared journey. Each of the others longed for her even as they accompanied her. They did not join her along the path to the Rapture, but they would accompany her to the beginning of the task.

The Creature settled on her shoulder and the container was burdenless in her hands. Silence rested among the company, as though they lacked the strength or will to make another sound. Hu opened her ears to the sounds of the Realm. She could hear the sound of the distance like the blowing of wind in faraway places. She heard the Mystery of Creation making its way towards the abyss. There are many things in creation which remain unknown. The Mystery of Creation is one of those things. The Glorified had travelled its many paths without uncovering its secrets. They did not know that the sound it made was its tongue. They did not know the Mystery told a story of creation, beginning much like the History of Creation. The Glorified, since their beginning, used the Mystery of Creation as the First, the Self-Generator, uses 'nothing'. Hu had spent many whiles with the Mystery. She would hold it, letting her Rapture's particles become one with it, drifting in whichever direction it flowed. As the company walked towards the seal, Silence reclined in its place; the Glorified, looking ahead, had no more thoughts to share.

The Glorified knew this section of the Realm. Each had spent more than a while within it. The company journeyed past the place where Hu had stationed herself during the first Rapture. She recalled how the whole section was bathed in the colour of her Rapture. This was the section where she would find herself standing after wandering throughout the Realm. It was the place where the *'other'* said she was journeying towards her destiny. The seal was to be found close to where she would stand by the Mystery of Creation after her wandering. She could hear the footsteps of the company, drumming their way towards the seal. Since the tale of the announcement had been shared, she had begun to consider again the form to use in breaking the seal.

Silence laid its burden down around the company. Seh reverted to considering how the others could share the task. The others did not know the location of the seal. They knew this was the section where the Mystery of Creation began its journey. It fell upon the mount after being created out of 'nothing'. It followed a path, falling into the abyss only to spring forth or fall from above in other parts of the Realm. The Glorified explored it, and with the particles of their Rapture, became one with it. They tried to uncover its source and purpose. In their beginning, they held their first circular assembly in this section in front of it. They entered and followed the path to where the Mystery of Creation fell upon the mount. The path Hu chose was the same the Glorified took when they first began to explore the Realm. They entered this section, ate the combed wafer that appeared out of nothing, and when they reached the mount upon which the Mystery of Creation fell, they drank it from their cupped hands.

The company continued as some of the others recalled the first circular assembly. They had seen the Mystery spring forth from the abyss or fall from above in other sections. In this section, the Mystery of Creation appeared different. It came out of the darkness. It seemed to pause, held up by nothing before falling upon the mount. It was not clear to the Glorified whether the Mystery was falling from above or if it was springing from the mount and flowing up towards the darkness. 'It is sharing', they said, as they wondered about the location of its source. 'It gives and it receives.' After drinking, they held a circular assembly. Before any questions were asked or any thoughts were shared, the Glorified searched the endowment. They were searching for references to the Mystery of Creation, but the endowment provided no information other than its symbol.

The Mystery appeared to wait and seemed to flow to and from itself. They were looking at it when the Glorified whose place was two positions on the right side of Hu, asked, 'If the darkness overhead is made from the Mystery of Creation?' The others did not know, but thought if that were true, the Mystery would fall from above everywhere in the Realm. The Glorified, one position on the right side of Hu, said, 'Everything is possible for the First, the Self-Generator.' That was the first, a Glorified had mentioned the First, the Self-Generator. She was not referring to the 'nothing'. She was referring to the truth of creation in the endowment. 'For that reason', she said, 'it could be the darkness overhead is made from the Mystery of Creation.' 'Everything is possible, but it is not known', Hu added. "The endowment says the Realm and everything in it has been created from 'nothing'." Again, they searched the endowment before asking, "What is 'nothing'?" That first circular assembly had more questions than the Glorified knew how to answer. They focused on the Mystery of Creation. It was suggested the Glorified should explore its path after they had explored the Realm. They thought they might be able to follow it throughout the Realm and back to its beginning. It would be a while before the Glorified could return to that suggestion. First, they would explore the thought that they, too, could be the creator of things. They knew from the endowment that things were created from 'nothing' but did not know what 'nothing' was. As the others accompanied Hu towards the seal, they thought about that first circular assembly—how it had led them to explore the endowment and to uncover knowledge in creation.

The Glorified explored the Mystery like they explored the Realm, yet they still did not know its source and had uncovered very little about it. They followed it from the mount to all the parts and places in the Realm. They sprang forth with it from the abyss or fell with it from above. The Mystery of Creation was there when they awoke into existence. It was not only part of the meal; it made the first sound that they recalled. Then they uncovered that it was part of everything in the Realm. They began to explore it because they wanted to understand its elements. Their exploration of it began in this section, where the seal is to be found and where they thought the Mystery of Creation began. They joined the Mystery and it carried them along its path towards the abyss. In the abyss, they were covered in darkness. There was no room, or space for any sound other than the tongue of the Mystery. The Glorified could not see; not even the Spark seemed to glow, but the Mystery of Creation knew its path. They thought it had one path—one path that leads to all the sections of the Realm. After falling into the abyss, the Mystery carried each Glorified along a separate path. Each of the Glorified travelled their path alone and sprang forth or fell with the Mystery into a different section of the Realm.

The section of the Realm each Glorified fell into could be thought of like their places in the circular assembly. Seh sprang forth from the abyss in a section that was three sections in one direction and four sections in the other direction away from the section Hu fell into. The Mystery placed Hu after it brought her forth from the abyss into the section with the seal. They did not know the Mystery would have placed each Glorified in a different part of the Realm. As they were brought forth, each Glorified waited for others to come forth. There were no others. Each was taken to another section of the Realm. Hu had been carried into the abyss, but she thought it was flowing upwards. She then felt she was drifting even though she did not know the direction in which she flowed. After a while, she found herself falling onto the mount. There, she waited for others to follow as the Mystery of Creation *began again*.

She did not know the others had been carried along separate paths and brought forth in other sections of the Realm. The others thought the abyss deepened further and, at whiles, it rushed as if falling from on high, then there would be a calm. They were always covered in darkness and accompanied only by the voice of the Mystery. In the calm, it seemed as if the Mystery was no longer in a hurry. The calm would slowly be overtaken by the sound of the Mystery. As the sound grew louder, the Mystery started to make haste, and the Glorified sprang forth from the abyss or fell from above. The outcome after their first attempt at uncovering the source of the Mystery was the knowledge:

there are many paths the Mystery follows. They held a circular assembly, and the question they asked but could not answer was how the Mystery of Creation had chosen the section for each Glorified.

They decided that the next attempt at following the Mystery would start not in the section with the seal but in a section that was three sections in one direction and four sections in the other direction away. That was the definition of the furthest distance between two points in the Realm. The Glorified wanted to *begin again* as far away from where they had first started. The experience of the Glorified in their second attempt at following the Mystery was similar. It was Seh who began in that section and followed a path back into the same section. Seh described the path as flowing upwards as Hu had done, and he said he travelled across 'the firmament' to *begin again*. Hu affirmed that this would describe what she felt as well. She agreed with Seh, that flowing back to the beginning felt like she was passing overhead. It was not known if she was flowing backwards or forwards; she was simply drifting or being carried in the darkness.

The Glorified then began the journey in each of the sections of the Realm. In each section, a different Glorified would have the experience of following a path that led him or her back into the same section. They did not know how the Mystery chose the path and selected the section for each Glorified. They held circular assemblies to discuss the firmament, as Seh had called it. They wondered if it could be the source of the Mystery of Creation, as the '*other*', two positions on the right of Hu, had asked at their first circular assembly. They did not know, and after many whiles of exploring the Realm and following the Mystery along its path, it remained an unknown. They thought either the firmament or the abyss could be the source of the Mystery of Creation. Each of the Glorified experienced the feeling of passing overhead to *begin again*. They knew the Mystery carried them along a path that led back to the section where they had begun. They could hear the sound of the Mystery; they could feel it all around them, but they could not see along its path. Whether they were in the abyss or drifting across the firmament, the path was wrapped in darkness; only the Mystery of Creation knew the way.

The same darkness that covered the abyss also covered the firmament. The Glorified were careful not to create a *false truth*. They did not know if paths flowed into the abyss and led from the abyss into the firmament and then back to the section, where they had begun. They followed the Mystery along its many pathways and from all the sections of the Realm, yet they did not uncover its source. After the Rapture, they would begin exploring the Mystery of Creation again. They would enter the Rapture and allow the particles to become one with the Mystery of Creation. The particles would be everywhere the Mystery would be at the same while. They would be in the abyss, falling onto the mount, and along all of its different pathways. They would flow up and down at the same while. They would be calm along one path and in haste along another. The Rapture allowed the Glorified to follow the Mystery along its path in a new way, but they still did not know its source, or whether the firmament was made of the Mystery of Creation.

The Glorified spent many whiles discussing the firmament. It would be pointed out that each Glorified had the experience of flowing upwards. They thought they crossed overhead before falling back into the Realm. Seh would lead this part of the discussion, saying that if the Mystery of Creation carried the Glorified overhead, then there was a path in the firmament made of the Mystery of Creation. The others listened; they did not want to create a *false truth*. The Seven, the Glorified whose contentment in being animates his voice, would say, 'It is unknown. If the firmament were created by the Glorified, it would be made from the Mystery of Creation.' He would then forbid Silence from taking its place with the most precious sound in creation before saying, "Creating things from 'nothing' means the things found in creation are not required. All that is known is the firmament was created from 'nothing'." He would always conclude with laughter, as though he had shared the secret to understanding creation.

CHAPTER 21

THE SEAL

Hu was listening to the sounds of the Realm when the company reached its destination. They were all standing at the edge of the Mystery of Creation. The Creature began jumping back and forth. Hu did not join the others in standing; she walked instead to where the Mystery fell from the mount, the place where they had first cupped their hands to partake of it. She said, while looking up at where the Mystery seemed to pause before falling, 'The seal is here.'

Seh looked at where Hu said the seal was to be found and knew he had been there. It was there he had collected the Mystery for the gathering at the *crossroads*. He waited to hear if the others would say they could see it. The others moved closer to the mount, as if to get a better look. Then, Seh suggested they should enter the Rapture to see if the seal could be seen with the Spirit's eye.

'The seal is not hidden', Hu said, but the others affirmed they could not see it. She gently put the container down, and the Creature settled atop it. She stretched forth her hands and, in a low voice, called the Mystery by its symbol. She let it flow over her hands, then cupped her hands to gather it and splashed it on her face as if cleansing her hands and face after a long journey. As she reached for the Mystery, all the others but Seh stretched forth their hands; the Mystery tumbled over them, but the seal was not revealed. They too cleansed their hands and faces.

Seh, standing apart from the others, felt the mysteries found along the way bubbling within him. They had arrived at the seal, and he did not know how to ensure Hu would not again be set apart. He wondered once more whether another Glorified could do the task, as his fingers rolled into tight balls and he planted his feet firmly. Seh's form was starting to feel warm, so he did not hear her explain how she would break the seal. She told the others she would enter the Rapture so she could look upon creation once more with the Spirit's eye.

As the energy flowed through Seh, Hu entered the Rapture, and all of the others but Seh followed. The seal was there. She did not know if it was newly created or whether it had been there since the creation of the Realm. She spread the particles so she could be everywhere in the Realm. She saw Seh looking at the Creature. Again, she could see that there was something different about the Spark within him. She put it aside to focus on the task at hand. She looked upon the rest of creation. She saw the golden sphere in the Realm and witnessed the everlasting plenty it brings forth. She saw the Presence in all things and the Mystery of Creation as it spread itself throughout the Realm. She let her particles become one with the Mystery, wondering whether any creature, other than the First, the Self-Generator, would ever know its full tale. She followed it into the abyss, and the particles were everywhere the Mystery of Creation flowed. She drifted in the calm along one path while making haste along another. She fell with it upon the mount and sprang upwards to where it appears to come out of 'nothing'. She thought about the outcome of the task and the pattern in the announcement. The Mystery was not found among them, and she wondered if it would have a place in the new realm. She gathered the particles and left the Mystery of Creation to carry out its purpose.

She then let her particles become part of sound. She accompanied it as Silence led it towards the 'keeper of sound', before gathering her particles in a straight and narrow way. She joined the others at the *crossing* and watched with new knowledge and understanding as the particles entered the *crossing* and came forth on the other side. The others had done the same; they formed straight and narrow pathways as in the first Rapture. It was the same colourful bow, and the golden halves of the Spark sat at each end. Hu joined them, and all but Seh were in the Rapture. As they crossed the particles of their Raptures, she told them that the forms of creation were not to be found in the Realm. They had flowed through the dark inner layer and passed over the silvery lining to rest with the 'nothing'. They all looked at the particles of their Rapture, flowing to and from the *crossing*. They were not thinking of their forms of creation. They knew she believed this to be the last journey in the Realm. 'If there were to be no more beginnings of journeys in the Realm, if the circular assembly were to be incomplete, then all within the Realm would be lessened.'

After that, they said no more. There was no more to be said. She told them she would transform into the form she had created for the gathering before the announcement. While in that form, she would reveal the seal so all of creation could look upon it, then she would break the seal before transforming back into her form of creation to enter the place, space, or time where the task is to be done. She left the others in the Rapture and *'remade'* herself next to the Creature in the form she had created.

The others did not *'remake'* themselves. They chose to look at the revealing of the seal with the Spirit's eye. The body of the form she created was sleek and supported by four muscular limbs. It had a long tail with a tuft of hair at its end. The others saw that the form was exactly as it had been at the gathering. She used the front leg of the form to swipe across the falling Mystery. She made the first swipe, and the Mystery of Creation parted. It began to flow around the mark she had made, and the others wondered what she had done to interrupt the Mystery's flow. Were there symbols to be said or thoughts to be had before making the gesture which caused the Mystery to part? They were listening with all of their being, but Hu made no sound. She drew a mark across the path of the Mystery, and it reacted. She made two more swipes; the three marks formed a triangle. She paused, then she used the other leg with a single motion to make another sign. The second sign was also a triangle; it was upside down compared to the first. There were six points where the two triangles crossed, and together they made a sign. If a line were drawn through the middle, whether the line was drawn from right to left or up and down, the two halves would be mirrored images of each other, which reflected the symmetry in creation. The Mystery flowed around the points of the sign, revealing the seal. She had parted the Mystery of Creation, and a certainty was made a truth.

The Creature flapped its limbs, then jumped up and down on the container, as it had done in the announcement. The Glorified in the Rapture could see the six points in the sign. Each point was displayed in one of the 'three colours of being'. After revealing the seal, Hu waited, but the points where the triangles crossed did not wait. They started to move, hopping from one point to another in the sign. At first, the Glorified in the Rapture could see each point moving and could distinguish the colour of each point. Then the points started to flow more quickly. Finally, they were flowing so fast they appeared to make a circle inside the sign.

As Hu made the sign on the Mystery, Seh drew closer to her. He saw that the Mystery parted. He stepped closer to her, looking at how the Mystery was flowing around the shape of the sign. 'It is true', he said to himself, 'there is a seal.' The others in the Rapture looked on as the six points became a circle, and they could no longer distinguish among them. After waiting as if she were awaiting additional 'know-how', Hu made three more marks upon the sign. She connected the points in the sign with the same colour. There were three lines connecting the six points and each line was displayed in one of the 'colours of being'.

The seal was a truth for all to see. Seh, refusing to set aside the notion that the task should be shared, acknowledged to himself that he had searched this section of the Realm, stood in front of the seal, yet he did not see it. He too wondered what she had done to cause the Mystery of Creation to part. He looked at her as she waited; she looked as though she had forgotten the path and did not know what the next step should be, but he chose not to intrude on her. As Hu waited, Seh stood by watching, thinking she would be set far above all others forever and a more. He had not entered the Rapture, nor had he searched the endowment. He wanted to focus on the task so he stayed close to her, looking at her, anticipating—if not expecting.

The others in the Rapture acknowledged the unknown about how the 'colours of being' should be displayed. The Spark always displayed black as the second, or the middle, 'colour of being', but which colour to be displayed first or third was unknown. As the others looked upon the seal, they saw on the left side the 'colours of being' displayed as red, black, and green, and on the right side, they were displayed as green, black, and red. While Hu waited, and Seh wondered if she had forgotten the path, the others thought that creation continued to be filled with unknowns. The point where the three lines crossed, in the midst of the seal, there was another unknown. The Glorified called it an unknown because they did not know it. It was the point in the middle of the seal where the three lines crossed—but it had no colour. The 'three colours of being' made a colourless crossing. They looked upon it, wondering how colourlessness could be made from the 'colours of being'. They thought of the colours of their Raptures, knowing they had not uncovered how they were created.

As they wondered, circles started emerging from the midst of the seal. The circles began to expand outwards. The Glorified thought the circles were like sound drifting off towards the 'keeper of sound'. As one circle emerged and expanded outwards, another would follow. Marking a sign on the Mystery of Creation is beyond the 'know-how' of humans, but any human being could witness the pattern of the circles in the seal by dropping a pebble in the Mystery of Creation. The circles emerged one after another, pushing outwards until the first circle was no longer inside of the sign. Hu was still waiting as the inner circle journeyed to the outer edge and surrounded the sign, as the First, the Self-Generator, surrounds creation. The sign was covered with colourless circles, from the midst of the seal to its outer rim, and the Creature positioned itself to bear witness to it.

Hu was preparing to make the last mark upon the seal. She brightened her face, thinking she might have no more beginnings in the Realm. She recalled the twelfth truth, reminding herself that she would never be alone. She waited, her thoughts drifting, listening on one side to the quiet and on the other to the sounds of the Realm. She reminded herself to let the Spark lead when she entered the place, space, or time of the task. As she waited, a colour appeared in the Mystery of Creation. It moved as though being blown by a gentle breeze. There were no symbols in the endowment to describe the image that the Glorified saw. In the human universe, it could be described as a flame flickering in the breeze. At first, the Glorified thought the flame—to use the human symbol—was upon the Mystery. Then, they thought it might be a reflection. Seh looked above to see if it was a reflection of some unknown object. Finally, they were able to see that the Mystery had changed. There was a colour upon it. The colour is common among humans. They refer to it as orange. There would be several different shades of orange among humans, but this particular orange is the colour made when the Mystery of Creation appears to have a flame upon it. Hearing this, humans would ask, how could flames have a place in water? The Glorified would explain that there were no flames in the Realm. That is why there were no symbols in the endowment. It was the colour and the movement of the Mystery that caused it to appear as if flames were on it. Each bounce or bump in the Mystery looked like a flame flickering in the breeze. The Glorified looked upon the Mystery as it transformed from the colour of its creation to the orange colour, but they did not know how to describe it.

The Glorified in the Rapture saw more than Hu and Seh in their physical form. They saw the growth in the colour. It grew from a light grey colour to a bright orange, appearing as a flame dancing on the Mystery of Creation. That was the first the Glorified witnessed what humans would come to know. Every colour in the human realm could be made to be grey. After what they heard about the announcement, the Glorified, looking at the Spirit of the Mystery—how it parted to reveal the seal, and then looking upon the seal, which was as colourless as the abyss was dark—did not think of the First, the Self-Generator. That was not the way of creation. They had not been enlivened to consider the 'nothing'. Such thoughts would deny the purpose of existence. They wondered, instead, if they could uncover the knowledge to make colourlessness out of the 'three colours of being'.

Hu waited a while longer before she made the last mark to break the seal. Seh was standing close to her, the Creature was on top of the container, and the others were in the Rapture. The sign, with its orange outline dancing, waited. Seh wondered again if Hu had forgotten the path. She should just break the seal, he thought! She started, as though she heard his thoughts to make the last mark. She began from the highest point and made a straight line down the middle, connecting it to the lowest point in the seal. As she drew the line, the Glorified in the Rapture wondered if the seal would simply fall apart. After Hu made the last mark, there was a *while of quiet*. The silence was filled with anticipation. For a while, the mark seemed to have no impact on the seal. Then, as though the circles had served their purpose, each circle started to gain a colour. Hu, waiting, the Creature and Seh anticipating, saw the changes in the same way as the others in the Rapture.

The Glorified in the Rapture saw the colourlessness of the circle first become misty or cloudy, as humans would say. Then, the circle became what humans would consider grey before finally gaining the colour of the inner layer of the Rapture. The circles, one after another, in the order they emerged from the midst of the seal, transformed from colourlessness to cloudy grey and then to the colour of the inner layer of the Rapture. That made it look as if the circles were flowing from the outer rim towards the midst of the seal, like humans returning from the marketplace to home. As they approached the centre of the seal, there seemed to be no more circles to be transformed. The point where the three lines crossed remained colourless. The seal had an orange circle around its outer edge, and it was covered in the same colour as the inner layer of the Rapture—except for the point in its centre. That point was colourless; it was made brighter by the darkness that surrounded it. Humans, hearing this part of the History, would point to the firmament and ask if it was the same as the twinkling of the stars. They would ask the Glorified if they knew what the colourlessness was. The Glorified would say it was the colourlessness in the midst of the seal. Humans would say they believed it was the First, the Self-Generator. The Glorified would brighten their faces, knowing that human beings—who had not yet grown to access the endowment—substitute belief for not knowing. So, the Glorified would simply say all they could affirm was—it was part of the *perfection in creation*.

The seal did not fall apart. The dark circles seemed to push the colourless point away from the Realm. The Glorified were not certain whether the circles were pushing or the point was pulling. It mattered not; it mattered only that the middle of the seal was drifting away from the Realm. It grew smaller, and the dark circles formed a gateway with the colourless point at the end of it. The gateway was covered in darkness. In the distance, the colourless point seemed bright and beckoning. The human universe would have no true representation of the colourlessness. The colour of the Mystery of Creation would be similar, but not the same; yet humans still referenced this part of the History. They used that moment from the breaking of the seal as a symbol of hope. They refer to it as a light at the end of a tunnel, meaning all is not lost. Like the abyss, the gateway was covered in darkness, but there was a light at the other end of it. Then, the colourless point— the light at the end of the gateway—could be seen getting smaller and smaller, before it could be seen no more. The circle of orange flames that surrounded the outer edge of the seal was still alight, outlining the entrance for Hu and the Creature.

The company waited, and the Silence was loud. Seh and the others wondered if the seal had been broken. He moved closer to Hu while the Creature flapped its limbs and chased Silence from its place with three cock-a-doodles. The sound filled the Realm, and the Creature swung its head—first to the left and then to the right—to signal: *begin again*. It jumped from the top of the container into the darkness of the gateway—then it was gone. It could be seen no more. The Creature leaping into the entrance caused no change in the gateway. There were no movements in the darkness. It was similar to a Glorified entering the Rapture. The Creature leapt, and vanished. Seh, stepping closer to Hu, thought the Creature was leading again. The Creature signalled, *begin again*, and Hu prepared herself as the others waited for her to follow the Creature.

She transformed into her form of creation and picked up the container with the orbs. She looked at Seh and then overhead; she stepped towards the gateway and said to the others, 'The purpose of creation is …'. Before she could complete her statement and enter the gateway, she lost her way. Seh, standing beside her, caught her before she fell. The others in the Rapture saw that Hu was unable to enter the gateway. They saw her falling into the arms of Seh. As she fell, they noticed something different about the Spark within Seh, even as he reached out to assist her. They wondered what could have caused her to lose the strength to complete the task. They 'remade' themselves so they could be with her, to explore what she needed to complete the journey. As the others 'remade' themselves, they too lost their way. Seh, still holding Hu, could not prevent them from falling. So, he watched as each of the other Glorified 'remade' themselves—lost their way and fell.

Seh laid Hu down and picked up the container. It was cool to the touch. It had more weight than he expected, and the orbs were no longer flowing around the dark centre. He wondered how a Glorified could fit in the design. Would the design expand and grow? He was trying to choose. He looked at the outside of the container, for Hu had mentioned that there was a design there. He looked, but he could only see a faint glow of a golden sphere, similar to the sphere in the midst on the human universe. In the container, there were a number of orbs, of similar size, surrounding a dark centre. That would be the place for a Glorified, he thought. A Seven might be able to sit there in the circular assembly position if the design expanded. Seh's knowledge of the task and how the orbs should be placed was limited. He had seen the orbs in the container as the others experimented with the Creature, but he did not know the outcome. He thought if the Creature led the way, he could assist Hu in completing the task.

CHAPTER 22

CALL OF SILENCE

Seh stood there with the container in his hands. The Glorified lay around him. He felt, for the first since they began existence that he was alone. It was as if the others had come to an end. He was tempted to enter the Rapture to see if the Presence in all things was still there. It was a new feeling for Seh. Since their beginning, the Glorified were almost never alone. Besides the twelfth truth, each Glorified knew that another was only three sections in one direction and four sections in the other direction away. They could always feel the presence of the others, as if they were being looked at, but after the others fell, Seh felt he was alone. In his aloneness, even the Realm became quiet. He recalled the second truth: 'There is only one First, the Self-Generator', and he tried to overcome the feeling of aloneness by saying, 'In the beginning, the First, the Self-Generator, was alone.' He wondered if this was how *It* felt in the beginning, when *It* was alone, when there was no consciousness beyond *Itself*.

The quietness that descended upon the Realm enveloped him. It called to him, but there seemed to be a space separating him from the rest of creation. Silence waited, as if it had asked a question and was listening for the answer. All of creation, other than the Glorified, was listening; everything waited to see what Seh would do. Would he follow the indications of the Spark? Or would he again choose a path not in the way of creation? He felt the weight of Silence as if it were standing on his shoulders. It was calling to him in the loudest voice possible; he did not hear it, or he chose not to listen. He had once before let his Spirit roam and had chosen a path not in the way of creation. That choice had left a mark on his Spark; and once again, as he stood in front of the gateway, surrounded by the fallen Glorified, his Spirit was roaming. It was roaming away from the indications of the Spark.

As he held the container in his hands, looking at the fallen, all of creation waited to see what he would choose. Everything waited to see whether Seh would heed the call of Silence and choose the way of creation. Seh had spoken of choosing—or choosing not. He thought that Hu could choose to do or to do not. He knew he had not chosen 'sharing of know-how'. He understood choosing; he sensed choosing could act upon and mould the Spirit. In pursuing transformation, the Spark could not follow where his Spirit roamed, and the glow of the Spark dimmed.

The Silence around him was loud, but he did not hear the true path calling; he did not see the way indicated by the Spark. 'She has lost her way', he said, adding that he would assist her. He gave no thought to the others as he took the container and tried to enter the gateway. The Glorified whose place in the circular assembly is three positions on Hu's left side—and whose contentment in being could be heard in laughter—had fallen just in front of the gateway. Seh, turning towards the gateway, stumbled over him and fell to his knees. That caused the container to fall from his hands into the gateway. He picked himself up, stepped over the Seven, and leapt into the gateway. Seh chose, and again, the Spark could not follow.

Here Ends the Beginning!

ACKNOWLEDGEMENT

First, I want to thank the voice, which always speaks up, reminding me that other people's beliefs—the things they do not know—are not a plan for my life.

I want to acknowledge the contribution of the brothers and sisters from the heady, hopeful days in Montreal, Canada. I thank the 'Black Muslims' who first spoke to me about Islam and showed me a picture of Elijah Muhammad, which caused me to ask, 'Why does god always pick someone who does not look like us?'

I thank the Rastafarians who introduced me to Marcus Garvey, Malcolm X, Walter Rodney, and of course Haile Selassie I, Jah Rastafari. Those days of grounding with 'I and I' in Coronation Park have never left me and contributed to the foundation on which 'I man' stands today.

Above all, I give thanks to my aunt, who was 82 years old the year I was born. For the first twelve years of my life, she gave me everything I would need before Canada stole me away. I remember well her words and her stories. The stories about the men and women who ran away just so they could spend a portion of their lives not serving the enslavers. I remember the things she said we did when we were in Africa.

You were such a light! Someone your age who was not ashamed or afraid of the word 'African'. But Tita, what I remember most is the piece of advice you gave me that moulded me into the person I am today. Oh, how I wish I still had that stone you put in my hand when you told me, *'No matter what you do, make sure it is built on a foundation as strong as this.'* You, Tita, are among the greatest of the ancestors!

jkm

ABOUT THE AUTHOR

jkm Mbdw is a reluctant writer. In many ways, he knows he does not have the right or the privilege to call himself a writer. He holds a master's degree, but it is an MBA in finance, not an MFA in creative writing. He has not been a closet writer, nor has he ever thought that after a career in finance, he would become a writer. He knows that writing, like finance, is a skill, that requires a lifetime of dedication.

Nevertheless, after being fired from Corporate Canada yet again, he felt the calling to write this book instead of looking for another job in Corporate Canada. jkm is an African who lives in Canada. *History of Creation: The Announcement*—an African/Black literary fiction—is his first book.

Thanks for reading, I dragged my feet writing this story; I almost didn't do it. I would love to hear your honest feelings about it. I look forward to your thoughts on Amazon or Goodreads.

jkm